Reckless Need

SCARLETT SCOTT

Reckless Need
Heart's Temptation Book 3

Dedication

To my fabulous former editor, Grace. I can't thank you enough for all the support you gave me over the years and for all you taught me. It was truly a pleasure to work with you.

Contents

Chapter One   1

Chapter Two   17

Chapter Three   37

Chapter Four   56

Chapter Five   70

Chapter Six   87

Chapter Seven   101

Chapter Eight   116

Chapter Nine   136

Chapter Ten   154

Chapter Eleven   172

Chapter Twelve   191

Epilogue   202

Preview of *Sweet Scandal*   207

About the Author   214

Other Books by Scarlett Scott   215

Chapter One

East Anglia, England, 1882

IF THERE WAS ONE THING IN THE WORLD THAT Tia, Lady Stokey, adored, it was parties. Give her a good *fête*, an army of new dresses, an entertaining assortment of guests and she was a happy woman.

Under ordinary circumstances, that was.

Grumbling to herself, she trekked through the maze at the Marquis of Thornton's hunting estate, Penworth, in search of her wayward charge. A mere hour after their arrival for a country house party, Tia had discovered Miss Whitney missing from her bedchamber.

"In need of a nap, my bottom," Tia grumbled, stalking around a corner. If only the hedges weren't so frightfully high and she so irritatingly diminutive in height. But of course, that would have rather nullified the purpose of a maze, she supposed.

The young Miss Whitney had declared the need for a respite after their travel through the countryside, and Tia had acquiesced. But suspicion had brought her round to collect the girl early, where she'd discovered only a note telling her that her charge had decided to take a restoring turn about the gardens instead.

"Restoring indeed," Tia scoffed, her ire growing with each step. She had a dreadful feeling that her charge was going to prove much more than a handful. After all, she recognized herself in the girl, and it was one of the reasons why she'd agreed to help introduce her to society.

The sound of gravel shifting interrupted her cantankerous musings. She stopped, holding her breath to listen. It sounded as if Miss Whitney was perhaps just around the next bend, behind the thick hedges obscuring Tia's vision. Smiling in triumph, she grabbed her skirts and hurried around the turn in the maze.

"Ah ha," she called out in delight. "I've found you now, you little minx."

But her moment of triumph was terribly abridged, for the noise-making culprit, seated on a bench before her, was not Miss Whitney. Nor, in fact, was it even a female. Quite the opposite.

Dear heavens. Eyes the same wistful color as a summer sky met hers, stealing her breath. She stopped, her heart thumping as madly as a runaway stallion's hooves. The man staring back at her, an open book in his large hands, a golden brow raised, was decidedly as far as one could get from the petite, Virginia-born Miss Whitney.

"I daresay I've been called a great number of things in my life, but never yet a little minx," drawled the Duke of Devonshire as he stood and bowed to her.

"I must apologize," she hastened to say, embarrassment making her cheeks go hot. "I mistook you for someone else."

A small smile curved his lips, drawing her attention to just how finely formed his mouth was. He had changed since she'd seen him last. He'd grown a beard. She swallowed, her heart continuing its mad pace. The duke had always been a handsome man, possessed of a rare masculine beauty that almost made him seem too perfect to be real.

But the neatly trimmed beard took the purity of his features and rendered them somehow sinful. Seductive. Her cheeks burned as she realized she was staring and, to her greatest dismay, he'd said something to her.

She had no earthly idea what.

Bother it all, what ailed her? She'd seen Devonshire scads of times before. The boring manner in which he conducted himself had long since rendered her immune to his undeniable good looks. He was quiet, uninteresting. For the most part, he didn't move in the same circles as she. In private, she referred to him as the Duke of Dullness. Why, then, was she turning into a silly schoolroom miss in his presence? A beard? An intense stare?

Tia released her skirts, allowing them to fall back into place as it occurred to her that she'd likely been revealing far more of her limbs than she'd intended. That bright-blue gaze of his followed her movement, making her feel almost as if he'd caressed her.

"By any chance, were you searching for a lovely young American, Lady Stokey?" he asked, saving her from further embarrassment.

She didn't know why, but she found it troublesome indeed that he thought Miss Whitney lovely. Tia shook the unworthy notion from her mind, reminded that she was charged with looking after the virtue and the conduct of a rather precocious young girl.

"I was, Your Grace," she acknowledged, dipping into a slight curtsy as her wits returned to her. "Have you seen her?"

"About half an hour ago," he confirmed, closing the distance between them. That smile still flirted with the corners of his mouth, almost as if he were enjoying a sally at her expense.

Half an hour. Tia frowned. The girl could be halfway back to America by now. "I don't suppose she told you where she intended to go next?"

"No."

A great lot of help he was. Tia tried not to notice how very broad his shoulders were, how lean his legs. She glanced instead to the book he held. It was a volume of poetry. She'd never had much patience for verse. "I'm sorry for the interruption," she told him, deciding the time for lingering was at an end. She needed to find Miss Whitney and bring the girl to task. England was not Virginia. She couldn't simply wander about as she chose, especially not as a young, innocent miss. She had a reputation to uphold.

"Think nothing of it, my lady." Devonshire still stood uncomfortably near to her, looking down with an unreadable expression upon his face. "I was merely enjoying a bit of solitude while I still could."

Solitude? Tia thought it an odd statement indeed but perhaps another indication of why she'd never been particularly drawn to the man. Aside from his undeniably arresting appearance, that was. She considered him now, her gaze dropping to his mouth of its own will before she forced herself to once again become ensnared in his riveting stare. "I confess I'm confused, Your Grace. Is not keeping the company of others rather the point of a country house party?"

He nodded, appearing a solemn, lonely figure suddenly. "I daresay it is, my lady. For most."

She couldn't help it. She knew she ought to be running after her errant charge, but there was something suddenly compelling about Devonshire. Here in the outdoors, the sun shining down upon him, the polish of his ordinary façade buffed away by the manner in which she'd caught him unaware…he seemed different to her. Almost dangerous. Certainly handsome. But sad too, as if he were a man who had never quite located his true place in the world.

"But not for you?" she asked him quietly.

"*Ça dépend*," he answered, stroking the binding of his book absentmindedly.

There was something about watching his long fingers that caused an ache deep inside Tia. It had been so very long since she'd been touched by a man. Too long, she reminded herself, else she wouldn't be mooning over the Duke of Devonshire. "On what does it depend?"

"The others with whom I'm expected to keep company," he answered cryptically.

"I see." She frowned again, supposing she really should have left well enough alone. She had the distinct impression he didn't want her there. "Then perhaps I should leave you to your seclusion after all. I don't wish to further inconvenience you. Good day, Your Grace."

She spun on her heel, determined to beat a hasty retreat before she made any more of a fool of herself, tarrying over conversation with a man who would prefer to be left alone. A man she didn't even like, no matter how attractive she found him. Yes, it was the beard, she decided as she hurried away. The beard had rendered him quite magnetic.

Lost in her round of self-chastising, Tia wasn't paying proper attention to her mules. They were delicate silk, horridly impractical for being outside and not at all the sort of things to be rushing about in. Her heel caught in the stones of the path, twisting her ankle and making her lose her balance at the same time.

Pain shot from her ankle up her leg as she landed in an inglorious heap on her hands and knees. She must have cried out, because the duke came rushing around the bend, all the better to prolong her humiliation. Her ankle aching, she stared at his trousers in misery, wishing she'd had the grace to fall somewhere out of his earshot instead.

He hunkered down at her side, his striking face coming back into her view. "Lady Stokey, are you hurt?" His voice was laced with genuine concern.

"Yes," she told him, grimacing when she flexed her foot and was met with another sharp twinge of discomfort. "My pride and my ankle are both grievously wounded."

He took her hands in his, turning them over to inspect her palms. They were bare because she'd been too intent on chasing after Miss Whitney to care. Devonshire was gloveless too, and the contact of his skin on hers gave her an unexpected jolt. He rubbed his thumbs over her lightly, lingering on the abrasions she'd earned in her tumble. "I'm afraid you're bleeding as well."

She glanced from her raw palms to his face. He was unbearably near, so near she had great difficulty catching her breath. Good heavens. She had to compose herself. "I shall mend," she said, trying for an air of unconcern. It wouldn't do for him to know the effect he had on her. Why, she didn't like the man. He was altogether unappealing. She preferred men who were eager and attentive, who knew how to kiss and woo a woman. Who were seductive and easy to understand and flirted with practiced ease. Men who didn't hide in the gardens reading poetry, of all things.

"Let me help you to stand," he said in a tone that allowed for no argument. "On the count of three. One, two—" He pulled her up without waiting for her compliance and without waiting to say "three".

Tia leaned into the duke as she stood, wincing when the pressure of weight upon her ankle produced more pronounced pain. Oh dear, perhaps she'd sprained it. However would she contain Miss Whitney if she were hobbled like an old dowager for the entirety of the party?

"I thought you said on the count of three," she groused, rather cut up about the entire situation.

First, her charge had disappeared. Then, Tia had reacted to Devonshire as if she were a smitten young girl straight off her comeout. Now she'd fallen in a heap before him. And she still hadn't located Miss Whitney. This fortnight was certainly off to a marvelous start.

"Put your weight on me," he ordered next, ignoring her. "I'll walk you to the bench, and then I'll take a look at your ankle to see what damage has been done."

"No." She tried to extricate herself from his grasp without success. "I don't require your assistance, Your Grace."

"Nonsense." When she continued to attempt her escape,

he caught her up in his arms.

Tia's hands went to his shoulders for purchase, finding them just as solid and strong as they looked. "Good heavens, put me down at once," she told him. If his proximity before had been tempting, it was now alarming. She could smell his scent, a deliciously masculine blend of soap, spice and the outdoors. She could feel the fine fabric of his jacket beneath her fingertips. His golden hair curled down over his collar, brushing against her as he moved. And she could detect the faintest flecks of gray in his otherwise perfectly blue eyes. It didn't escape her notice that he'd scooped her up without a bit of strain, as though she weighed little more than a handful of feathers.

He disregarded her request to put her back on her own two feet and carried her to the bench where he'd been sitting when she'd first interrupted him. He gently lowered her to its hard surface, and she had to secretly admit that she was somewhat disappointed to no longer be in his arms. When he sank to his knees before her, reaching beneath her skirts, her disappointment turned to dismay.

"Your Grace," she protested. "What are you about?"

"Hush," he dismissed her concerns, his hand closing around the ankle that was giving her pain. "I'm seeing to your injury."

"You needn't." She endeavored to pull her limb from his grasp, to no avail. His touch was warm and gentle through her stockings. A sudden rush of awareness threatened to swallow her whole. A wicked, luxurious heat settled between her thighs. She tamped it down. "For heaven's sake, I'm fine. I'm merely in a bit of pain, but it shall pass."

But his fingers were already gently at work, angling her foot this way and that. "It would be remiss of me not to make certain you haven't done yourself serious harm. You took quite a spill."

Oh dear. Little more than a dull throb plagued her ankle now, but another throb had taken up residence within her. A decidedly naughty one. She wet her suddenly dry lips.

"Truly, Your Grace. This is most improper."

He was insistent in playing the role of savior. "Does this hurt?" He pressed his thumb against her inner foot.

"No." Quite the opposite. It felt wonderfully good. Too bad he was not at all the sort of man for an inamorato. The wickedness in her pulled her skirts just a bit higher anyway, revealing the curve of her calf.

The duke's touch moved north as well, feeling suspiciously like a caress. "What of this?"

She flinched when he found the exact spot on her ankle where the soreness originated. "Yes."

He stopped his ministrations and glanced up, his gaze meeting hers. She wondered if he could tell she wasn't as unaffected as she pretended and hoped not. He moved her foot again with one hand while holding her ankle with the other. "I don't think you've broken anything, fortunately. But it does feel a trifle swollen. More than likely, you've sprained it. You'll need to rest for the remainder of the day."

Tia scoffed, doing her best to disregard his lingering touch. "I haven't time to rest. I have a wayward young American to locate and browbeat to within an inch of her wretched life."

"That sounds pressing indeed," he told her solemnly. "But I'm afraid you'll have to enlist someone else to help hunt your charge down for the life-threatening browbeating."

He released her ankle and pulled her skirts back into place. Tia felt the loss of his touch like an ache. This ridiculous reaction to him had to stop. She'd been a widow for several years, but she took great care with her lovers. She didn't simply set her cap for a man because he was beautiful and happened to touch her ankle and had a deliciously rakish beard.

Tia stared at him as he stood, an idea taking root in her mind. Yes, it was the perfect solution for her sudden, inconvenient and thoroughly foolish attraction to the Duke of Devonshire. After all, it would be a wonderful coup for

Miss Whitney to bring a duke up to scratch. "Perhaps you'll be so kind as to assist me in locating Miss Whitney?" she asked, giving the duke her most charming smile.

He nodded, picking up the book that he'd abandoned on the bench when he'd rushed to her rescue. "Of course, my lady. But in the meantime, I fear you'll need my aid to escape from the maze first." He offered her his arm.

Tia took it, allowing him to tug her to her feet. Her ankle still hurt but not nearly as badly as it first had after her inconvenient spill. "Thank you, Your Grace. You're most kind." And easily trapped, she hoped. For it would certainly be a boon to her if she could settle the troublesome Miss Whitney with a suitable gentleman at the first opportunity. A man very much like the Duke of Devonshire.

Heath aided Lady Stokey back to the main house, mindful of her limping gait and his painful arousal both. Had he known that touching her would prove so bloody dangerous to his restraint, he never would have so much as laid a finger upon her hem. But he'd been carried away by his concern, the need to make certain she hadn't broken a bone. From the moment he'd caught her up in his arms, he'd had a troubling suspicion that he was walking down a path from which there would be no return. Lady Stokey was an ethereal beauty, as golden as an angel with finely formed features, lush red lips and wide eyes the color of a meadow in spring. She'd smelled of violets.

He could still smell her now if he leaned near enough.

But the greatest folly of all had been lifting her skirts to reveal her trim, lovely legs. He'd stolen a peek all the way to her knees when he first lifted her silk and petticoats aside. He hadn't been able to help himself. And it had been worth it. Touching her had been intoxicating. He'd never before caressed a woman's limbs through her stockings, but he would now forever find the act unbearably erotic.

Unless he missed his guess, she hadn't been immune either. He'd caught the way her lips had parted, the way the green of her eyes had deepened, the way she'd lifted her hem even higher. It was too bad, really, that he was in search of a wife and not a mistress. If it had been a mistress he was after, he would have escorted Lady Stokey to her chamber and then joined her inside. To the devil with her nuisance of a young charge.

Instead, he was playing the role he'd honed well over the years. Perfect gentleman. "How is your ankle faring, my lady?" he asked, still desperate to distract himself from the inconvenient state of his cock.

She turned to him, her elaborately styled blonde locks glinting in the sun. In her haste to chase after her charge, she'd neglected to wear a hat and he was grateful for it. "In truth, it's still paining me, but I daresay it shan't be the death of me."

He'd always thought Lady Stokey something of a flighty woman. Though on occasion he'd traveled in the periphery of her circles, they'd never truly engaged in much conversation. That she was clever surprised him. In his experience, there ordinarily wasn't much substance to a woman of beauty. He'd known a few exceptions, of course, but they were just that. Exceptions.

A distinct expression of pain now furrowed her brow as she limped through the maze. He disliked seeing her suffering. "I would be more than happy to carry you to your chamber, Lady Stokey," he volunteered out of a combined sense of duty and desire. He had to admit that holding her in his arms once more would not precisely be a hardship.

"Heavens no," she objected immediately. "If I sap all your strength, you'll have none left to pursue Miss Whitney, wherever she may be."

She'd gone back to watching the ground before them, giving him her profile. He instantly regretted his hasty offer to locate her charge. Miss Whitney had indeed ventured past him in the maze, and though she was but a slip of a girl, he suspected she was a wily foe if the way she'd flummoxed Lady Stokey was any indication. He hadn't the patience for silly young girls.

"You'll not sap my strength so easily," he reassured her. Lady Stokey, for all her layers of dress, had been as light as a bird in his arms. And like a bird, she was a tiny, gorgeous creature.

"Oh," she exclaimed suddenly, her expression crumpling as she clenched his arm in a rigid grip. "Oh dear."

He stopped, sliding an arm round her waist, the better to give her purchase and keep weight off her injured leg. The maddening scent of violets enveloped him. "Perhaps you'll permit me to carry you after all."

"No," she denied even as she clutched his arm and her eyes glistened with unshed tears. "You mustn't. I can walk on my own. I may lack grace, but I'm no weakling."

A weakling she was not. A stubborn woman, however, she was. He decided not to allow her the opportunity for further argument. Heath tucked his book inside his coat, then bent and once more scooped her up.

"Your Grace," she remonstrated, her tone one of surprise mingled with disapproval. Her hands linked around his neck. Her lovely Cupid's bow of a mouth was so very near to his. If he but dipped his head, he could take her lips.

No, damn it. He could not. He forced himself to stare straight ahead and carry them from the maze. He'd come to Penworth in search of a wife, and he was determined to stay the course. Lady Stokey, tempting though she may be, was not the woman for him. Her reputation preceded her, and he didn't want a butterfly as his mate. Rather, he wanted a bookworm. A woman of substance. A woman of loyalty who was willing to respect her husband. Not a dazzlingly seductive widow with a string of lovers in her past and a penchant for throwing wild soirees. Regardless of how delicious she smelled and how alluring she felt in his arms.

"I'll not have another word of protest," he informed her coolly. "I cannot in good conscience allow you to carry on while in such obvious pain."

As he entered the house, Lady Thornton, his hostess and Lady Stokey's sister, appeared before him, having been interrupted in directing her housekeeper. The sisters were opposites in appearance, one dark, the other light, but both equally lovely. Worry clouded the marchioness's face. "What has happened?"

"I merely sprained my ankle. Tell this insufferable man to put me on my feet," Lady Stokey demanded in a queenly accent.

Heath exchanged a commiserating glance with Lady Thornton. "This insufferable man is attempting to keep her ladyship from doing herself further harm. If you'll be so kind as to direct me to her chamber?"

His hostess raised an inky brow at his request. He knew he could have simply deposited Lady Stokey in the drawing room, but he was on a mission now. He couldn't very well abandon his damsel in distress partway through his rescue. But if she thought his actions odd, in the end Lady Thornton chose to keep her misgivings to herself. "The east wing, third door to your left."

He nodded to her. "Thank you."

"You cannot be serious," Lady Stokey chimed in. "I'm perfectly capable of walking. Cleo, tell him."

"You mustn't take any chances," her sister called after them as Heath stalked in the direction of the stairs. "You'll not want to be injured for the party, dearest sister."

Heath gave his reluctant armful a victorious glance. "You see? Finally, a voice of reason. Listen to your sister if not me." He took the steps with ease, grateful that all the hard labor he'd been performing on his estate had finally rewarded him. He wasn't even winded.

The same could not be said for Lady Stokey, whose cheeks were pink and whose breath seemed too quick for a woman at rest. Her eyes snapped emerald fire at him. He had to admit she was even more captivating when irritated. "Voice of reason indeed." She tipped up her chin in a show of defiance. "Since when is carrying an able-bodied woman about as if she were a sack of turnips considered reasonable?"

"I would never carry a sack of turnips with such great care," he told her solemnly. There it was again, her heavenly scent, teasing his senses and his cock both. He forced himself to keep to the matter at hand. "Though I must confess I wonder what circumstances in life would require one to carry a sack of turnips to begin with."

"Bother." Her lips compressed and she turned her head away from him again, apparently too cross to even continue berating him.

She was pricklier than a cornered hedgehog. He rather enjoyed nettling her and a sudden, wicked impulse to continue hit him just then. "Oh dear," he said, feigning worry.

That deep, warm gaze swung back to his. "What is it?"

"I fear I'm going to sneeze," he told her.

"Good heavens." Her eyes widened and then narrowed as the grin he couldn't quite contain emerged. "You're not serious."

"No." He reached the top of the stairs and headed down the hall.

"That was not a kind jest, Your Grace," Lady Stokey chastised him.

He stopped before her chamber door. "Perhaps not kind but certainly humorous. Would you be so obliging as to turn the knob for me, my lady?"

Making a sound of irritation, she did as he asked. Something within him stirred as he stepped over the threshold into her private rooms. He pushed the door closed with his shoulder, trying to ignore the awareness creeping over him. Damn it, what was it about the small woman in his arms that made him want her so much? He'd seen more than his fair share of beauties. He'd long thought himself immune to the lure of a lovely woman. The lust coursing through him made little sense. He hadn't been so moved by the mere presence of a woman since Bess. The thought of the sweet, innocent woman he'd loved made his blood run a bit colder. She could not have been more different than the willful, decadent Lady Stokey.

Heath stalked the last few feet to her bed, stopping to carefully lower her to it. Lady Stokey's eyes were on his. Their noses nearly brushed. Her lips parted. The desire he'd been doing his damnedest to dash away returned, hitting him in the gut with the force of a punch.

"Thank you," she said softly. Her hands were still on his shoulders, burning him through his jacket, waistcoat and shirt.

"You're most welcome," he returned in a voice gone rough. He knew he should straighten, put some distance between them, ring for her maid and leave the chamber. But she was a temptation he couldn't resist. From the moment she'd rounded the bend in the maze and he'd caught sight of her, the sun glinting in her golden curls and twin patches of pink on her cheeks, her curves molded in a scarlet day dress, he'd been thinking of kissing her. Undoing the line of buttons on her bodice. Peeling her out of her gown to see if her breasts were as full and luscious as they appeared beneath her proper layers.

Before his conscience allowed him to change his mind, he lowered his mouth to hers. She opened to him and he took advantage, sweeping his tongue inside to taste her. Her fingers slid from his shoulder to his neck, sinking into his hair. An arrow of heat shot directly to his cock, making him instantly hard. One of his hands moved to her elaborate coiffure, itching to undo it and unleash her long blonde curls. With his other hand, he cupped her breast. She arched into him, filling his palm with the curve of her breast that wasn't contained by her corset, making a throaty sound of appreciation deep in her throat.

He wondered if her nipples were hard, and if they were the same pretty pink as her soft lips.

Damnation.

He hadn't meant to give in to his baser instincts. But now that he had, he couldn't seem to stop. He wanted more of her. Couldn't help himself from pressing his knee to the bed and leaning over her, the better to kiss her senseless. When her tongue ventured against his, a shot of unadulterated, reckless need blazed straight through him as if it were an inferno. He dragged his mouth down her throat, kissing the creamy skin he'd admired in the gardens. She even tasted of violets, sweet and floral, and for some reason, he found it incredibly erotic. The high lace collar of her gown served as an impediment for further exploration, so he released her breast to find the line of fabric-covered buttons keeping him from what he desperately wanted. He slipped them from their moorings, returning to her mouth for another deep, passionate kiss.

One, two, three, four. He counted each button he freed in his mind, eager to see and touch the skin he'd revealed. He wanted her so badly he ached with it. And if her response was any indication, she wanted him back with every bit as much fervor. Five, six, seven, eight.

Heath broke the kiss and raised his head to gaze down at his handiwork. Her red bodice had gaped over her breasts, exposing two generous swells above her white embroidered chemise. He met her gaze then, sensing her watching him. Her mossy eyes were glazed with passion, her lips swollen from his kisses. Several of her curls had come free of their pins, tumbling about her shoulders. Even mostly clothed, she was the most gorgeous creature he'd ever seen. He wanted to toss up her skirts, find the slit in her drawers and slide home. Deep inside her.

"Is this why you insisted upon carrying me to my chamber, Your Grace?" she asked, her voice breathless. Dazed. Slightly on guard.

He couldn't blame her. Her words sliced through the haze of yearning clouding his brain. Dear God. What had come over him? He'd meant to aid her, to keep her from harming herself. Instead, he'd closeted himself inside her chamber and all but ravished her. She was an incapacitated woman, for Christ's sake. It wasn't as if she could flee him.

"Of course not," he murmured, furious with himself for his weakness. He had not stooped so low ever in his life. He always treated ladies with care. He certainly never all but made love to them a mere half hour after chatting with them in a bloody maze. "I must apologize, my lady. I have no idea what came over me."

"I'm sure I do," she said, the saucy woman. She lowered her gaze to the obvious bulge in his trousers, which hadn't had the courtesy to abate even a bit. The minx. He should have been scandalized by her boldness, but it only made him harder. Damn it all.

As much as he wanted to continue what he'd begun, he knew he could not. It wouldn't be fair or right. Not for Lady Stokey and certainly not for himself. He was here to acquire a wife. Not a mistress. Even if that mistress was as ravishing and deadly to his sensibilities as the woman before him. He removed his knee from her bed and straightened, knowing he ought to keep his distance from her or else he'd be drawn back into her charms.

"Once again, I apologize. I shall ring for your maid to see to your ankle."

He bowed and turned on his heel, not waiting for her response. The need to flee was just as strong as the need to stay and finish what he'd begun. And Heath knew he must never embark on a seduction with a woman like Lady Stokey. It would only lead to ruin. He'd closed the door to passion a long time ago, and he had no intentions of reopening it now.

Chapter Two

"THE DUKE OF DEVONSHIRE?"

Tia looked at her incredulous sister Cleo, the Marchioness of Thornton, and wondered if she looked as guilty as she felt. Guilty as sin. "What of him?"

"You always called him dull," Cleo reminded her, helpful soul that she was.

Yes, and devil take it, she didn't find him dull any longer. Not one bit. His tongue had been in her mouth. And that had rather changed everything. She blinked, realizing that her sister was awaiting a response. "I never said anything of the sort," she denied.

"You most certainly did. The Duke of Dullness, you called him." Cleo's blue eyes narrowed. "But it scarcely matters. What does matter is that you cannot be inviting scandal upon yourself now. You've Miss Whitney to consider."

Ah, yes. The little American who had been the cause of all her troubles today. With the aid of the duke, Cleo had finally found Tia's wayward charge in the kitchens and had immediately dispatched her back to her room. "I do hope you've posted a guard at the girl's door. I can't have her running about like a common dairy wench all day long." She paused as the implications of her sister's admonishment sank in. "Scandal? How can I possibly be doing anything scandalous? I merely twisted my ankle, and that jackanapes of a duke took it in his head to carry me off."

"And undo your bodice," Cleo hissed. "You're quite fortunate I happened upon you before your maid."

Oh yes. There was that. Heat rushed to Tia's cheeks as she recalled the duke's fingers on her buttons, his hot, wet mouth upon her throat. Who knew that a man as seemingly staid as Devonshire was a man of such overwhelming passions?

"I was having difficulty breathing," she lied. "Bannock laced me too tightly this morning."

"You seemed to be breathing perfectly fine when I saw you downstairs," her sister observed.

Sisters could be such a bother sometimes. Bannock had been sent away to fetch a poultice for Tia's smarting ankle, leaving Tia at Cleo's mercy. She frowned. "Precisely what are you suggesting, my dear?"

"I'm suggesting that when I first happened upon you here in your chamber, you looked as if you'd been thoroughly kissed and half a dozen of your buttons were open. Your chemise was on full display, for heaven's sake."

Well, she *had* been thoroughly kissed. It rather rankled her to admit it, but the duke was a wickedly skilled kisser. Perhaps even the best she'd ever experienced. With his mouth upon hers and his fingers making short work of her bodice, she'd been ready to throw up her skirts and invite him to her bed. It was alarming, her reaction to him. Horrible, in fact. She had already decided to settle him with Miss Whitney. She couldn't very well take him for herself. No matter how delicious a prospect having him in her bed would be. She couldn't deny it now, not after what had happened between them. It was as if she'd been cast into flames. Her heart still thumped madly just to think of him.

"Tia?" Cleo brought Tia out of her musings. Her sister

glared at her. "Truly, I'm beginning to think you injured your brain and not your ankle."

"That makes two of us," Tia grumbled.

"What can you have been thinking?"

"I wasn't thinking, obviously." Tia tested her ankle, hoping she could simply do away with the need for a poultice and for listening to her sister's dressing down both. "He kissed me first, if you must know. I didn't mean for anything untoward to occur. But I admit that I was rather swept away. It's the blasted beard, I tell you. It makes him look so deliciously wicked."

Cleo pressed her fingers to her temples, looking much aggrieved. "Tia, darling. You cannot get swept away, as you call it, now that you've Miss Whitney in your care. Bella will have both our heads if we bring any hint of scandal the girl's way."

Bella was the stepmother to Miss Whitney, sister-in-law to Cleo, and dear friend to Tia. Heavy with child, Bella was not currently able to squire about her stepdaughter. Tia had been happy to step in and help her friend, in no small part because doing so involved procuring an entire wardrobe for the girl. There were few things Tia loved as much as commissioning new gowns.

She raised a brow at her sermonizing sister now. "I must confess it's rich to hear you preaching about propriety and avoiding scandal. You created one of the biggest scandals of our century."

Cleo wrinkled her nose. "Certainly not the century, and we've done away with all that now. Thornton and I are quite respectable and boring."

"Respectable and boring," Tia scoffed. "I daresay those two words shall never be spoken in connection with you."

Cleo and her husband Thornton, a respected advisor to Gladstone, had embarked on a wild affair while Cleo had still been married to the Earl of Scarbrough. The resulting scandal had been enough to nearly ruin Thornton, but in the end, Scarbrough's demise—he'd been drunk and struck down by an omnibus—had enabled Cleo and Thornton to wed. They were deeply in love, and Tia had to admit harboring more than a trifling amount of jealousy at their devoted union. If only her life had not gone so hopelessly awry, perhaps she too would have been happily in love.

But that hadn't been meant to be. The love of her life, the Earl of Denbigh, had wed another. And Tia had married the much older, rather cantankerous Baron, who had left her with a handsome widow's portion when he'd died but little else. He'd certainly never loved her, nor she him.

"You needn't be a bear," Cleo told her, once again interrupting her thoughts. "I'll leave you here to nurse your ankle for the entirety of the party if you can't be nice."

"I don't mind limping about," Tia countered.

Cleo harrumphed. "Nonsense. My maid shall instruct Bannock on the poultice. She's got a marvelous head for herbs, and you'll be right as rain in a trice. I can't have my sister languishing abed when there's a party underway, now can I?"

"I daresay you can't." But Tia had to wonder if perhaps it wouldn't be safer. She didn't think she could be trusted to be in the duke's company after what had transpired between them. She hadn't wanted him to stop. And while she didn't care for being chastised by her sister, Tia knew Cleo was right. She wouldn't dare harm Miss Whitney with her own ill-advised actions. The quicker she found a husband for the girl, the better.

"But heed me well, Tia. You must stay away from the Duke of Devonshire. For your sake and for the sake of Miss Whitney both. I wouldn't dream of seeing either of you hurt." Cleo gave her hand a sisterly pat.

Tia sighed. "You have my word that I shall stay far, far away from the duke. I haven't the slightest desire to see him again."

Liar, accused her inner voice.

Tia promptly told her inner voice to stubble it.

Heath knew he should keep his distance from Lady Stokey. And he'd tried. For three whole dreadfully troublesome days. Following her about like a lovesick swain would only leave him looking the fool, with nothing to show for his efforts save a hard cock. And yet in the drawing room after dinner that evening, he found himself going to her side where she was carefully seated on a gilded settee, her ankle propped on a small stool. Her wily charge Miss Whitney was within eyesight but beyond earshot, and her sister had just beat a hasty retreat to her husband's side, leaving Lady Stokey alone for the moment.

He bowed to her, thinking she looked exceptionally lovely in a black-and-gold-striped silk-and-velvet evening gown. "Lady Stokey."

Her gaze met his, sending an inadvertent jolt through him. "Duke."

He thought of how she'd looked in her chamber, her bodice undone, creamy skin on display, and it nearly undid him. She had been so beautiful, and he'd wanted nothing more than to stay with her, open the rest of her buttons, divest her of every inch of her clothing. Make love to her. Damnation, he never should have approached her, but it was too late now. She was looking at him expectantly, waiting for him to speak.

"How is your ankle, my lady?" he asked at last.

"It's recovering quite nicely, thank you." She seemed ill at ease, her effortless wit from three days ago nowhere in sight. "Do sit down. You're hurting my neck, forcing me to gaze up at you."

Heath sat next to her on the settee, leaving enough room between them so that her voluminous skirts barely brushed his trousers. The scent of violets teased his nose. The twin diamond stars she wore clipped in her hair twinkled at him. "You've received injuries enough of late, I daresay," he drawled, aware that his conversation was appallingly boring.

But he couldn't seem to think of a single worthwhile thing to utter.

"It would certainly seem so." She paused, seeming to consider her next words with care. "I suppose I ought to thank you for your kind assistance the other day."

He'd never heard a more grudging attempt at gratitude in his life. "You suppose you ought to? Pray contain your enthusiasm, my lady or else it shall go straight to my head."

Her eyes widened. "I didn't mean to sound ungrateful."

"Nor did you mean to truly thank me," he returned, suspecting that it wasn't often that anyone dared to oppose her.

Her lovely mouth worked for a few moments, and he thought he'd left her speechless. Finally, she found her voice. "I meant to apologize just as surely as you meant to unhook my buttons, Your Grace."

Heat slid through him at the reminder of what had almost been. He hadn't expected her to refer to his lapse of judgment, particularly when they were in mixed company. "I suppose I ought to apologize for my imprudence," he said, intentionally repeating her phrasing.

She cast him a sidelong glance. "Do you regret it?"

A surge of lust crashed over him as surely as waves on a storm-tossed sea. He couldn't look away from her. "No."

Lady Stokey inhaled, her only reaction. But it spoke volumes. "Perhaps you should."

"Yes," he agreed. "But we cannot always help what we feel."

Her left hand slid from her lap to rest on the cushion of the settee, almost touching his trousers. "And what do you feel, Your Grace?"

Christ, he didn't know what he felt. That was the crux of it all. One moment, he'd been engrossed in a volume of poetry on a sunny day, and the next he'd been ensnared. From the instant he'd look up to see her standing before him, whatever it was inside him that had shifted had yet to settle back into place. He feared it wouldn't.

The need to touch her again was a fierce ache pulsing within him. But he wasn't free to be bold with her as he'd done in her chamber, not with so many other revelers lingering about, waiting for the slightest hint of gossip. Instead, he inched closer to her hand, slowly covering it with his. "I could ask you the same," he said lowly, careful to cast his eyes about the men and women surrounding them. None seemed to be looking their way. He laced his fingers through hers, tightening his hold on her, hiding their entwined hands in the billowing folds of her skirt.

"You're being most unfair, Your Grace."

"Heath," he said, wanting to hear his given name from her lovely lips even if he didn't quite know why.

"Pardon?"

She hadn't removed her touch from his. It pleased him, a reaction that was even more ludicrous than his sitting at her side like a dutiful suitor. Hadn't he just told himself to keep his distance? Hadn't he decided to attend Lord and Lady Thornton's country house party for one purpose, to find a wife? Well, that and the shooting, at any rate. Hadn't he decided there wasn't a lady more unsuitable for that position than the woman whose hand he was now holding?

Yes to all three questions. But none of that slowed him down a bit. "Your Grace sounds so very formal. Call me Heath, if you please," he told her. He was completely, foolishly dim, he thought. Fit for the madhouse.

"Heath," she said softly, considering him with a sidelong glance that drove him wild. "It suits you."

He knew then that he had to have her. He could damn well find any wife he wanted. But Lady Stokey stirred feelings in him he'd thought long dead. As a young man, he'd been ruled by his passions. He'd been heedless, careless. He'd been devoted to his paintings and Bess and little else. Admittedly, he'd thought he'd had all the time in the world to marry the woman he loved. He'd gone abroad to study painting. And then Bess had grown ill. He hadn't made it back to England in time to see her before she'd died.

As he'd watched her coffin sinking into the earth, he'd sworn to himself that he would never again allow his passions to rule him. And he hadn't, restricting himself in the years since Bess' death to women who slaked his needs but made him feel absolutely nothing.

Tia was different, and he knew it down to his bones. She was not the sort of woman it would be easy for a man to forget. But what could the harm be in just one time? One night of desire? He could assuage his desires and then resume his search for a wife. Why not?

"Why are you suddenly so silent?" she asked, dispelling his tumultuous thoughts.

He ran this thumb over hers, toying with her smooth nail. "I suppose I'm bemused."

"By what?"

He saw the instant her protective sister spied them together and read the determination on her face as she caught up Miss Whitney and headed in their direction. "By the things you do to me," he murmured.

"Good heavens," she said, her voice sounding thick.

He slid his touch to her wrist, feeling the rapid beat of her heart there. "I want you, my lady."

"Oh dear." She was breathless now. "You mustn't."

He released her hand as Lady Thornton and Miss Whitney sailed their way. "And unless I'm mistaken, you want me too."

"I very much fear I do," she whispered.

Tia was shaken. The duke's words echoed in her mind long after she had doused the gas lamps and ventured to bed. She waited in the darkness for sleep to claim her, but such a respite was not forthcoming. Her entire body was aflame. She didn't recall ever feeling so aroused, her every sense heightened. The ache that had settled low in her belly, migrating to between her thighs, had not stopped. If anything, it had only been spurred on. Mere thoughts of him, of the way he had kissed her earlier, the way he had opened her bodice, the way he had touched her hand, haunted her. Dear God, the way he had told her that he wanted her. Blatant and bold, as if it were a completely appropriate statement to make to a lady in the midst of a drawing room. As if it hadn't been a statement that would change everything for her.

I want you, my lady.

The sweet, deep voice returned to her, making moisture gather between her thighs. Such simple, stark words had never affected her more. No man had ever been so blunt with her. She'd been wooed and charmed. Men were always eager to ply their charms upon her and win her over. But no man had ever taken the chance to hold her hand before a drawing room of people and tell her exactly what he required of her.

Passion. Desire. Him claiming her, much the way he had with their kiss.

Dear God, she had to admit that she wanted him too. She wanted the Duke of Devonshire, as impossible as it seemed. Cleo had warned her away from him. Tia herself had once thought him staid. Dull. She had Miss Whitney to consider. She couldn't afford to take a lover. Not now.

But she wanted him. She wanted him, and at five-and-twenty, she had to wonder why she couldn't have him. She'd had all the dresses she wanted. All the flirtations. All the lovers. Would it be a sin to take one more without anyone being the wiser?

Tia's eyes fluttered open, staring at the painted ceiling above her. The moonlight crept in from behind heavy drapes to cast her chamber in an ethereal glow. She could barely discern the figure of Cupid, his ready bow and arrow.

And then she heard the unmistakable sound of the door closing on the neighboring bedchamber. She sat up in bed as if she'd just been dealt the blow of the arrow promised her. Miss Whitney had been given the chamber alongside

Tia's, which meant that her troublesome charge was once again about the business of causing mayhem.

Making a sound of exasperation, she threw back the bedclothes and slid from her bed, mindful of her still-sore ankle. The bright shine of the moon enabled her to locate a candle and light it. Hastily, fearing that Miss Whitney would damage her reputation by wandering the house without a chaperone, Tia threw on a dressing gown before grabbing up the candle and hurrying out into the hall.

Miss Whitney, *naturellement*, was nowhere to be seen.

"Drat that girl," she muttered to herself, wondering which direction she ought to try first. What had Tia been thinking to undertake the onerous task of chaperoning a girl who was hell-bent on sending her to an early grave with her flighty antics? Very likely, she'd been charmed by the waifish girl's startling beauty and her rebellious nature, so like Tia's at that age.

And if Tia had been determined to disappear when she'd been a precocious sixteen-year-old, where would she have gone? The library seemed the obvious answer. Tia had never been the voracious reader her sisters were—indeed, she rather found the act of burying one's nose in a book to be deadly dull—but as a young lady, hiding in libraries had been an excellent way to avoid her mama's hawk-like gaze.

In fine dudgeon by the time she limped her way to the library and caught sight of the illuminated cracks around the closed door, Tia stalked inside with as much circumstance as she could muster given the state of her ankle. Her irritation melted, however, at the sight of a wilted-looking Miss Whitney, whose shoulders were hunched in defeat as she browsed a shelf. She spun about, eyes wide, knowing she'd been caught.

"Miss Whitney, would you care to explain what you're doing in the library when you ought to be sleeping safely in your chamber where I left you?" she demanded, though not with as much force as she would have liked. Soft-hearted she may be, but she'd prefer for the girl not to know it.

The sheen of tears marred Miss Whitney' cheeks. She blinked and swiped at them with the back of her hand. "I couldn't sleep, Lady Stokey," Miss Whitney said, her Virginia drawl laced with a defiance that belied her sadness.

She suspected that Miss Whitney was suffering from homesickness and grief combined. The girl's mother had passed away just before her father had brought her to England. But none of that meant she could allow Miss Whitney to continue flouting the rules of polite society. "My dear, I must insist that you either remain in your chamber or seek me out in such a circumstance. While we're in mixed company at a house party, it simply won't do for you to be wandering about. Your reputation depends upon it."

She knew Miss Whitney had come from a genteel upbringing in Virginia, that she'd been raised in a manner befitting a proper young lady. When her father had brought her to England, her comportment had been a trifle rusty, but her stepmother, Lady Bella, had made short work of that minor flaw. The girl's failure to comply with propriety was not from ignorance but rather willfulness.

"What if I don't care for my reputation?" Miss Whitney asked.

"You must," Tia advised, feeling very much like her mother in that moment. Feeling too that perhaps she'd do well to heed her own counsel. "Your virtue is of the utmost importance. Ruin it, and you'll ruin your chance at making a good match."

"Was yours a good match, my lady?" her charge startled her by querying.

No one had ever been so forthright with her before. Indeed, from anyone else, it would have been considered dreadfully ill-mannered. This plucky American was an odd little creature. Tia folded her hands together at her waist, as if in prayer. "I'm sure it was, my dear."

"I reckon that means it wasn't," drawled the cheeky thing.

Tia thought of her marriage to Lord Stokey, a man she

had not particularly cared for, and a man who had not particularly cared for her either. It had been a lonely existence. Widowhood, though equally solitary, suited her far better than being a wife ever had. "It was a good match in terms of title and wealth," she elaborated. "That is all that must be considered."

"What of love?"

Ah, matters of the heart. Tia had been in love once. She hadn't seen the Earl of Denbigh in years. She'd taken great care to avoid him. She'd been young and naïve then, easily given to romantic notions she now knew didn't exist for most. "You'd do well to avoid it at all costs, Miss Whitney. Avoid it as you should avoid sneaking from your chamber without a chaperone." A chill crept through her then, reminding her that they were both far from their warm beds. "Come now, we need to return to our chambers before we wake someone."

"I'm not certain I can sleep," her charge revealed, an embarrassed thread of honesty in her voice.

At last, some truth. Tia thought it promising. Perhaps if she could crack the shell the girl had built around herself, her inclination toward mischief would also abate. Miss Whitney was a slight, depressing figure, so Tia closed the distance between them, putting an arm around the girl's thin shoulders. "When next you can't sleep, come find me, my dear. I have three sisters, you know, and when we were growing up, I was forever having one of them at my door."

"Truly?"

Tia guided Miss Whitney from the library. "Truly. Sad lot of wretches they were. I've always been brave enough to chase the ghosts away."

"You've never seen my ghosts, my lady," Miss Whitney said.

"Perhaps not, but I can assure you I'm brave enough to make anyone's ghosts flee in terror," she promised the girl. After all, if there was one thing she could claim besides her looks and her frivolous lifestyle, it was her bravado. It was also the very thing that, more often than not, landed her in trouble.

Heath had admittedly imbibed too much of Thornton's deceptively delicious whiskey. That was the reason he was walking, not to his chamber where he belonged for the evening, but in the direction of Lady Stokey's chamber instead.

Tia. The mere thought of her, her golden curls, tempting breasts and sweet violet scent, was enough to stiffen his cock. After all his years of staid living and doing penance for allowing his passionate nature to rule his head, it was too damn ironic that one woman could so easily undo him. She made him weak. Made him want what he ought not want. Made him hot with desire, eager to fall back into passion's fiery grip.

Most definitely, he should be turning about at once and venturing back to the safe confines of his chamber. He could put his hand to work just as well and it would lead to a far more sensible outcome than tangling with Tia ever could. But it wouldn't be even close to the same, and he knew it. Knowledge was a horrible thing at times, for he also knew which door belonged to her. And his feet were intent upon carrying him to it.

He reached the hall where Tia's chamber was a mere few feet away. The creaking of a door stilled him. He snuffed the candle he'd been carrying just as an undeniably feminine form sailed into the hall, illuminated by the candle in her hand. The gas lamps had long since been turned out for the night, leaving the inhabitants of Penworth no better than their predecessors centuries before. Divested of its technologies, humanity was all the same, regardless of time.

Heath held his breath as the flickering glow bathed the woman's face. She limped in his direction, oblivious to his presence. The moment recognition slid through him, an

SCARLETT SCOTT

arrow of unadulterated lust shot straight through him. He swore he caught the faint scent of violets. Her hair was unbound, the golden curls she ordinarily wore elaborately styled hanging freely almost to her waist. He swallowed, wondering what it would be like to have her riding him, her hair a gilded curtain around him.

"Jesus," he muttered to himself, thinking he must be beyond inebriated to be standing in the darkness, watching Lady Stokey as if he were a common thief waiting for the household to go to bed so he could pilfer the silver.

She stilled, apparently having heard his self-chastising. Hell. He'd supposed himself too far away for her to eavesdrop. She held the candle higher, peering in his direction. "Who's there?"

Her taper cast a half-moon before him. It stopped just short of revealing him. He debated the wisdom of stepping forward, entering the light. If he had a modicum of sense, he'd spin on his heel and disappear into the darkness from whence he'd come. He would leave her alone. Purge her from his mind. Settle on a nice biddable young lady for his wife. Forget the desire casting a heady spell over him. Never again think about the luscious body hiding beneath her dressing gown. Or peeling the dressing gown from her while he kissed her senseless.

Devil take it.

He took several steps forward, stopping only when he was a mere foot from her. Her eyes were wide, meeting his and sending a new jolt of awareness straight through him. "Heath?"

Hearing his name on her lips was his undoing. If she'd called him "Your Grace" or even "Devonshire", he'd have been able to resist her. At least, that's what he told himself as he closed the final distance between them, his hands going to her waist as if they belonged there. And perhaps they did. Tonight, if not every other.

"What are you doing here?" she demanded, sounding breathless.

"That should be obvious," he whispered, his gaze lowering to her seductive mouth.

"You're mad," she returned, but she licked her lips, giving herself away.

He knew she felt the same reckless need burning between them. He knew she was equally as powerless to resist. "Perhaps I am," he agreed, his hands sliding to her bottom, round and firm. Thank God she wasn't wearing a bustle. He filled his palms with her soft flesh and gave her a gentle squeeze. She gasped. "But somehow, I rather think you don't mind."

"We cannot do this," Tia hissed. But her body gave her away. She arched her back, driving her softness against his erect cock.

He leaned down, wanting to kiss her. He felt more intoxicated in her presence than he'd been on the whiskey he'd drunk. "Why not?"

"My ward is in the chamber next door," she said, surprising him with her response.

He'd expected her to say that they shouldn't dally with each other. That a quick tumble at a country house party was beneath her. But he hadn't expected Miss Whitney to be her sole objection. He would have cursed the girl if she hadn't been the reason for bringing Tia into his arms in the first place.

"Come with me to my chamber," he suggested, amazing even himself with the bold proposal. "I haven't any inconvenient wards as neighbors. Merely old Lord Tuttleworth, and he's quite deaf."

She smiled, and he knew she wouldn't require much convincing. She cast a furtive glance over her shoulder, as if she suspected someone to suddenly appear and demand to know what they were about. When she turned back to him, she caught her lower lip between her teeth. "I'm afraid only one sort of thing could happen were I to follow you to your chamber, sir."

"Precisely." He couldn't resist the temptation another

instant. He lowered his mouth to hers, kissing her as he'd done in her chamber. She responded instantly, opening to him, her tongue sliding against his. He broke off the kiss with great reluctance, knowing that if he didn't stop he'd soon be ready to rip off her dressing gown and have her right there in the hall where anyone could happen upon them. "I believe we've already had this discussion, my lady."

"So we have, Your Grace." She paused, her big eyes searching his. "I'm not certain it's wise."

"What has wisdom to do with it?" He ran a finger over her smooth cheek. "If it's wisdom you're looking for, you aren't going to find it lingering here in a darkened hallway with me."

That she was lingering at all told them both that she was tottering on the edge the same as he was. One small push, and they'd both fall headlong into the passion that threatened to consume them both.

"I'm not looking for a lover," she told him, as if it mattered.

Perhaps it did to her, but he didn't give a damn. "Nor am I." No need to mention he was looking for a wife. At the moment, all he was looking for was a blonde siren with curls to her waist and the sweetest lips he'd ever tasted.

She swallowed. "What if someone should hear?"

He grinned, sensing the scales had been tipped firmly in his favor. "Tuttleworth snores like a bear."

"Very well." Her lashes lowered before she gave him a penetrating, direct stare that aroused him every bit as much as her proximity had. She was a woman to be reckoned with, his Tia. "I'm sure I shall regret this in the morning, but I'm in the mood to be wicked tonight."

It was all he needed to hear. He grabbed her hand in his before she could change her mind. "Let's be wicked together."

Tia didn't know what worm had decided to infiltrate her brain. But it was most assuredly a devious one, the sort that caused her to fling all sense of propriety out the nearest window. For it was half past one in the morning and despite all logic, all common sense, all warnings from her sister, Tia was holding the Duke of Devonshire's hand, slipping through the shadowy hallways at his side as fast as her ankle would allow.

On her way to his bedchamber.

The very notion should have sent her running in the opposite direction. Instead, it made her heart race and sent moisture between her thighs. A delicious ache of anticipation bloomed within her. She'd never done something so foolish. At any moment, they could be caught. Her reputation would be in shreds.

Somehow, the danger of being caught only heightened her desire for him.

She couldn't help herself. Something had happened the moment their eyes had met in the gardens. It all seemed fated that this wild, carefree moment should be unfolding. Nothing in her life had ever felt more dangerous. But nothing in her life had ever felt more right either.

As she followed the duke into the west wing of Penworth, a door suddenly creaked open. He reacted faster than she, dousing her candle and swinging her into a nearby alcove. He shielded her with his body, holding her in his strong arms. A woman's throaty giggle mingled with a man's low, rumbling voice not far from them. Tia's heart hammered against her breast at the possibility of being seen. She held her breath.

The duke's hands were on her waist, anchoring her to him, heating her even through the layers of her dressing gown and nightdress. She felt as if she were a young girl, hiding from her parents and chaperones. It was ridiculous to be wrapped up in the Duke of Devonshire's arms, sneaking about in the darkness, risking everything for the possibility of passion.

He kissed her again then, and she realized that it was also wonderful. His lips angled over hers, firm and demanding. Claiming. Taking. Her hands went around his neck, her fingers sinking into his hair. The scrape of his well-trimmed beard on her sensitive skin was incredibly erotic. His tongue sank inside her mouth, making her ache with want.

One night indulging her desire, that was all she yearned for. Give her tonight, and by morning she would be perfectly ready to behave. Well, to mostly behave, anyway. It wasn't as if she could turn into her prudish grandmamma overnight, after all.

His palm slid up, over her waist to her left breast, cupping her. Her nipple hardened instantly, her body's response reminding her that the likelihood of her ever becoming prudish was frightfully minimal indeed. She moaned against the duke's lips, shifting so that her leg hooked round his hip, her nightgown and dressing robe the only barrier between the hard ridge of him and her willing flesh.

Dear, sweet heavens.

If she wasn't careful, she'd allow him to take her right here in this darkened alcove. The thought brought at least a modicum of sanity to cool her ardor. She broke their kiss with great reluctance, tipping her head back to allow the drafty air of the corridor to bathe her heated cheeks as she caught her breath.

He dragged his mouth down over her throat, nipping and licking at her skin as he went. His fingers found her nipple beneath the layers of fabric separating her from him, rolling and pinching. Pleasure swirled through her, sharp, swift, and sweet. She didn't recall ever wanting another man as she wanted Devonshire.

Heath. For he would forever be Heath to her now. He would never again be simply the duke. They had crossed boundaries, trespassed in ways that could not be undone. And before the night was over, they would venture across even more lines. They would become lovers.

The reminder brought a jolt of reality back to her. She had followed him this far. But her conscience reminded her that she couldn't afford to act with such a blatant disregard for societal rules. She had Miss Whitney to consider, and her ward had shown her a weak side tonight that had melted Tia's cold heart.

"We could be seen," she whispered, trying to cling to her rapidly dwindling ability to tell him no.

"Damn it," he muttered, pulling his lips from her neck. "You make me lose my head."

She could easily say the same, but she kept silent, releasing him and stepping back as far as the alcove would allow. She listened for the sound of the lovers who had interrupted their impromptu race to Heath's chamber. It seemed they had found their way to wherever they'd be spending the night.

His fingers entwined with hers. "How fares your ankle?"

His concern touched her. She thought inexplicably of the Cupid fresco on the ceiling in her chamber. Perhaps the arrow had found its mark after all. Tia forced herself to speak. "It pains me a bit, but it shall do."

"I'll carry you," he said in august, ducal tones that brooked no argument.

"Nonsense," she said anyway, not cowed a bit. He'd already played the role of savior with her.

"Stubborn woman," he murmured, scooping her up into his arms before she could offer further protestation.

"Stubborn man," she countered.

"Hush," he ordered before taking her from the alcove.

Tia clung to him, rather enjoying the way he so effortlessly carted her about. His strength was infinitely arousing. Being near enough to breathe in his scent and sink her fingers into his silky, golden hair wasn't precisely a chore either. She kept silent as he stalked down the darkened length of the hall. Her candle was long forgotten. She supposed she'd dropped it back in the alcove, but it hardly mattered now, for the man carrying her off had apparently reached his chamber door.

He opened it, crossed the threshold and kicked it closed at their backs. The lamps had been left lit, presumably by his manservant. Heath lowered her to her feet. They were well and truly alone, no chance of being seen or overheard now.

His maddening words returned to her in that moment, and she wasn't sure if it was a warning or a herald. *Let's be wicked together.* Tonight, it would seem she was prepared to be wicked indeed.

Chapter Three

HEATH STARED DOWN AT TIA. DEAR GOD, she was beautiful, gazing up at him with her emerald-colored eyes, her long hair framing her face, her lips swollen from his kisses. He could scarcely believe the goddess before him was in his chamber. That she had accepted his mad, half-drunk proposition. But the alluring scent of violets reminded him he wasn't dreaming.

For the last few years, he'd lived a life of quiet respectability. He'd thrown himself into duty, into repairing his estate, into living a life that was above reproach. And now he was about to cast his time of penance into the wind. His reaction to Tia shook him, he couldn't deny it. He'd never experienced a pull so strong.

Except for his painting.

The unwelcome thought gave him pause. He hadn't taken brush to canvas in five years. After Bess' death, giving up the passion that had once consumed him had seemed the only fitting punishment for leaving her to die alone. In all that time, he'd never once missed creating the artwork that had once driven him. But he couldn't keep himself from noticing the way the light played across Tia's lovely features, bringing her burnished curls to life, rendering her a sultry Venus before his eyes.

The old itch returned. He wanted to paint her. Nude. In his bed. Waiting for him to take her. The mere thought of it had him so hard he could scarcely form a coherent sentence. Good Christ, what was wrong with him?

"Is something amiss?" she asked quietly, apparently sensing the change in him.

He took a breath, trying to rein in the wild emotions stampeding through his chest. He hadn't brought her to his chamber to paint her. He'd brought her here to have his wicked way with her. "No," he lied. There wasn't a need, after all, to unburden his darkness upon so light and gorgeous a creature. "I was merely admiring your beauty."

Her eyes narrowed, but if she didn't believe him, she chose not to say so. "I very much like your beard," she startled him by revealing as she reached up to caress his jaw.

Her simple touch sent another surge of desire through him. He caught her hand, pressing a kiss to her fingers as if they were meeting in a drawing room rather than his chamber. "Do you?"

"Oh yes." Her lashes fluttered over her eyes, briefly shutting him out. "I like its rasp against my skin."

Heath kissed a path to her wrist, turning her palm up. Her heartbeat was a steady thrum against his lips. He rather enjoyed employing a slow, unhurried seduction on her, and he fancied she felt the same. He rubbed his beard against her inner wrist, testing her reaction. "Do you like this?"

She licked her lips. "Yes."

Heath found the fastenings of her dressing gown, pulling them open to reveal a white nightgown beneath, and stepped closer to her, running his beard along her throat. "And this?"

"Yes," she said, her voice a throaty murmur. Her hands fluttered to his shoulders as she rubbed her cheek against him in response. "Oh my, yes."

Her scent invaded his senses again. His fingers went to

the line of buttons on the front of her nightgown, pulling them from their moorings. Slowly, inch by inch, her creamy skin was revealed to him. The tempting curves of her breasts came into view. Damn, but he wanted her naked. He cupped the heavy mounds in his hands, gratified when her hard nipples poked hungrily into his palms.

Heath lowered his head and ran his beard over her nearly bared bosom. "What of this?"

"Mmm."

He liked the sound of that, so he flicked open a few more buttons and peeled away her gown, pulling it down her shoulders and arms so that every inch of her was visible to him from the waist up. Her breasts were full and round, the taut peaks the same luscious pink as her lips. A slight flush tinged her skin where he had rubbed her with his beard. He liked seeing his mark on her. The signs that, for tonight at least, she was his.

She was watching him through half-closed eyelids. "Kiss me, Heath."

The sound of his name in her throaty voice was as erotic as her standing half-nude before him. "Where?" he asked, framing her breasts with his hands as he once more lowered his head. He pressed a kiss on one stiff nipple. "Here?" He moved to the other, kissing it too. "Or here?"

"I'm not certain," she murmured. "Perhaps you should try it again."

The naughty thing. He glanced up at her as he drew one of her nipples into his mouth, sucking. The open, unabashed expression of passion on her face was nearly enough to make him gather her back up in his arms and take her straight to bed. But he couldn't do that. Not yet. First, he would make her mad with wanting.

He used his teeth, gently tugging, gratified when he won a moan from her. Her fingers sank into his hair. He sucked again before dragging his mouth away at last, her nipple leaving his mouth with a wet, lusty-sounding pop. "Shall I try it again?"

She didn't answer him. Instead, she pulled his face to hers, fusing their lips in a passionate, open-mouthed kiss. He ran his tongue against hers, his cock going even more rigid. He wanted to be deep inside her in exactly the same way. Heath's ability to leisurely woo her was about to disappear faster than a gold pocket watch in White Chapel.

With a groan, he tore his mouth from hers before going to work on shedding his evening attire. His jacket went first, flung to the floor, followed by his waistcoat. She helped him with his necktie, seemingly as eager for him as he was for her. He didn't even bother with the buttons on his shirt. He rent them, tearing from end to end and shrugging his shirt away.

"I fear you've done it irreparable damage." Tia's gaze lingered on his bare torso like a caress.

He caught her to him, starving for the feel of her bare flesh pressed to his. He wasn't disappointed. The tempting points of her breasts poked his chest. "I don't give a damn," he told her, just before taking her mouth once more.

They moved as one toward the bed, he leading and she taking steps backward. In those few steps, he tried to summon his conscience, to remind himself that he had not come to Penworth for a dalliance but to find a wife. That he had come so far only to fall back down into the abyss once more. That the glorious woman in his arms deserved more than one night of reckless lovemaking.

But his cock was a hard reminder in his trousers that this night could only end in one way. He and Lady Stokey may have begun the house party as strangers, but they would end it as lovers. When they reached the bed, he stopped them, reminded of his need to remove her nightgown the rest of the way. He pressed kisses down her throat, stopping only when he reached the hollow between her breasts. His fingers located the thin line of buttons keeping him from heaven.

Tia, perhaps sensing his urgency, grabbed both sides of her half-discarded nightdress and shimmied her hips, pulling it down until it landed in a puddle of fine linen at her feet. She stood before him, naked and lovelier than he could have possibly imagined. The urge to paint her rose again within him, stronger than before. Her form was impossibly perfect, her waist nipped, her hips full, her mound flanked by pale, exquisite thighs.

His mouth went dry as he stared at her, and he knew in that instant that despite all his promises to himself, despite his not having created so much as a charcoal sketch in the last few years, he would paint her. It was inevitable. As inevitable as this moment between them now had been. From the second she'd wandered around the corner in the maze, prettier than a butterfly and every bit as delicate, Fortune's wheel had dealt him a turn that was as thrilling as it was dangerous. Because he could very easily lose himself in the passions he'd once known. And no other woman had ever brought him so close to pitching himself back into the flame.

"Do you not like what you see?" Tia asked then, interrupting his weighty thoughts with her hesitant voice.

He realized then that she must have misread him. If he hesitated, it was merely because of the weight of his thoughts, not because she wasn't the most breathtakingly gorgeous woman he'd ever seen nude before him. Because she most assuredly was. No other could compare to her.

"On the contrary," he reassured her, catching her hand in his and pressing it to his brick-hard cock. Her fingers found the outline of his arousal, skillfully working him from root to tip through his trousers. The breath fled from his lungs.

"Do you like this?" Her tone turned teasing, sultry, as she repeated the very question he had asked of her not long before.

She was a woman who knew what she wanted, a lusty woman with an unapologetic sense of who she was. She knew what she wanted and wasn't afraid to take it. To follow him through the halls of Penworth when at any second a door could've opened or a servant could've rounded the bend, catching them. Damn if her forthright nature, her willingness to meet him seduction for seduction didn't arouse him even more.

"Perhaps you would like this," she murmured, pulling open the fastening of his trousers.

His cock sprang free and he'd never been happier that he had a habit of eschewing small clothes. He couldn't abide by the extra layer. Never had. Now the lack of a barrier seemed fortuitous indeed. Especially when Tia gripped his shaft and sank to her knees. Dear, sweet Christ. She was going to take him into her mouth.

Her brilliant gaze fixed firmly on his, she licked a circle around the tip. "What of this?"

"Jesus, Tia." The gentleman in him reminded him that he ought not to simply abandon all sense of proper conduct and allow her to suck him as if she were no better than a common doxy. But he couldn't summon the restraint. Her lips parted and she took his cock deep into her mouth. He couldn't suppress the moan that escaped him, couldn't stop from jerking into her, couldn't keep his hand from sifting through the soft cloud of her hair, wrapping it around his hand.

She sucked him back into her throat, then retreated to lick along the underside of his shaft, circling him with her tongue. The sight of her before him, her bare feet peeking from beneath the swells of her sweetly rounded bottom, her full breasts grazing his thighs as she worked his cock, was enough to make him fear that he would spend himself right then and there. She cupped his balls as she sucked and took him back into her throat. Every part of his body clamored for release.

No, damn it. Not yet.

Before he lost himself entirely, he used the hand he'd fisted in her hair to hold her still when she reached his tip again. "Stop, darling."

She flicked her tongue against him, giving him a look

that was part siren, part innocent. "You don't like it?"

"I love it." Damn it all. One night of her would never be enough for him. He saw it for what it was. He was hopelessly, helplessly in her thrall. "But I want to give you pleasure."

He wondered then what sort of other lovers she'd had. The kind who had accepted her gift of pleasure without returning it? Very likely. He would show her what she had been missing. He caught her arms and pulled her to her feet before guiding her to the bed and giving her a hand up. She lay back, watching him wordlessly.

"Open your legs for me," he said, part command, part request. It was his turn to ply sensual torture, and he'd never wanted anything more in his life than he wanted to make Tia come on his tongue.

Tia was sprawled across the Duke of Devonshire's bed, her body on fire for him. He stood before her, dropping his trousers, his eyes a possessive brand that never left her. His cock was magnificent and hard, jutting from between his thighs. She had taken him in her mouth, and it had aroused her beyond belief. Never before had she been so bold and wanton with a lover, but something about the man before her brought out a wild streak she hadn't known she possessed.

His demand that she open her legs to him made a new ache of desire pulse there. She was already wet for him, utterly ready. Tia watched him as he joined her on the bed, his figure all lean angles and rigid muscle. He must have indulged in a great deal of labor to have such a fine form, she thought before he lowered his head to press a kiss to her inner thigh.

Good heavens.

Then, all thought ceased to exist, for his wicked mouth moved next to the plump nub peeking from between her folds. His tongue shot out to tease her, playing over her with a practiced skill that had Tia jerking off the bed as pure pleasure shot straight through her. She moaned as he sucked hard on her, the same way he had her nipples earlier, drawing her very near to the edge of release. No one had ever pleasured her in this way, loving her with his lips and tongue until she was frenzied beneath him.

He sank a finger inside her, probing deep as he continued licking and sucking. The breath left her lungs and she arched into him, wanting more. Deeper. All of him. Suddenly, the sensations were too much. She was spiraling helplessly out of control. Her release was swift and hard as he slid a second finger inside her, making her body quiver as white-hot bliss blossomed from her core, spreading to overtake her.

Heath rose over her, his mouth glistening with her wetness, unbearably handsome. He looked in that instant, with his blond hair, powerful body and masculine beard, like a Viking conqueror of old come to take her. She reached for him, pulling him down atop her, thinking that she could live the rest of her life and never forget this night, the raw desire, the heights to which he had taken her.

He guided his cock to her slick entrance, the tip grazing her in a maddening way. She wanted him inside, buried to the hilt. A crude word rose in her mind then, one ladies dared not say or think, but one that seemed to fit in its elemental way. Fuck. Yes, that was it. She wanted him to fuck her. The sentiment was so wicked she didn't dare say it aloud.

"Please," she said instead. "I need you inside me."

Tia was not a woman who begged. Indeed, she was quite proud, oftentimes to a fault. But he had brought her low. Made her into someone she didn't even recognize, someone willing to thumb her nose at propriety, someone willing to risk scandal and follow a man she barely knew to his chamber and his bed all for a taste of passion. Even if it had been worth it. Every delicious second of it.

"Not yet," he told her in a voice low and laden with promise.

He took her nipple into his mouth again, drawing on the taut peak until she cried out, forgetting that she ought to keep quiet. He licked a lazy circle around it before glancing up at her. "Hush, darling. We don't want to wake Tuttleworth."

And then he caught her sensitive nipple between his teeth, tugging. Oh, the wretch. How did he expect her to keep her silence when he was tormenting her so? She bit her lip, trying to keep her cries under control. But he was hell-bent on driving her wild, and it was increasingly difficult to rein herself in.

The tip of his cock sank inside her then, and she couldn't help it. To the devil with Tuttleworth. She moaned and jerked against him, wrapping her legs around his hips, welcoming him into her. Tia didn't want to go slowly. She wanted fast and hard and deep. She wanted to be claimed. Devoured.

"Damn it," he muttered, surging inside her another measure.

She knew he'd wanted to go slowly, and she had to admit that she rather enjoyed his inability to deny himself. It meant that he wanted her as much as she wanted him. It gave her a sense of power. "Is something amiss?" she asked, keeping her tone deceptively innocent as she moved again, bringing him deeper.

"Minx," he accused without heat. He sucked her other nipple and then braced his arms on either side of her head, gazing down at her. "I wanted to give you pleasure."

"Oh, you have," she assured him, jerking her hips once more. "And you will."

"Sweet Jesus." He groaned, and then he lost himself completely, surging into her so swiftly that it quite took her breath. He was buried inside her to the hilt before withdrawing only to sink inside her again.

Her fingers tunneled through his hair, pulling his mouth

down to hers for a lush, open-mouthed kiss. His tongue tangled with hers. She was very close to reaching another climax. The combined sensation of him within her, his mouth on hers, his hard body pinning her to the bed, was enough to undo her. He seemed to know precisely how and what she wanted, thrusting into her, consuming her with his mouth and his cock both.

She kissed him back, matched his rhythm thrust for thrust. Their coupling was fast and furious. Decadent and thrilling. Everything she wanted. Suddenly, she couldn't get enough of him. He reached between them to toy with the plump nub hidden within her folds again, flicking it back and forth with just the right amount of pressure. Pleasure shot through her. The combination of it all was too much. Too potent. She was going to lose herself.

"Heath," she cried out, climaxing so quickly it was as if a bolt of lightning had struck her. Potent, powerful. But oh so wonderful.

He pounded into her, still nipping at her lips with small, quick kisses. And then, suddenly, he lost himself inside her, his seed spilling deep into her womb with a series of rapid strokes. Tia twisted up off the bed, taking as much of him as she could.

"Tia," he said against her mouth. "Ah, sweet Tia."

She had never felt closer to another human being in her life. An exquisite sensation enveloped her. She knew well enough to know the bliss that washed over a woman after a skillful bout of lovemaking. But this was different. Different enough to excite her and frighten her all at the same time. He kissed her again, deliberately and open-mouthed. Possessive. And any misgivings Tia may have had were banished. For the moment, at least.

Heath woke to the earliest glimmers of morning sunlight filtering in through the drawn curtains. He blinked and rolled over, stretching. Damn, he hadn't felt this bloody good in quite some time. His body was relaxed, satisfied and replete. A deep sense of satisfaction filled him all the way to his bones, something he hadn't felt in as long as he could recall.

Not since Bess.

Thoughts of his betrothed now brought reality to him with an uncompromising jolt. Tia. Good God. He had fucked Lady Stokey last night as if she were no better than a well-practiced whore. Had carted her back to his chamber with shocking disregard for her injured ankle, stripped her bare, sucked and licked every delicious inch of her beautiful body before burying his cock in her hot, tight cunny.

And he had spent himself inside her.

He never acted with such an alarming lack of self-control. He knew well enough to avoid siring bastards. His own grandfather was rumored to have had as many as a dozen scattered throughout the countryside, perhaps more, in his lifetime. He'd seen his fellow lords fall into that trap too many times to count. He'd vowed to never be the same.

And indeed, in the last few years, while he'd slaked his needs where he could, he had certainly never acted with such complete, foolish disregard for what was right. For what he'd always believed was right.

Groaning, he cast a glance about the chamber to confirm that Tia was truly gone. Aside from the dent in the feather pillow alongside him and a lone strand of waist-length golden hair, it was as if she'd never been there at all. But he remembered. Good Lord did he remember.

Every searing second of the night before. He didn't know how they could ever go back to polite exchanges. What they had shared was too all-consuming and far too powerful. He didn't know what it meant. They had been strangers, traveling in the same circles of society without ever truly knowing each other. And now they were lovers.

"Shit," he muttered, passing a hand over his face. She must have wandered back to her chamber in the cold dark of the night, her injured ankle making her progress unbearably slow.

He should have been a gentleman and at least escorted her back instead of rutting and then passing into oblivion. What the hell was the matter with him? He didn't carry off women he scarcely knew and make love to them at house parties. He'd been determined to find a wife. Instead, he'd found a woman he should never want. A woman he should have never touched.

A woman who could, at this moment, be carrying his child.

Oddly, the thought didn't alarm him in the way it undoubtedly should. Rather, it warmed him. Tia had surprised him. She was sensual and giving. Beautiful to be sure. Open to pleasure and passion in an unashamed manner that made him want her all the more. She was everything he should never want in a wife.

But somehow, he couldn't shake the odd sensation that maybe, just maybe, he'd found what he'd been looking for all along. And then he couldn't resist rolling back over and burying his face in the pillow opposite him.

Ah, yes.

Violets.

It was only the fourth day of Cleo and Thornton's house party, and Tia had already gone down the path of no return with the Duke of Devonshire. She'd woken up in the inkiness of the night in his bed, her head on his chest. They'd both been naked, entangled as though they were longtime lovers. It hadn't escaped her just how perfectly they fit together.

Regret unfurled within her later that morning as she sat in her sister's sitting room alongside Cleo and Miss Whitney, attempting to appear normal to them. Attempting to appear as if she hadn't been ravished the night before by a man she'd once mistakenly supposed to be boring as a bowl of porridge.

Dear Lord, the mere thought of what he'd done to her, what they'd done together, was enough to make her cheeks flame. She held her breath, praying Cleo was too engrossed in her discussion of the entertainments she'd planned for the unfolding house party to notice.

"Tia, darling, I daresay you're looking quite flushed," her sister commented suddenly.

Drat. "I find it excessively warm in here," she offered in her most flippant tone. "I thought country estates were all supposed to be rambling, draughty affairs. It feels like summer in here."

"I find it cold," drawled Miss Whitney, no help at all.

Tia glared at the girl. "It's warm for England, I tell you."

Cleo's eyes had narrowed upon her, and Tia knew a sinking sensation in her stomach. She suspected she'd been caught. "Perhaps you're feverish, my dear."

Tia made a show of fixing the draping of her silk skirt. "I'm the picture of health."

"Perhaps it is merely your ears that are the problem then," her sister suggested. "I was just telling you that I have the most brilliant plan for this evening's entertainments."

Tia didn't wish to think about something as trivial as house party entertainments at the moment. She felt as if she were walking about with a sign around her neck proclaiming to all what she'd been about the night before. Wickedness.

"Oh?" she managed, desperately distracted.

"Indeed. We're to have duets before dinner. Miss Whitney has a lovely voice, and I've come up with just the thing. We shall partner her with the Duke of Devonshire," Cleo proclaimed, giving Tia a knowing look. "It is a wonderful idea, is it not?"

"No," she snapped before she could think better of it. "It is an altogether horrid idea."

Dear God, she couldn't very well attempt to marry off her charge to the man she'd shamelessly bedded the night before. Everything had changed. Two pairs of eyes pinned her to her seat. She felt rather as if she were a pressed flower in a botany display.

"Why ever not?" her sister asked before sipping at her tea.

"He's too old," Tia managed. "And boring. A young thing like Miss Whitney requires someone more of an age with her."

"He doesn't seem terribly decrepit," Miss Whitney ventured. "I do find him handsome as well."

"His whiskers are making many of the ladies here sigh," Cleo agreed.

Tia contemplated kicking her sister in the shins but thought better of it. She'd likely only injure her own toes, and her ankle was still paining her. "I don't find his whiskers at all alluring," she felt compelled to say. "I would imagine they're quite abrasive to the touch."

In truth, his beard was lovely. She knew firsthand just how delectable it felt upon her skin. The memory of it rubbing between her thighs was particular cause for the leap in her pulse and a renewed flush over her cheeks.

"If I didn't know better, I'd say you're smitten with the duke yourself."

Her sister's all-too-perceptive assessment robbed the breath from Tia's lungs. Was she smitten with Heath? Dear heavens, Cleo made it sound as if she were a young girl in short skirts, sighing over her first love. Tia's had been a handsome stable boy. When her mother had discovered her infatuation, the lad had been promptly moved to their Scottish estate, and that had been the end of Tia's lusty sighs over a man she shouldn't want.

Until now.

She was aware of Cleo and Miss Whitney awaiting her response. "Don't be foolish," she forced herself to say. "I couldn't give a fig for the Duke of Devonshire."

Cleo muttered something beneath her breath that sounded suspiciously like *liar*.

Or maybe it was merely Tia's own heart betraying her.

Tia stopped outside the yellow drawing room, casting a glance over each shoulder, her hand poised over the knob. No one was about, everyone apparently having been otherwise occupied by Cleo's lavish entertainments. But she knew one man who was not so distracted. Or at least she hoped she did. For after wrestling over what she ought to do next since that morning, she'd finally decided to summon him. Her lady's maid, Bannock, was infinitely trustworthy for the delivery of important missives. And fortunately for Tia, she knew Penworth well enough by now to know which rooms would not be in use.

The yellow drawing room had been an easy choice. Asking the Duke of Devonshire to meet her within had not been. With a deep, fortifying breath, she turned the knob and crossed the threshold lest she change her mind and flee.

He was waiting for her within, his back to her as the door closed behind her with a gentle snick. He spun about at her entrance, his blue gaze searing her. Gads, he was handsome. Looking at him now brought back all the sins he'd wrought upon her willing body. Lying with him had been stupid. Wonderful, but wholly foolish. Because she could not look at him without thinking about every delicious act in which they'd engaged.

He was looking at her expectantly. Understandable since it was she who had called upon him to join her. *Say something riveting*, she told herself. *Something alarmingly witty.*

But nothing would come to her weakened mind.

"It is a lovely day," she said lamely, inwardly cursing herself for not being capable of managing more intelligent speech. He rather overwhelmed her.

He inclined his head. "It is indeed. You wished to see me?"

The formal tones underlying his voice coupled with his

debonair appearance made her unaccountably ill at ease. She clasped her hands at her waist and considered him with as much composure as she could muster. "Yes. Thank you for meeting me."

He stared at her, and she swore she could feel his gaze as surely as a mark upon her skin. "I gather you've something of more import on your mind than the weather."

"Of course." *Stupid woman*, she cursed herself. She had meant to appear utterly unmoved by him. Instead, she was acting as brainless as a miss who'd fallen in love with her first dancing partner at her comeout ball. She forced herself to recall why she'd brought him here in the first place. "I wished to tell you that we cannot carry on in this manner."

Heath raised a brow, every inch the impeccable, arrogant duke. "And what manner is that, Lady Stokey?"

Oh dear. She, who had always prided herself on her remarkable aplomb and composure in polite circumstances—her sister's presence not withstanding—blushed so furiously that her cheeks burned. "You know very well the manner," she managed to say.

"Oh?" He strode toward her, closing the safe distance that separated them and taking with him her defenses.

The nearer he stood, the easier it was to allow his gaze to melt her insides. Being in his presence was very much like standing too close to a raging fire. And she feared she'd get burned. She licked her lips. "Yes."

"Would you care to elucidate?" He took another step closer, until the tips of his shoes almost brushed the hem of her handsome dress.

Had she ever thought herself bold? Something about the way he was looking at her, as if he wanted to devour her, made it difficult indeed to make sense of the thoughts careening wildly through her head. But he was expecting her response, and she was willing to rise to the occasion. If it was an elucidation he wanted, an elucidation he would get.

"I cannot come to your bed again," she said bluntly. "There. You've made me say it."

A slow smile spread across his sensual mouth. "What if I should come to yours?"

Her breath fled from her lungs. He was close enough to touch. So close that she could feel the warmth emanating from his big body. So close she could see those gray flecks in his eyes again. Could smell him. The way he had made love to her last night had been the perfect blend of tenderness and fierce passion. He made her feel as if she were wound as tightly as a pocket watch. She looked to the paintings hanging on the wall behind him, trying to steady herself.

What if he should come to her bed, he had asked her. And he knew the answer as well as she did. She would not deny him. But she'd made up her mind that she needed to put distance between them. That she could not allow herself to indulge in an affair, not with Miss Whitney so near. Not at her sister's home. Not when Tia herself was so incredibly drawn to the man before her after just one night in his arms.

"Tia? You haven't answered my question." His voice was low and insistent, washing over her like a caress. He reached out and caught her chin in his fingers, tipping it up so that she was helplessly caught in his gaze.

"You know we should not," she forced herself to tell him, even as her body cried out in protest. Every bit of her was clamoring for more of his touch, more of his kisses. More of him.

"You're perfectly right," he surprised her by saying. "What we did last night was bloody foolish."

"Yes." But she was robbed of the ability to further speak by his thumb's gentle exploration of her lower lip.

"It must never be repeated," he added, his head dipping lower until his breath fanned over her mouth.

"Never," she agreed. His thumb continued to run in a slow swipe, from left to right, tantalizing her. He cupped her face with his other hand. She couldn't have been more still had she been carved of marble. The anticipation coursing through her threatened to overtake her. To break her resolve to resist him.

"I certainly shouldn't kiss you again then, should I?" he asked, his gaze searing.

"No," she breathed.

In the next instant, his mouth was on hers, open and demanding. With a moan, she gave in, kissing him back with every bit of the yearning sweeping over her. Her hands went to his shoulders. The whiskers she had so recently mocked provided a delicious abrasion on her sensitive skin. When his tongue tangled with hers, her nipples hardened beneath the layers of fabric and boning separating them.

As if he sensed the need ricocheting through her, he cupped her breast. She wished they were naked together in his chamber again, free to touch and tease each other, no barriers between them. No fear of being discovered by an unsuspecting fellow guest.

He kissed a path down her throat, his other hand sinking into the elaborate knot of her hair. She felt her coiffure loosen and knew that he was sending her hairpins cascading to the floor. She knew too that she should have cared, should have stopped him before he sent her curls flowing down her back and anyone who passed her in the hall would know precisely what she'd been about. She walked a dangerous line between dalliance and scandal, and she very much feared she was beginning to lean to the side of scandal.

One of the buttons on her bodice popped open. Then another. Heath pressed a kiss to the hollow of her throat, his tongue flicking against her thumping pulse. Another button slid free.

Suddenly, the sound of breaking porcelain intruded on their idyll. Tia pulled away from his embrace, spinning to find the source of the noise. A vase had fallen from a nearby table, taking with it some red conservatory roses. Her bustle must have brushed against it, bringing it tumbling down. And bringing a return to her sanity.

She looked from the shattered vase to Heath, who stood

not even two steps away, his gaze dark with the passion burning through her as well. Tia knew in that instant that if she didn't retreat from the room, she'd wind up allowing him to do far more than remove a few buttons from their moorings and take down her hair. She had to get as far away from him and his delicious kisses as she possibly could.

"This is madness," she said. "From this point forward, I shall do my best to keep my distance from you. Neither of us can afford to bring a scandal down upon our heads, which is all we'll manage by continuing in this fashion."

"Tia," he said, taking a step forward. "I'm sorry. I didn't intend for that to happen."

"Nor did I. You were right when you said this is bloody foolishness. It cannot happen again." She turned her back on him and quit the chamber as quickly as her feet would carry her. Lest she forget her good intentions and go back to him to finish what they'd started.

Chapter Four

*C*HRIST, HE VERY BADLY WANTED TO FINISH WHAT they'd started.

Heath watched the tail end of Tia's pink silken skirts disappear behind the closing door. His gaze dropped to the mess of porcelain and roses marring the floor. Perhaps it was an omen of sorts. A sign that he ought to listen to his common sense and Tia both and avoid her at all costs for the remainder of the house party.

But he couldn't.

That much was as apparent as the rigid cock tenting his trousers. When he'd received Tia's summons to meet him, he hadn't known what to expect. He'd been surprised at such a bold move, but intrigued as well. When she had entered the room, her demeanor reserved and cool, as if she hadn't been aflame in his arms the night before, he'd been sorely tempted to ruffle her feathers. To make her come alive for him again. Make her realize she couldn't simply forget any more than he could.

He shouldn't have kissed her. Shouldn't have taken her back into his arms. The damage had already been done, however, and now he needed to clean up the mess, both literally and figuratively. The first was easy. Summon a maid. The second seemed nigh impossible.

Before he could compose himself enough to venture into the maze of Penworth's halls, the door clicked open again. This time, it wasn't a golden-haired siren breezing over the threshold but the Marquis of Thornton, his host. Thornton, for all that he'd been mired in a scandal involving the marchioness some time back, was a good sort. Heath rather liked the fellow.

"Devonshire," the marquis said, sounding startled to find someone where presumably no one should have been. "Am I interrupting? It looks as if you were just going a round with my wife's roses."

He grimaced, realizing the picture he must present. He was sure he looked every inch as guilty as he was. "My apologies, Thornton. I'm afraid I'm rather clumsy this afternoon."

Thornton raised a brow, but if he didn't believe the lame explanation, it was the only outward sign. "Nonsense. I'll have one of the maids sent round to tidy it up." He stalked into the room then, looking about him. "Have you seen a book of songs? Lady Thornton wishes to have duets for entertainment this evening, and apparently she's in desperate need of the bloody thing."

"I'm afraid I haven't." Fortunately, the interruption had caused his heated blood to cool, saving him from further embarrassment.

"Did Lady Stokey have it in her possession, by any chance?" Thornton asked next, startling him. "I saw her leaving the room just a moment ago, but she was headed toward the east wing in rather a hurry, and I couldn't catch up with her to ask."

Hell. It would seem he'd been caught. "I don't believe she did."

He stayed where he was as he knew a gentleman should, not about to run. The marquis was roughly the same size as he, and he had no doubt he could deliver a powerful punch.

Lord knew he deserved it after the way he'd been dallying with Tia. It was altogether out of character for him. Wholly unacceptable. But yet, he couldn't very well *not* touch her, and that was a deuce of a thing.

Thornton approached him, his expression unreadable. "I wouldn't like for my house party to become a den of scandal, Devonshire. I've done enough to cause tongues to wag on my own, and I'm now doing penance for my wife's sake. Penworth and all who are guests here must be above reproach."

Jesus. He was far too old, far too intelligent to be receiving a lesson on propriety from a fellow peer of the realm. He inclined his head, inwardly cursing himself and his stupid cock. "I understand, my lord. You have my word that I have no intention to sully your reputation during my stay here. Indeed, I've always prided myself on possessing a reputation that is above reproach as well."

"I'm well aware of that," the marquis said, giving him an assessing look. "That's what makes this so damn bewildering."

At least Heath wasn't the only one mystified by his sudden reaction to Tia. "I agree." He shook his head, wondering at the state of his sanity. "Trust me, Thornton, I wholeheartedly agree."

His host nodded. "And trust me on this: if you upset Lady Stokey in any way, I will be forced to answer for it."

He understood well enough what Thornton threatened. A sound drubbing. Perhaps it was exactly what he needed to cure what ailed him.

Tia pled a headache and skipped her sister's evening musical entertainments. The last thing she wanted to endure was the sight of Heath paired with Miss Whitney, especially not with her emotions in such horrid tumult. Instead, she remained in her chamber, taking a late tea alone and trying to figure out what in the name of all the heavens was wrong with her.

She had allowed him to kiss her again when she had sworn she would not. Had allowed him to once more shake her composure and undo her buttons. Damn it all. Although she'd always been the sort to follow her heart rather than her head, she wasn't ordinarily so reckless when others were concerned.

With a sigh, she took a sip of her tea only to discover that it had gone cold during her prolonged musings. She detested tea that wasn't perfectly hot. Tia returned her cup to its saucer and stood to pace the length of her chamber.

How was she to carry on for the remainder of the house party? She wasn't certain she could keep her distance from the duke as she'd vowed she must. Wasn't certain that she even wanted to do so. If only she could leave, it would all be so much simpler. But she had committed to chaperoning Miss Whitney, and she was firmly mired in East Anglia for the duration.

Her chamber door flew open without so much as a warning knock. Cleo sailed inside, looking formidable in a navy gown, her black curls piled artfully atop her head. Her blue eyes flashed with her annoyance.

"Tia, what were you thinking?" she demanded after the door slammed closed at her back.

Oh dear. She supposed her sister's ire wasn't merely caused by her lack of desire to listen to duets. But she decided to play innocent all the same. "I was thinking that my head was pounding dreadfully," she said.

"I'm not referring to your decision to eschew my entertainments," her sister snapped, planting her hands on her wasp waist. "Is there something you wish to tell me?"

"Thank you for looking after Miss Whitney in my absence," she tried.

"You're most welcome, but that wasn't what I had in mind either. I'm speaking of you being alone with Devonshire earlier. What were you about?"

Drat. "I was—"

"No," Cleo interrupted. "I've thought better of it. Don't tell me. I'm sure I don't want to know."

A telltale flush crept over Tia's cheeks. "How did you hear of it?" She'd thought she'd been discreet. She should have known that her sister would have eyes and ears everywhere at Penworth.

"Thornton saw you leaving the yellow drawing room, and when he entered, he found Devonshire within looking wholly guilty." Cleo raised a brow. "What can you have been thinking of, Tia?"

Well that was quite simple. She had been thinking of the lovely way the man kissed her, how he set her at sixes and sevens with a simple touch, how she wanted to be in his bed again. She winced, knowing she very well couldn't share that with the disapproving sister before her.

"I'm not certain," she said lamely. "I meant to tell him that we needed to stay as far away from each other as possible for the duration of the house party. And instead, I allowed him to kiss me."

"Thank heavens that is all the liberty you allowed him."

Tia studiously avoided her sister's probing gaze. "Yes, thank heavens."

"Tia?"

She busied herself with adjusting her skirts. "Yes?"

"You look guilty as a thief holding a sack of the family silver."

Tia swallowed and glanced back at Cleo. "I acted with great foolishness, I'm afraid."

Cleo's gaze narrowed. "Just how foolish were you?"

She didn't want to reveal all to her sister, but she'd already revealed too much. And she'd always been abysmal at prevarication. "As foolish as a woman can possibly be."

"Oh dear God." Cleo's hand fluttered to her brow, quite reminding Tia of their mother in that moment. "Hypatia. How could you?"

Tia loathed her full name. No one ever called her by it other than her sisters and her mother. Its use was reserved for august tones of disappointment, and sadly she'd heard them far too many times in her life. "It was a moment of weakness," she defended. Or rather, many long, profound moments. But no need to stoke the flames of her sister's angry fire.

"Indeed it was. I trust it won't be repeated?"

Heath's passionate kisses of earlier rose to her mind, tempting her all over again. Dear, sweet heavens. "Of course it won't." And it wouldn't. Just as long as she could keep at least several hundred miles between herself and the duke at all times.

Cleo appeared to soften a bit. "It cannot, Tia. You know that as well as I. Beyond your responsibility to Miss Whitney, there is something else to consider. It's common knowledge that the duke is hunting for a wife, not just the pheasants he's come here to shoot. I should hate to see you hurt."

Heath was seeking a wife? The revelation struck Tia in the region of her heart as surely as Cupid's arrow. She knew as well as anyone that gentlemen didn't dally with women they wanted to wed. If he had come to East Anglia looking for a suitable mate, he certainly hadn't found one in Tia.

"I hadn't realized," she murmured. He'd told her he wasn't looking for a lover, and she supposed that much had been true. But he had been looking for someone else. Someone who was not a widow willing to follow him to bed for a night of passion.

Cleo patted her arm. "You see why no good can come of this?"

"Of course." And Tia did, now more than ever. The trouble was, she still wasn't certain if it would be enough.

The morning sun shone bright as Heath returned to Penworth the next day. The shoot, ordinarily a sport he enjoyed, had left him with the same nagging sense of incompletion that had been plaguing him ever since Tia had left him in the drawing room the day before. She had been avoiding him, bowing out of the evening entertainments. At dinner, she'd been seated far away from him, a situation no doubt owed to the glares Lady Thornton kept directing his way. It would seem the marquis had shared his discovery with his wife, and she wasn't pleased.

As he entered the main hall with his fellow shooters, Lady Thornton herself swished into their midst. She looked to be in high dudgeon, and Heath hoped like hell he wasn't the source of her ire this time.

"Lord Thornton, I hate to bombard you so soon after your return from the shoot, but I need your aid," she said, her voice colored with worry. "Lady Stokey went for a ride hours ago, and she still hasn't returned. Her mount did, however. Without her."

Jesus. Real fear unfurled in Heath's gut. There was only one reason why her mount would have returned to the stables without her. Tia had been thrown. And if she'd been thrown, she could very well be lying out in the chill autumn air, injured.

Or perhaps worse.

"I'll ride out to find her," he volunteered, not even bothering to think twice. To hell with propriety and repercussions and their mutual vows to stay away from each other. If Tia was out there somewhere, he was bloody well going to scour every bit of Thornton's estate until he located her.

"You?" Lady Thornton looked at him as if he'd just suggested he saddle up and ride to the moon.

"Yes." He dared her to naysay him. "Me."

"Thank you," the marquis interrupted. "The more men we have out there, the greater our chances of finding her."

He inclined his head. It would seem that Thornton was at least a man of reason, warnings about drubbings or no. "We shouldn't waste any time."

"The sooner we get to her, the better," his host agreed,

turning to the other members of their shooting party. "Gentlemen? Are you with us?"

A chorus of assents rose, and they passed off their guns to waiting servants, heading for the stables. With each step, worry ate at him. He couldn't bear it if something had befallen Tia. He didn't stop to contemplate why that was, simply got on his horse and rode as if the hounds of hell were at his heels.

It would seem that Tia's luck had gone from bad to worse. She leaned against the trunk of a large old tree, trying her best to ignore the pain shooting from her ankle and her wrist and radiating through her body. Devil take it. She'd only meant to go for a nice head-clearing ride this morning.

And then her horse had been spooked by a fox. She'd been so consumed by her thoughts that she hadn't been holding onto the reins properly. Sidesaddles were complete rubbish, in her opinion. But a necessary evil, and one that had caused her to go flying to the mud.

Though she'd done her best to catch her fall, her already sprained ankle and her wrist had caught the brunt of her weight. Her brutal landing had taken the breath straight from her lungs. By the time she'd gathered her wits and managed to wrangle herself into a standing position once more, her frightened horse was long gone.

To make matters worse, she'd ridden for so long and for so far that she wasn't quite sure which direction she ought to head back in. Her ankle was horribly painful. And it had begun to rain.

Yes, if she wasn't falling in the gardens and acting scandalously with a duke she scarcely knew, she was stranded in the wilds of East Anglia charged with the Sisyphean fate of limping back to Penworth, wherever that might be. At least it was the beginning of the day and not the end. Presumably, someone would notice her absence and come searching for her. She certainly hoped she wouldn't be forced to spend the evening curled up at the base of a tree as if she were a common woodland creature.

She shivered at the thought, looking around her for some sign of civilization in the dense forest. Then she saw it, the silhouette of a small building almost hidden in the undergrowth. She guessed it to be a hunting hut of some sort. Whatever it was, it would definitely provide shelter from the cool rain pecking at her skin through the layers of her riding habit and dolman. She knew she couldn't remain in the rain for much longer for fear a chill would set in.

Gritting her teeth against the pain, she pushed away from the tree and began limping her way to the building. The steady rain turned into a raging torrent as she made painstakingly slow progress. Her skirts were soaked. Her hat was a crumpled, dripping wreck and the chill in the air was cutting her straight to the bone. After what seemed like a century of miserable, laborious navigation through thickets and trees, she reached the door of the cabin.

From up close, it was a sad, tumbledown affair with a sagged roof and shrouded windows. She didn't suppose it had been used in some time, but it would have to do. Anything was better than remaining in the cold and the downpour, hobbling about like an invalid.

Thankfully, it was unlocked. The door swung open with a lusty creak, the dark interior of the cabin scarcely lit by the gloomy light of the day. She hesitated only a moment before ducking inside. After all, what choice did she have? She only prayed that she wouldn't get a face full of cobwebs or step on a mouse. She pulled back the drapery from a window, allowing meager light to filter inside and illuminate the contents of the cabin just a bit.

As her eyes gradually adjusted to the dim lighting, she could discern a fireplace with an open hearth and logs in the grate. A shiver swept over her then, the effect all those layers of sodden fabric clinging to her skin. Her teeth chattered. She prayed there would be a source of ignition somewhere, left behind along with the wood by the last hunter who'd made use of the shelter. Because if she didn't soon get out of her wet clothes and into the heat of a fire, a swollen ankle and a painful wrist would be the least of her worries.

Heath almost rode straight by the old hunting shack tucked away in the woods. At the last moment, its dark silhouette caught his eye and he slowed his mount, wondering if perhaps Tia had found it as well and taken shelter inside. It was worth at least a cursory inspection, he decided. He and the other gentlemen in the shooting party had split up in all directions, the better to cover more ground and locate Tia.

Worry sat in his stomach as heavy as a rock and every bit as impenetrable. He hadn't seen so much as a sign of her yet. The rain was giving him a lashing, and if she was stranded somewhere, it was no doubt chilling her to her core. The cold and the rain would make her terribly vulnerable to pneumonia.

And the last woman he'd known to contract pneumonia had died before he'd made it home from Italy.

Damn it all, he couldn't bear to see that same fate befall anyone else. He urged his mare through the thicket and toward the building, dismounting when he spied a small lean-to. It wasn't in the best shape, but it would do to keep his horse out of the rain. After tethering his mount, he hurried to the cabin, hoping Tia would be safe and sound within.

He opened the door and froze on the threshold.

She was within, all right. And she was bloody well half-naked, standing before a crackling fire in nothing but her corset and chemise. Her lovely hair was unbound, hanging to her waist, her delicious curves on full display from nipped waist to lush hips and bosom.

Her gaze caught his. "Heath," she said softly. "I should have expected it would be you."

He wasn't certain if she meant that in a good sense or in a bad sense. Belatedly becoming aware of the wind and rain at his back, he stepped all the way into the cabin and closed the door behind him.

"Are you injured?" he demanded, closing the distance between them easily.

Relief coursed through him, banishing the very real fear that had taken up residence within him ever since learning of her disappearance. He wanted to take her in his arms, but after their last discussion, he hardly knew where they stood.

She caught her lower lip between her teeth in that way she had that he already found mesmerizing. "Once again, I landed with an appalling lack of grace. I'm afraid my bad ankle rather bore the brunt of it."

She convulsed with a violent shiver then, her teeth chattering. To hell with the walls she wanted to build between them. "You're cold." He shucked his wet coat and wrapped his arms around her, drawing her into the warmth of his body. She didn't protest, snuggling against him like a little kitten. He tucked her head beneath his chin, the sweet perfume of violets wafting up to tease him. "Better?"

"I suppose it depends upon one's definition of the word," she quipped.

He was grateful that she didn't seem at all rattled. She was herself, with a rapier-sharp tongue always at the ready. He'd never met a woman quite like her, and he was increasingly drawn to her despite his every good intention. "Are you warmer?" he clarified.

"A bit." Her teeth chattered again. "How did you find me?"

"Luck." Or perhaps a lack thereof, because surely the fates were laughing at him now. How the hell was he to keep his wits about him when his cock was pressed against her tempting body? The gentleman in him had promised to keep his distance from her. But all he could think about was sliding inside her, taking them both to the edge of reason all over again. He knew it would be foolhardy. He knew he was compromising himself by even touching her. He couldn't seem to stop. Devil take it all. Reason was an elusive thing when the woman he wanted more than any other was half-naked and pressed against him.

"I suppose I should thank you."

A reluctant grin tugged at his lips. Her manner of expressing gratitude was peculiar as ever. "It's nothing," he dismissed easily. "The entire hunting party's been searching for you ever since our return from the shoot. I was simply the first to stumble across your path."

"The entire hunting party? Oh dear." Another shiver racked her frame. "I feel the fool. I simply meant to go for a ride. The day looked clear when I left. Then my horse spooked and left me limping through the rain."

He threw a glance around the dingy room, searching for a wingback chair and finding none. The sole pieces of furniture decorating the sparse one-room building were a table and a bed tucked into a corner. The bed would have to do. He released her and then scooped her up into his arms. He was beginning to think she belonged there.

"What in heaven's name?" Her palms pressed against his chest. She stared up at him, her beauty sending a sharp pang of desire through him. "Why must you forever be carrying me about, Your Grace?"

Because he liked the way she felt. Because she was forever injuring herself in one way or another. Because he couldn't seem to keep himself from touching her, no matter how much he knew he should.

"You shouldn't be standing on that ankle," he told her firmly as he stalked to the bed. It was covered with a quilt, which was no doubt dusty but better than nothing.

"Dear God, not the bed," she protested, giving him pause.

Could she sense the tumult within him? The want warring with his sense of what was right? Good Christ, he hoped she didn't think he would attempt to seduce her right here in the ramshackle cabin? Of course, he couldn't really blame her if she did. He couldn't deny that he'd had the thought more than once already.

He cleared his throat. "You have no need to fear me, Tia. I'm not seeking a repeat of last night. You and I both know that would be the worst sort of folly."

"Yes," she agreed, though she had stiffened. "It would. However, I was merely in fear of rodents, Your Grace. Of the four-legged sort rather than the two-legged."

Let it never be said that Lady Stokey couldn't deliver a crushing setdown, even stripped of her silk gowns and wet as a fish. "How kind of you to imply I may be confused with the despicable creatures," he intoned, rather enjoying their verbal sparring. At least it distracted him—albeit in small measure—from the hardness in his trousers and the twin creamy swells of her breasts above her corset. "The bed appears relatively lump free."

She shuddered. "I'm afraid that isn't at all heartening."

"And I'm afraid our choices are severely limited," he pointed out as her shudder turned into another shiver. "You need warming, and while I'm quite impressed you were able to build yourself a fire, this draughty old place is taking most of the heat straight up the chimney."

"This rotten cabin is dreadfully frigid," she agreed, her teeth once more clacking together as a violent tremor racked her entire body. This time, the shivering didn't stop. It became uncontrollable. "I'm so cold, Heath."

Her use of his given name softened him. He realized then that even though she'd done away with most of the layers of her clothing, the remainders she wore were still sodden as well. There was only one way she would truly be warm. And it was with his body heat radiating into hers, both of them divested of their wet fabric.

"Bloody hell. I'm sorry, Tia." He set her back on her feet as gently as he could, gripping the top of her corset and forcing the first hook and eye closures apart. "You need to do away with this as well."

Her icy fingers latched onto his hands. "But—"

"No arguments," he interrupted. "I don't want you to take ill, and the only way we can avoid that is by getting you out of these wet undergarments."

"I'll be too cold," she protested.

He ignored her, working the fastenings of her corset until it fell to the floor and she stood before him in only a chemise. Then, he started on his shirt. "I shall warm you."

Chapter Five

*T*IA KNEW HEATH WAS RIGHT. SHE DIDN'T recall ever being colder in her life. And the fire she'd begun wasn't its strongest, the damp wood producing just enough warmth to tease her. Her wet garments were an impediment. So were his.

I shall warm you.

The trouble with allowing Heath to warm her was that involved the both of them fully nude and in the same bed. She wasn't so naïve to believe that either of them would be able to resist giving in to the desire smoldering between them even now, regardless of what either of them said. Despite any noble intentions.

But she also couldn't deny the fact that she couldn't stop shivering and if she needed to suffer the fate of the certainly dusty, possibly mouse-infested old bed, at least she could do so with the help of a naked and far warmer Heath.

"Very well," she muttered, giving in and throwing back the covers to slide inside.

The bed clothes smelled a trifle musty, and they were certainly cold. But blessedly, her bare feet didn't meet with any suspicious fur. Her teeth clacked together as she watched him hurriedly disrobe. Although she told herself to avert her gaze, she couldn't keep her eyes from him. Couldn't help noticing his generous cock was hard and full. It would seem he wasn't entirely unaffected.

And, frozen though she was, she couldn't help but revel in a feminine swell of satisfaction. Good. At least she wasn't the only one to be so bedeviled.

"Turn 'round, please," he ordered, startling her.

She met his gaze, her face going hot. She knew then that he had caught her in the act of ogling him, but she wasn't certain she cared. Her body—with the exception of her scalding cheeks—was cold as Wenham Lake ice. She had seen him naked the day before. And by God, she was Hypatia Harrington, a woman who prided herself on her boldness and her refusal to force herself into the mold of a mild society widow.

She arched a brow at him. "Have you forgotten that I've already seen your wares, Your Grace?"

He stared at her, and she knew then that she'd shocked him. "My wares? Good God, woman, you make me sound like a bloody shop."

Another shudder shook her, taking with it the sudden burst of naughtiness he'd inspired with his unfairly delectable male nudity. He truly was a gorgeous specimen of manhood. When he wasn't being irksome, that was. Her patience went the way of her mount earlier, galloping across the countryside never to be seen again. "Get in, will you, and cease your dawdling. This disgusting bed is colder than a snow drift."

"Such a tempting invitation," he teased. "How can I resist?" But he slid into the bed just the same, his hip pressing into hers beneath the blankets.

She scooted nearer to his warmth instantly and for precisely two reasons. His body radiated the heat hers so desperately needed and she was unbearably drawn to him. How could she not be? He was gorgeous. He smelled divine. He'd brought her body more ecstasy than she'd known existed in a mere night. And she wanted more. Yes, she wanted more despite what she'd promised her sister and despite what she'd told the duke himself earlier that day. She didn't want distance. What she wanted—what she craved— was Heath. More Heath. As much as she could get. She couldn't keep her hand from skimming over his taut stomach, seeking the cock she'd seen standing at attention just a moment before.

He groaned. "None of that. Lie on your side facing away from me, you stubborn wench."

His words rather stung, so Tia snatched her hand away and did as he'd directed, giving him her back. "Very well. You needn't be so cruel, you know."

"I'm not being cruel," he gritted, his lips so near to her ear that they grazed the delicate shell as he spoke. "I'm being practical. You need warming, and this is the best way to accomplish that without causing a repeat of last night."

"Oh," she said simply, stiffening as his arms wrapped around her. His broad chest branded her back, but he kept his lower body away from her. It would seem that, as much as he might clearly want her, he was equally determined not to give in to his baser instincts. Disappointment skewered her. She couldn't help it. She knew it was likely for the best for both of them, that further lovemaking between them would only be pure folly. But that didn't mean her body didn't long for him just the same.

"Good Christ, woman. I'm doing my damnedest to be noble," he muttered.

He wanted to be noble, did he? She shimmied backward, not stopping until her bottom connected with his groin. His cock remained hard and ready, pressing against her. "It's a tad late to be noble."

"You agreed that a repeat of last night would be foolishness," he reminded her. But as he said the words, he thrust his cock against her bottom. "Are you warming, Lady Stokey?"

"Slowly," she said, biding her time. Something about the

remote nature of the cabin banished all thoughts of propriety and promises from her mind. All that existed for her was the duke at her back, hot and hard and, most importantly, hers. It was as if they were removed from the sphere of the house party. There was no one to interrupt them, no one to berate them, no one to remind them that sanity and society both dictated that they behave as strangers in a drawing room and not as feverish lovers.

He rubbed his palms over her arms. And then he kissed her ear. "How about now?"

"A bit." She feigned another shiver when one wasn't easily forthcoming. Perhaps it was subterfuge, but she deemed a minor, harmless deception a fair weapon in her arsenal. After all, her distracted state was what had led her to be thrown from her horse earlier, and that had been wholly his fault. If he had been noble from the first moment they'd crossed paths in the garden, she would never have known the fire that she was missing.

He continued rubbing her arms, even throwing one of his long legs over hers. His breath was hot against her neck. "And now?"

"Slightly." In truth, he was warming her more than any mere flame ever could. But he needn't know that.

He kissed her ear again and then her throat. "Are you trying to torture me, darling?"

She shivered, but this time it had nothing whatsoever to do with being cold. "Of course not. Did you not say you were trying to be noble?"

"Yes," he gritted. His thumb skimmed over one of her nipples.

"But you just kissed my ear twice," she argued. "And I'm certain that touch I just now felt was not unintentional."

"What touch?" His tone was one of feigned innocence.

Perhaps she wasn't the only one reveling in their game. She caught his hand and pressed it to her breast. "One like this."

"Tia." His voice was low, seductive and rough, at once

whiskey and silk to her senses.

He was warning her, she knew. If she pushed him one inch more, he'd fall off the ledge and take her with him. "Heath," she returned, enjoying his name on her tongue. "I don't think I want you to be noble just now."

"You don't?"

"No." She guided his other hand to the apex of her thighs.

He made a low sound in his throat, his fingers expertly dipping into the folds of her sex to find the sensitive bud hiding within. "I thought we agreed further behavior of this nature would be inadvisable."

"Indeed." It would seem she could only manage one-word responses now. The things this man did to her, rendering her little more than a weak-willed wanton in his arms. He flicked his thumb over her in a tease that was as deliberate as it was delicious.

"Perhaps you've changed your mind?" He kissed her neck again.

She most certainly had. Where he was concerned, she possessed not a shred of resistance. Not when he was nude and hard and utterly tempting at her back. How could she? What would be the harm in one more time?

"For the moment," she said on a moan as he continued to tease her.

"You seemed so determined earlier," he observed as one of his fingers slid inside her.

She was wet and ready. Her hips jerked. She wanted more of him. All of him. "I was trying to avoid scandal," she managed to say.

"And now?" He toyed with her, withdrawing and slicking the moisture over her nub.

He was taking her dangerously close to the edge. "I," she began, only to falter when he sank back into her. "Oh."

"To hell with scandal and to hell with being noble," he said. "I want you, Tia."

So many words teemed inside her. But all she could

muster up was one. "Yes."

He rolled her gently onto her back, and then he was atop her. The musty blankets were slung about his shoulders like a cape, and he was careful to keep the cold air from touching her even as he lowered his mouth to claim hers.

Their kiss was fierce, filled with mutual longing. His tongue sank into her mouth in that slow, bold claiming she loved. Her nails sank into his sleek, strong shoulders. She raked them down his skin, following the contours of his back to the firm swells of his arse. When she reached his bottom, she grasped him to her, wanting completion. Fulfillment. A joining. Nothing else would satisfy her. Gone was the cold that had been plaguing her body. Gone was any hint of guilt, of propriety hanging over her shoulder, of the promises she'd made, of the people she could hurt by following the whims of her heart and body.

All she knew in that moment was that she'd lived an entire lifetime without knowing a man who made her feel as if she couldn't exist without him in her bed. Until Heath. As illogical as it was, the man she'd once dubbed the Duke of Dullness was the only man who could set her aflame, who could make her want until she could scarcely think, who could bring her the kind of pleasure she'd never even dreamed existed.

She broke their deep kiss, desperate for him. "I want you so very much, Heath. Please."

"God, darling. What you do to me." He guided his cock to her entrance, rubbing his hard length over the bud that so ached for him. "Tell me what you want."

What she wanted was him, deep inside her. She knew that it was the gentleman within him that wanted a response. A way to assuage whatever guilt would plague him later for eschewing his efforts to be noble. "I want you inside me," she elaborated, aroused even further by saying the forbidden words aloud. It went against everything she'd promised herself. Everything she'd told him. Everything she'd sworn to repay the debt she owed those around her, from Cleo to Thornton to Miss Whitney. But she couldn't help herself. Here in the quiet, far-off world of the hunting cabin, it was incredibly easy to forget about all the weights holding her down. In this moment, she was merely Tia, a woman following her heart. And the man atop her was Heath, not the duke, not someone seeking a wife who was not a jaded, wanton widow like herself.

No, they were simply man and woman. Aflame.

He kissed her again before dragging his sensual mouth down over her throat. He nipped at her delicate skin with his teeth and tongue. She wrapped her legs around his waist, opening to him, inviting him. Showing him what she wanted far better than mere words ever could. He surged against her, dragging his mouth down her neck to her breast. When he sucked a hard nipple into his mouth, she moaned and arched into him, wanting more. Needing more.

"Harder," she directed, longing for something she couldn't even quite comprehend. All that she knew was that as far as he'd pushed her, she wanted to push him further. As far as they both could venture. "Use your teeth."

He bit her nipple then, gently but with enough force to send a rush of wetness between her thighs. Anticipation was for girls. She was a woman grown, and she wanted satisfaction. Now.

Heath released her breast and moved to the other, sucking that nipple too. And then he thrust, his cock entering her. She moved, loving the sensation of her body stretching to accommodate him. Tia felt as if she'd waited her entire life for this, the life-altering, completely delicious sensation of Heath sheathing himself within her. He was deep. Hard. But she wanted more, so she arched against him, urging him deeper, guiding him into a rhythm that was as tantalizing as it was fast.

Oh dear God, yes.

"Tia," he groaned against the swell of her left breast. "I'm going to lose my head."

"Good," she told him, "for then we shall be even."

Because surely she had already lost her head or else she wouldn't be once again making love to the Duke of Devonshire despite the vows she'd made to her sister. Nothing about what she was doing made sense other than in the elemental way. Her lust for him she understood—a mere necessity for all human nature. But her willingness to put those around her in danger for another kiss, another thrust of his cock…it was shameful. Her lack of control was shameful. Embarrassing. Troubling. Horrid. Heath rendered her a complete fool.

He began a fast, wicked rhythm, pumping into her in the way she loved. He sucked her nipple, occasionally tugging with his teeth, making her mad for him. By the time his lips fused with hers once more and his thumb was yet again flicking her tender nub, she was well beyond the ledge. She'd leapt, in fact, hoping for something to catch her fall. He thrust into her again and again, his cock unrelenting. She loved every second of it.

Finally, he flicked her sex, thrust home deep within her, and sucked her nipple simultaneously. She lost whatever tentative grip she might have had upon her ability to control herself. Tia threw back her head, moaning and allowing the waves of pleasure within her to build to a crashing crescendo until she reached her pinnacle. Pleasure licked at her as Heath increased his pace, pumping into her again and again. It didn't take long for him to reach his completion as well, but just as he tipped back his head, sliding so far inside her she wanted to come again, the door of the cabin burst open.

Cold air swept inside. Grasping at Heath's shoulders, Tia looked beyond him to discern the thin, forbidding shape of one of their fellow revelers. Lord Trotter, to be specific, a man who was old, self-righteous, and possessed of a tongue that delighted in gossip.

Heath seemed unaware of their visitor, continuing to thrust into her until he moaned, his angle changing within her. She felt a spurt of something hot and wet and couldn't help but be aroused all over again, even if the thin, hawk-eyed viscount was watching them as if he'd just caught the devil about to don a lamb's skin.

"Good sweet God," announced Lord Trotter, ruining their idyll and making Heath stop in mid-thrust as he lost himself within her.

"Jesus," Heath said, clamping the bedclothes firmly to the bed to protect her modesty and tossing a look over his shoulder. "What the devil are you doing here, Trotter?"

"I've come in search of her ladyship," Trotter intoned, his voice tainted with self-righteous fury.

"Oh dear," Tia whispered, a sinking feeling entering her gut. It was much the same one she'd had when her mother had sent the poor footman to Scotland. She had a horrible feeling that reality was about to intrude upon her and Heath both, just as surely as Lord Trotter had. They were clandestine lovers no more, and there would need to be an answer for what they'd done. Society needed appeasing, after all. The old world required placating, even if the story told wasn't true. But in this instance, Tia feared there would be no return from the path down which she and the duke had happily trod. A peer of the realm stood on the threshold of the hunting cabin, completely aware of what they were about.

"Get the hell out of here, Trotter," Heath ordered in his most arch, ducal tones. "Or I shall trounce you to within an inch of your life."

Before Tia could so much as blink, the door to the hunting cabin slammed shut, leaving her alone once again with Heath. But the niggling sensation that there would be ramifications intolerable to both she and the duke lingered long after the thud of the closing portal.

"I'm sorry," was all he said as he slid from her body.

Not the most comforting words. Not at all.

"I regret to inform you that while I've discovered Lady Stokey, I've also discovered the Duke of Devonshire. It gives me great pains to be forced to divulge such dark news, but I fear I have reason to believe that their relations were...improper." The last was said with a horrified shudder.

The Marquis of Thornton stilled his restless mount and cursed his particular luck to the devil. Rain sluiced from his hat onto his trousers as he tipped his head forward, hiding his expression. Damn it all. He should've known Cleo's troublesome sister couldn't be trusted to behave. And Devonshire. By God, he would make good on his threats to thrash the blighter.

After weathering the scandal he'd created with his darling wife, he'd just barely earned back his place in the political and social worlds. He'd managed so far by taking the *ton* by storm with the help of Cleo, who was the most perfect woman he could have ever asked to have by his side. After the birth of their son, she had worked diligently to reenter polite society with a series of lavish entertainments. This house party at Penworth was to have been the culmination of all their labors. They'd invited an impressive assortment of august old lords, fusty politicians, family and friends.

One of those august lords, Viscount Trotter, was facing him now, red-faced and outraged. Seated atop one of Thornton's mildest mounts, Trotter resembled nothing so much as an irate parsnip drowning in hunting tweeds. Thornton stared at the man, wondering why, of all the guests at Penworth, Tia would have had to be found by the biggest sanctimonious prude. And apparently in *flagrante delicto.*

Bloody, bloody hell.

"Perhaps you misunderstood what you saw," he suggested firmly to the man, praying that he would take pity and observe the age-old method of keeping gossip where it belonged. Behind bedchamber doors.

"I saw them in bed together, my lord. There is no doubt," Lord Trotter said succinctly, banishing Thornton's hopes.

When it rained, he supposed. "You're utterly certain?"

Trotter nodded emphatically, his voice trembling in his self-righteous fervor. "I know what I observed, my lord. I cannot say I'm entirely shocked that this sort of egregious behavior would be unfolding within your midst. But I did hope for better from you."

Thornton gritted his teeth. "I can assure you that I in no way espouse such conduct. Lady Stokey and the duke will both be called to answer for their actions."

Trotter appeared somewhat mollified. "What will be done?"

There was no hope for it. Only one solution existed, one that would preserve his fragile reputation and dampen the flames of scandal at the same time. "They will marry, of course," he said. "In the meantime, I suggest we all ride back to Penworth and await their return."

Without waiting for Trotter's response, Thornton spurred his mount forward. He was going to wring Tia's neck for this. And beat Devonshire to a pulp. And then, his wife would likely box his ears for promising her sister to the first unfortunate chap to be caught in bed with her.

Bloody, bloody hell.

"Devonshire."

Heath met Thornton's gaze without flinching. They stood not two feet apart in the marquis' study, two men squaring off much as prizefighters would in the ring. Apparently, Trotter had been swift with his inability to keep the winds of scandal subdued. The bastard had gone straight to the marquis with what he'd seen, which had admittedly been damning indeed. Heath had been summoned for his reckoning, and he knew it.

"Lord Thornton," he greeted in turn, equally formal. What did a man say to the brother-in-law of the woman he'd just been caught fucking in an abandoned hunting cabin? The very woman he was to have been rescuing, to boot.

Thornton's expression was grave, his eyes as hard as the stones of a castle wall. "I presume you know why you are here for this unfortunate interview?"

Heath clasped his hands at his back and nodded, feeling like a lad in leading strings getting punished for sneaking into the kitchens and eating Cook's tarts. Only the sin he'd committed this time was for worse. Far, far worse and with a more severe consequence. "I do."

"Interesting choice of words," the marquis said, grinning in the way he imagined an executioner might as he fit the noose over the prisoner's head. "Have a seat, Your Grace. I'm not going to resort to fisticuffs." He paused. "Unless I find it necessary to."

Ah. He was being given options. Of a sort. He seated himself in a chair opposite Thornton's escritoire and watched guardedly as his host did the same. His ride back to Penworth with Tia had been quiet. They'd both been lost in their own thoughts, the ramifications of what they'd done. Heath hadn't known precisely what to say, how to broach the subject of what must happen.

Marriage.

They had no other alternative now that Trotter had caught them. The damage to all their reputations would be too severe. He had no wish for Tia to be snubbed in society on his account. He had been searching for a wife. It would seem he'd found her. And why not? He couldn't deny that the prospect of having Tia in his bed was a thoroughly pleasant one. Good Lord, she'd all but set him on fire. He couldn't wait to have more of her. All she had to give.

Of course, there remained the small, niggling notion that she wasn't at all the sort of wife he'd intended to procure for himself. He had never meant to wed a woman who was as beautiful as she was maddening, as silly as she was seductive. A woman who knew what she wanted and wasn't afraid to achieve it. Yes indeed, there was something about Lady Stokey that rendered her a dangerous woman.

"Would you care for a whiskey?" Thornton asked, interrupting his thoughts. "You look as if you could use it." He splashed some amber liquid in a glass and nudged it in Heath's direction without bothering to wait for his response. "Besides, it'll dull the pain of my fist connecting with your jaw. Supposing it's required, of course."

"Naturally." Heath took the glass and tossed back a gulp. "I'm no fool, Thornton. I know I deserve a sound thrashing."

"Yes," his host said agreeably, having a healthy sip of his own whiskey. "You do."

"But I hope we can dispense with the formalities," he pressed onward, not truly relishing the thought of the marquis giving him a drubbing, regardless of how justified one would be. "Since Lady Stokey's father is not present, it would seem I must ask for her hand in marriage from you."

"I would be happy to act in Lord Northcote's stead," the marquis said, raising a brow. "I trust your offer is a serious one?"

In for a penny, in for a pound. He took another sip of whiskey. "Yes. It's no secret that I've been looking for a bride. I would be honored to take Lady Stokey as my wife."

"Honored?"

Bloody hell. The man needn't sound so dubious. "I realize that circumstances have necessitated this proposal, but I do hold her in high esteem."

"Good. As my wife's sister, Lady Stokey's future happiness is my chief concern," he said. "Do you promise to make her happy?"

The question startled him. Ordinarily, peers of the realm discussed finances and dowry when arranging alliances. Even his interview with Bess' father had been no exception. Happiness was not a prerequisite. Indeed, it wasn't even a consideration. "I shall do my utmost," he said simply, meaning the words.

It wasn't his intention to wed Tia and make her miserable. After Bess, he'd given up on the idea of finding love again. It had taken him some years and a hell of a lot of guilt-banishing to realize Bess' death didn't mean he couldn't find a comfortable union with another woman. He wanted a woman in his bed, a lady in his drawing room, a mother for his children. Tia would wear all those roles exceedingly well, he felt. That he wanted her more than he wanted his next breath didn't precisely hurt either. He hadn't wanted a cold, chaste marriage of duty only. He had no fear he'd suffer that fate with Tia.

The marquis nodded. "I'll take you at your word, Devonshire. There is one more thing. My wife requested that I remind you that Lady Stokey is possessed of some funds of her own. I'm given to understand she would likely prefer to retain access to them during her marriage to you."

It was another odd request, but one which didn't trouble Heath in the least. He had his own funds. If Tia required funds for baubles and fripperies, he had no objections. He wasn't marrying because he needed gold in his coffers. He was marrying for necessity and heirs. "She may retain her funds and dispense with them as she likes."

"Excellent." Thornton stood, his expression changing to one of relief. "Welcome to the family, Your Grace."

Heath stood, knowing he'd done the right thing by Tia. Now all that remained was to get his little spitfire to agree to marry him. And he had the distinct feeling that it would prove quite a feat.

"I must what?"

Tia stared at her outraged sister, aghast. Cleo's expression was most forbidding. Perhaps unforgiving as well. Tia knew this time she had gone beyond the pale, but that didn't mean anyone could expect her to simply bow to the whims of society as if she didn't have a free will.

"You must marry him," Cleo repeated, folding her arms over her chest and glaring at her in the same way their nasty old governess, Miss Hullyhew, had whenever they'd been naughty. "There is no other alternative."

She supposed a smarting ankle and wrist had become the least of her problems. "You cannot order me about as if I were your vassal, Cleo." But of course, she knew her sister could and would, both because she was a sister and because Tia herself was a captive audience, trapped in her bed thanks to her latest misadventures.

"Lord Trotter saw you and the duke in bed together," Cleo said, her voice accusatory but scarcely above a whisper, almost as if she feared someone would overhear them although they were alone in Tia's private chamber with the door closed.

Tia winced at the reminder of their unwanted guest at the hunting cabin. "The duke was warming me. I caught a chill after being stranded in the rain. That is all the man could have seen."

"Darling sister, please dispense with your protestations of innocence. You and I both know quite well that you weren't innocently singing hymns in bed with Devonshire."

"Of course we weren't." Tia sniffed. "I'm a dreadful singer."

"Cease being obtuse," her sister ordered, apparently not willing to allow her to brazen it out. "I warned you about your behavior with Devonshire. You know that Thornton and I are treading on extremely thin ice with society as it is. Not to mention the ramifications for poor Miss Whitney. And Bella. Dear heavens. Bella will slay you if you don't do the proper thing and wed the duke."

Marriage.

To Heath.

Tia frowned, considering the previously inconceivable prospect. She'd never thought to marry again, and certainly not if it wasn't for love. Lord Stokey had quite cured her of the notion that marriage was an institution in which she would care to trap herself once more. Her widow's portion was respectable. She flitted through life much like a butterfly, floating when and where she would with no man to demand her time. No troublesome rules. No tiring emotions. Not a single expectation.

She treasured her independence. It was a possession few women could claim to fully own. She wasn't prepared to so quickly raise the white flag of defeat and simply bow to Cleo and Thornton's wishes. There was also the matter of the duke not having asked for her hand.

"Devonshire hasn't asked me," she pointed out. "You said yourself that he came here to hunt for a bride. Men like the duke don't wed a woman like me." As she said the last, a pang crept through her heart. It was true, of course. But a small part of her rather wished it weren't.

"You say that as if you're a French whore." Cleo's eyes narrowed. "The lady doth protest too much."

Damn it all. Why did her sister have to be so perceptive? Why couldn't she have been blessed with a meek and dull-witted sibling instead? Tia sighed. "I'm merely speaking truth. Devonshire is likely searching for a young, innocent miss. I'm a widow. I've had lovers. I adore parties and dresses and the city, and he adores books and crumbling estates in the country. We're quite opposite." Most of these things she knew from what she'd heard of Heath, back when she'd traveled in the same circles without ever being kissed senseless by him in her bedchamber. Or carried in his arms. In truth, if she was honest with herself, she would admit that she knew very little of the man himself, other than that he was the best kisser she'd ever known and that he could make her weak with wanting by merely catching her in his blue gaze.

"Yet apparently none of the things you've just listed kept you from becoming lovers," Cleo observed wryly, bringing Tia back to the conversation at hand. Or to be more precise, to her sister's berating.

Well, yes. There rather was that. But lust could do powerful things to a woman. "Bed sport is different from an offer of marriage," she insisted. "It's one thing to have a spot of fun and quite another to be chained to a man as his chattel for the rest of my life."

Cleo raised a brow. "You should have thought of that before you went about cavorting in hunting cabins with the Duke of Devonshire."

"I wasn't cavorting. A lady of my age doesn't cavort." Of course, she did allow a wicked duke to have his way with her. Bother it all.

"You were, and you were seen." Her sister's frown was ferocious, letting Tia know she couldn't easily cajole her way out of the predicament in which she now found herself firmly mired. "And I've heard enough of this claptrap that you're too ancient for misbehavior and marriage. You're only five-and-twenty."

Drat Cleo for being so persistent. Tia's head was beginning to ache. She needed some time alone with her thoughts. Some time to figure out her next course of action. Some time that didn't involve being berated by her sister. "If you're finished railing at me, I should like to get some rest. I've had a devil of a day."

"You?" Cleo's tone was indignant.

Tia winced. "It isn't a trifling matter, getting caught out in the wilds of East Anglia in the midst of a raging rainstorm, you know."

"Enough," Cleo bit out. "I won't entertain any further attempts on your part to garner my pity or to otherwise distract me. Thornton is having an interview with Devonshire at this very moment. Your fate is sealed, my dear. You will wed the duke, and that is that."

Dear, sweet heavens.

Chapter Six

*T*HE LADY WAS BEING STUBBORN.

Heath cooled his heels in the yellow drawing room later the next evening, waiting for Tia to deign him worthy of her presence. Despite Lord and Lady Thornton's most fervent efforts to oversee a meeting between Heath and Tia the day before—ostensibly to both ward off further scandal and to ensure a union was indeed forthcoming—Tia had pled a headache. She'd been unable to leave her chamber, thanks to her grievous injuries. After many frustrated attempts at coaxing Tia from her haven, Lady Thornton had conceded defeat. Her eyes had been snapping with fire as she'd announced to Thornton and Heath both that the lady would not be joining them.

Heath had considered sneaking to her chamber and persuading her in the best way he knew how, but he'd thought better of it, not wishing to do any further damage. Thus far, Lord Trotter had been willing to keep his knowledge to himself thanks to the clever manipulation of the marquis. But their time of reprieve was limited. Trotter's silence was dependent upon an announcement being made.

An announcement that it seemed Tia wasn't willing or

ready to make.

He paced the length of the room, wondering if he'd be forced to simply go to her chamber and extract her from it himself. She had finally agreed to a meeting *sans* the marquis and marchioness. Thornton and his wife had acquiesced, seemingly at their wits' end.

But that had been—he consulted his pocket watch—an hour ago. His patience was thinner than Lord Trotter's hair at the moment. The minx had certainly put him through his paces. He was of half a mind to tell her—when she finally appeared, that was—that he'd like to ask for Miss Whitney's hand in marriage. It would be worth it just to see her eyes flash with fury.

The door to the drawing room clicked open at last, revealing the source of his irritation. She looked, despite his irritation with her, beautiful as ever. She wore a dashing day dress of silk and cut velvet in a deep shade of burgundy that set her golden locks off to perfection. Her bodice was high-necked, lined with a formidable row of buttons he longed to undo. She wore a diamond star in her hair, a brooch at her throat, and glittering diamond earrings.

She was not smiling. And she had only a slight limp to detract from her otherwise august figure. The result of yesterday's adventure, no doubt.

He bowed, deciding to be formal. She would need wooing, that much he knew from the short time he'd spent in her company. "My lady."

She stopped halfway across the room, leaving a good amount of distance between them. A safe amount of distance, he presumed. She met his gaze then, her expression guarded. "Your Grace. I understand you wished an audience."

He thought of how she'd felt beneath him the day before, warm and soft and eager for him. She could don a mantle of ice if she chose, but he knew how to thaw it, by damn. He stalked closer to her, cutting the space between them by half. "I did."

She clasped her hands at her waist and raised an imperious brow. "If you're intending to offer for me out of some misplaced notion of being a gentleman, you can stubble it right now. I'm a widow, not some silly virginal miss you've ruined."

A different tactic occurred to him just then. He moved toward her with slow deliberation, stopping only when he was near enough to catch a whiff of violets. "That wasn't my intention."

Her eyes widened ever so slightly, her cheeks turning the pale pink of a rose in bloom. "It wasn't?"

He shook his head. "No."

Tia licked her lips, staring at him. "Why in heaven's name are you standing so near to me?"

"What's the matter, darling?" He reached for her hand, running his fingers over her smooth skin, stopping only when he reached her wrist. Her pulse beat steady and swift. "Don't you trust yourself?"

She flinched away from him, giving him his answer more surely than any words could. "You're certainly familiar for a man who isn't intending to propose marriage. If it's a mistress you're after, you can stubble it just the same. I'll not be a kept woman."

In truth, he'd never thought of making Tia his mistress. Why would he want her temporarily when he could have her forever? Twice with her hadn't been enough. He very much doubted that forever would be.

"That wasn't my intention either," he told her. He could read the confusion in her pretty eyes. Good. He liked having her thrown off balance. It gave him the upper hand, a position he needed when it came to her.

"Then what was?" she asked, her voice hesitant.

At the moment, all he truly wanted to do was kiss her. Kiss her senseless. Kiss her until her rapier wit was dulled by desire. He planted a hand on her cinched waist and pulled her flush against his chest. "Simply this."

Before she could protest, his mouth was on hers. She

sighed and melted against him, not even bothering to fight it. When she opened for him, he deepened the kiss. His cock went instantly hard, and if he'd had any lingering doubt that marrying the woman in his arms was the right thing to do, they were banished in that instant. She was his. And he was going to show her precisely that.

He kissed her with all the passion raging through him, so thoroughly that by the time he broke away, he felt as dazed as Tia looked. Her delectable mouth was swollen and berry-red. Her eyes glistened. A handful of her curls had come undone. Save for the fact that she remained buttoned up as a temperance spinster, she appeared utterly debauched and utterly delicious. Oh, yes. She was his, damn it.

"Christ, Tia," he said, his breathing as ragged as hers. "When we're wed, I'm going to keep you in the bedchamber for a fortnight."

His words seemed to return her to the present. She blinked, raising a hand to her mouth. "When we're wed? You just said you had no intention of offering for me."

"I said I had no intention of offering for you out of...what was it you called it?" He stopped to capture her precise phrasing. "Ah yes, my misplaced notion of being a gentleman."

She frowned at him once more. "I confess, I'm quite confused."

He kissed her again, just to erase that frown. "I'm offering for you because I want you."

"I'm not your first lover," she said. "That's rather apparent. Why would you choose me for any reason other than necessity? You seek to avoid scandal, and that is all."

"No." Of course, that had been his initial motivation. But he'd had time to think upon it as he awaited her over the course of the last day. He knew that he would never find a more perfect wife than Tia. She was everything he'd never thought he'd wanted. And yet, he couldn't resist her, didn't wish to. "I seek a woman who drives me wild with desire, a woman who isn't afraid to be passionate in my bed, a woman who is beautiful and maddening and in need of a man who knows how to give her pleasure."

She was quiet, considering him with a searching gaze that he had the distinct impression saw more than he would have preferred. "You speak of desire but not of love."

Ah. She hadn't struck him as a sentimental female. He didn't honestly believe he could ever love again. Losing Bess had cured him of that ailment. Love was for fools and the incurably young. "I won't insult you by claiming to be hopelessly in love with you in such a short amount of time. But I do believe that we can build a mutual affection for each other."

"I can't claim to be impressed by either love or marriage," she said, surprising him again. "I was in love once, and I was hopelessly disappointed. When I married, it wasn't for love, and I was hopelessly disappointed then as well. Tell me, why should I give up my independence now when I know I'm bound to be disappointed either way?"

The lady had a point. She could continue flitting about society as she pleased, taking lovers as she pleased, attending parties and commissioning dresses. But he had a feeling that eventually she'd find that life just as disappointing. She wasn't meant to be alone, and neither was he. Maybe in each other, they'd found the perfect match.

"I can't speak for your past," he said honestly. "But I can promise you that I will do my utmost not to disappoint you as your husband. I've also spoken with the marquis regarding your personal funds. They shall remain yours to dispense with as you please even after we wed."

She looked away from him, lowering her gaze to study the intricate pattern on the rug at their feet. "I don't wish to be married to simply avoid a scandal. I'm made of stern stuff. I daresay I could weather any scandal that came my way."

"While the potential for scandal precipitated the situation in which we now find ourselves, I wish to marry you for another reason entirely. And it makes no sense for you to attempt to weather a scandal on your own when I've done my fair share to help create it." He reached out then and tipped up her chin, unable to keep from touching her again. She was too damn tempting. Too beautiful.

"I couldn't bear to be the object of your pity," she said quietly, her eyes back upon his.

"I don't pity you, Tia," he reassured her, taking her mouth in another long, sweet kiss. "I want you." He trapped her hand in his and lowered it to his trousers and his rigid cock. "Feel how much."

"Want can dissipate," she whispered.

"Or it can grow stronger," he countered. "Even a fool would know that what we share is rare indeed."

She caught her lip in her teeth, looking conflicted. "Your Grace, you should be marrying a sweet, innocent girl. Someone like Miss Whitney."

Bloody hell, she was stubborn. "I don't want Miss Whitney, and the evidence of that lies beneath your hand, my dear."

She flushed and snatched her hand away. "To think I once thought you proper and dull."

She'd thought him dull? He supposed he ought to be offended, but he couldn't blame her. He'd cultivated his reputation. He'd been careful to throw himself into restoring his estate and forget about painting and the creative force that had once ruled him. But he hadn't been completely able to stifle the passion in his soul, a passion Tia had wakened into a blazing fire.

"Marry me, Tia," he said simply, half question, half ducal decree. He couldn't help it. She would marry him, one way or another. There would be the easy way or the hard way. He hoped she would choose the former rather than the latter.

"I shall think on it," she informed him as regally as Queen Victoria herself before turning on her heel and giving him her back.

Damn it to hell. She was quitting the room as abruptly

as she had appeared—a feat, given her limp—not even allowing him the last word. He watched her leave, not bothering to stop her. She'd think on it? The saucy woman. It would seem she'd chosen the hard way after all.

"I hope we can make a happy announcement at dinner this evening."

Tia stared at her sister, thinking the grit in her voice belied the outward pleasantness of her words. Cleo wasn't merely telling her she hoped there would be an announcement of her impending nuptials to Devonshire. She was telling her there would be. Or else.

How to broach the topic in a politic way and tell her sister that she'd just turned tail and run like a spooked horse, leaving the duke without an answer in the yellow drawing room? She was seated on a *Louis Quinze* settee in her chamber, her throbbing ankle propped on a pillow, rendering her quite trapped. She didn't like being a captive audience, especially not when her sister was in high dudgeon.

"Precisely what sort of announcement were you hoping to make?" she asked, hedging. "That you've decided to cancel the fish course?"

"That you're marrying the duke, you dreadful thing." Cleo's frown was most ferocious.

"If I told you that you rather resemble Thornton's mother at the moment, would you attempt to do me harm?" Tia blinked in feigned innocence. Actually, irritating her elder sister was an entertaining and much-needed distraction from the troublesome thoughts plaguing her. And she knew that her sister and the dowager marchioness blended as well as tea and parsnips. Which was to say not at all.

"I should give you a sound drubbing," Cleo threatened with enough force to suggest she was deadly serious.

"And here I thought our sisterly hair-pulling days were over," she teased.

Cleo crossed her arms over her chest, affecting a posture that was at once forbidding and motherly. "I'm not in the mood for levity, Hypatia. I'm in the mood to hear that my minx of a sister has finally conceded to reason and will put an end to the scandal she's threatened to bring down on all our heads."

Tia winced. "You know I detest being called by my full name."

"Tell me that you've accepted the duke's proposal," Cleo demanded, ignoring her.

"I'm afraid I cannot."

"I'm certain I misheard you just now." Cleo stalked closer to her, within bodily harm-causing range. "You could not have possibly said such a hopelessly dull-witted thing to me."

"I haven't accepted Devonshire," she elaborated.

"A handsome duke wants to wed you. And you've told him no?" Cleo's voice was so high-pitched in her fury that Tia feared for the safety of the windows.

"I didn't tell him no, precisely." She eyed her sister warily. "I merely didn't tell him yes either."

Cleo threw up her hands, apparently frustrated enough to finally lose her composure. "Why in heaven's name did you not accept him immediately?"

There was the rub. Tia didn't know why she hadn't simply acquiesced and made everyone happy. She'd had some time to think on it, and the prospect of marrying Heath wasn't at all horrid. Quite the opposite. While they'd only spent a few days together, she couldn't deny she'd never been drawn to another man in the same elemental way. Not even Denbigh had made her feel such a heady tumult of desire and need, no matter how dangerous or how foolish. She wanted him. Desperately. His kisses in the drawing room had proven that. She'd been all but ready for him to haul up her skirts and bend her over a settee. If he had pressed her, she didn't know if she'd have been able to resist.

And he'd been painfully honest in his proposal. There had been no careful flattery or honeyed lies. There had only been stark truths. His words came back to her now, taunting her. *I seek a woman who drives me wild with desire, a woman who isn't afraid to be passionate in my bed.* For the first time in her life, a man wanted her for who she was, for the flamboyant nature she'd never been able to repress. Denbigh had thrown her over for another for reasons she'd never know. Others had wanted her merely as a bedmate. The duke wanted her as his wife. In his bed.

Marriage to him would not be boring, that much she knew. He'd promised to keep her in the bedchamber for a fortnight when they wed, and she couldn't say she'd offer much protest.

So why then had she made him wait for her response? She supposed it was because she could. He had seemed so assured of himself, plying her with kisses and standing so near to her that she could smell his delicious masculine scent. Making her helpless in his arms to say anything but yes. The answer he'd wanted to hear had been on the tip of her tongue. But the devil in her had decided to make him wait just a bit more.

"Tia?" Cleo's voice intruded on her thoughts, bringing her back to the present with a jolt. "Are you going to sit there like a ninny, staring at the wall, or are you going to answer me?"

"I didn't give him an answer because I wanted to make him wait," she replied, even though she knew it would only irritate her sister even further. "He seemed so very sure of himself. I took a bit of pleasure in leaving him there, wondering what I shall decide."

"Blessed angels, Thornton was right. You are the most infuriating female to ever live." Cleo punctuated her declaration with an unladylike stomp of her foot.

"Thornton said that of me?" She was sure she ought to

be insulted, but the urge to laugh overcame her instead so she gave in, tilting her head back and indulging.

"Are you completely mad?" Cleo was staring at her, incredulous. "I find no cause for laughter."

"Oh, pooh." Tia waved a dismissive hand. "Pray don't act as if you're the soul of propriety yourself. I seem to recall a house party where Thornton was routinely within your chamber. And he was not then your husband."

Cleo sank down on the settee alongside her with a weary-sounding sigh. "Dearest sister, I'm more than aware that Thornton and I created a scandal of our own. But we've done a great deal to repair our reputations. We've made things right. You and Devonshire need to do so as well. I've seen the way you two look at each other when you think no one is watching. Trust me when I say that, my frustration for you aside, this is a match that was meant to be made."

Tia considered Cleo's words for a moment. "Perhaps. But I have much to lose."

Cleo gave her shoulder a sisterly pat. "But you also have so much to gain if you only allow yourself to take a chance."

"I dislike chance immensely," Tia grumbled, fearing she was being won over. "I prefer the absolute to the possible."

"And I dislike tarrying immensely," her sister returned. "Go to him, Tia. You know what you must do."

Tia knew it was the hour that he would have returned to his chamber to dress for dinner. And she knew her way to his chamber by heart. "I shall think on it," she promised Cleo.

"Excellent." Cleo rose and settled her silk skirts back into place. "But do be quick about it. You haven't that much time left before the dinner gong, and as I said, I expect to make a happy announcement."

Tia certainly hoped it would be a happy one. And that marrying the Duke of Devonshire would be the right decision. If he would still have her, that was.

Heath had just dismissed his valet when a furtive rap on his bedchamber door startled him. He raked a hand through his hair, undoing all the attempts his man had made at setting it to rights. Christ, he hoped it wasn't Thornton come to deliver a flogging for his failure to acquire a betrothal. But when he stalked across the chamber to see who had knocked, he was pleasantly surprised by the stunningly lovely woman staring at him with big green eyes and a sweet Cupid's bow of a mouth.

"Tia," he said, shocked as hell to see her but every bit as delighted. She was dressed for dinner, wearing a red silk gown that showed off her mouthwatering bosom to perfection. Her hair was perfectly coifed, twin diamond stars twinkling at him from their place nestled in her curls instead of the lone star she'd worn earlier. He couldn't look at her without wanting her.

His cock rose to attention instantly, and he knew the moment her gaze lowered to discover the effect she had upon him. Her nostrils flared ever so slightly. "Devonshire. Let me in, will you? I can't very well have someone see me standing in the corridor outside your chamber or Cleo shall have my head on a pike."

He stepped back, gesturing for her to enter. Ever the saucy one, his Tia. He could honestly say he'd never met another woman quite her equal, and he wasn't certain if that was a good thing or a bad thing. Heath watched her as she cast a glance both ways before gathering up her skirts and hurrying over the threshold. This was certainly an interesting turn of events. He hadn't expected to see her so soon and not in his bloody chamber of all places. Didn't she know he couldn't very well be near her without wanting to strip every inch of fabric off her delicious body and take her until they were both mindless with release?

Damn. He took a deep, calming breath. He couldn't very well take her to bed again. Not here and not now. If she was to be his wife, he little wanted to cause any more tongues to wag than they already had. He forced himself to think of something that would cure his raging hardness. Lord Trotter's bulbous nose. Thornton's fist crashing into his jaw. A pheasant. Anything but how much he wanted to tear open her bodice and suck her pink nipples until she came.

Double damn. Nothing could force his cock to soften or his mind to stop replacing boring thoughts with thoughts of seducing the woman before him. It was a hopeless task.

"Your head is far too pretty to be on a pike," he quipped, trying to distract himself with dialogue instead.

"Not in my sister's draconian estimation." Tia said with a raised brow. "I assure you, she's quite the virago ever since I was caught without a stitch of clothes on in an abandoned hunting cabin with a wicked duke."

He found himself grinning at her, probably like the fool that he was. "A wicked duke, was it?"

"Very wicked indeed," she said, slowly sidling closer to him until her skirts brushed against his trousers. "He came upon me in the woods and ravished me."

Ravished her, had he? He caught her waist and pulled her against him, unable to resist touching her. "You were completely unwilling?"

She nodded, tilting her head so that her lips were just a breath from his."Of course."

The urge to kiss her was strong but he refrained. "Do you know what I think, my lady?"

"No," she whispered, her gaze lowering to his mouth.

"I think you're lying," he told her.

She feathered her lips over his in a delicate, tantalizing kiss."Perhaps just a bit."

His control was disappearing faster than a runaway horse. "I distinctly recall you telling me that you didn't wish me to be noble," he reminded her.

She caressed his face, rubbing lightly over his beard in a gesture that was at once gentle and incredibly arousing. "Dear me. I'd forgotten."

He pressed a kiss to her palm, then flicked his tongue against her skin. "I hadn't."

"Do you still wish to be noble?" she asked him, her tone hesitant.

Her reason for daring to appear at his chamber suddenly occurred to him. She had decided to give him an answer. If the drawn expression on her beautiful face was any indication, she was hoping he hadn't rescinded his offer for her hand. Which meant that her answer was yes.

If anything, the realization only served to make his cock even stiffer than it had been before. The urge to bury himself inside her was strong and tempting. But there remained a hint of the gentleman in him, reminding him that he ought not to act so rashly. Not this time.

No, instead he would toy with her and make her wonder as she had with him. Two could play at her game. "In what way, Tia?"

"You know very well, you scoundrel." She pinned him with a frown.

He wanted to kiss it away. "No. I don't. I'm afraid you must say the words aloud."

She sighed, clearly not pleased with having to raise the flag of surrender in their small war of wits. "I wondered if you still want to marry me, you insufferable man."

There it was again, that fierce nature of hers. Theirs would not be a boring union. Not at all. "When you phrase it so sweetly, how can I deny you?"

"Oh, bother. Perhaps you should just kiss me, then," she said, half suggestion, half command.

He did, slanting his lips over hers and tasting her when she opened for him. She kissed him back with the same fiery passion that threatened to undo all the good intentions he'd just so carefully built up in his mind. He tore his mouth from hers before he took things too far, gazing down at the woman who was to be his wife.

"You've decided you'll marry me, Tia?" he asked, even though it was already a foregone conclusion. He rather wanted to hear her say the words.

She paused, as though reluctant to relinquish her final

bit of power over him. "Yes. I will be your wife, Heath."

His wife. The small, gorgeous creature before him was to be his wife. The mother of his children. The lady of his estate. He had come to East Anglia intending to find his duchess, and find her he had. Even if she wasn't at all the sort of wife he'd meant to find. Even if she brought him perilously close to the man he'd once been, the fervent young man who'd been driven by passion and painting, who'd been hopelessly selfish. Who'd left the woman he loved to die alone. He could never, would never, forget what he'd done. The memory of Bess would haunt him until the day he too took his last breath.

But there was no room in this moment between him and Tia for ghosts. He knew that in his heart as surely as he knew she would make a good wife to him. He desired her, but more than that, he needed her. And she needed him in much the same irrevocable way.

"Thank you." He released her waist and took her hands in his, bringing them both to his lips for a kiss. "You've done me a great honor."

He vowed to himself as he looked down on Tia that he would do whatever he must to ensure the reckless man he'd once been remained buried. He would never again betray another woman he cared for. The last time had very nearly been the death of him.

Chapter Seven

FTER NEARLY FIVE YEARS OF HAPPILY living as a widow, she was once again a wife. Tia shivered as she awaited her new husband in her new chamber. They had remained in East Anglia at Thornton's estate after the house party, deciding that they would not delay their nuptials. Cleo had been thrilled to throw together an impromptu wedding. Even the wayward Miss Whitney had offered to stay and help before returning to her father and stepmother's care. Tia's other sisters, Helen and Bo, had joined them, along with their parents the earl and countess of Northcote. Her no-account brothers had been too busy gadding about, as brothers were often wont to do.

The wedding had been lovely if not a touch bittersweet, for Tia had known that at the end of the wedding dinner, she'd be leaving the comfort of her sisters behind for a new adventure and a new life as the wife of a man she'd known for little more than a fortnight. It had decidedly not been her intention in attending Cleo's house party to leave a married woman. But then, she'd stumbled in the gardens and had been saved by a man who kissed like the devil and knew his way around a lady's buttons. She'd been trapped by her own inability to resist temptation.

She stared at her reflection now, wondering that she didn't look different. For six years her identity had been Lady Stokey, and now she answered to a new name. It would take some time to accustom herself to the change, much as it would take her some time to feel as if Chatsworth House was her home. She had traveled through much of the day to Devonshire's family seat, had gone through the necessary introductions before the servants, had enjoyed a late meal and had retired to her chamber where her lady's maid had attended her.

There was no outward difference in her at all, she concluded. She possessed the same unbound blonde curls, the same eyes, same nose, same mouth she'd always despised for it was shaped far too awkwardly. She wore a silk-and-lace nightgown that had been prepared for just this occasion.

Her wedding night.

Ever since that day in the hunting cabin, Heath had forced a respectable distance between them. The proprieties having been observed and scandal neatly avoided, Tia was eager to be alone with him once more. She missed his kisses and knowing touch. In truth, she'd grown frightfully fond of him over the last few weeks as he'd courted her. He was surprisingly considerate, as evidenced by the efforts he'd clearly made to ready her chamber for her. It was beautifully decorated, with touches of bright color and not even a hint of dust to show it had been unused for the last few years. She knew it would have been an undertaking and that he'd given thought to her tastes when he'd directed its preparation. A lovely lithograph of a butterfly hanging on the wall had made her smile when she'd first entered.

A knock on the door adjoining her chamber to his startled her from her reveries and sent a jolt of anticipation snaking through her. Her husband awaited her. She gave her reflection a last look, smoothing down her hair before she turned to greet him.

"You may enter."

The door swept open to reveal Heath, looking unfairly handsome in a silk dressing gown. A slow smile curved his sensual mouth as his gaze met hers. "Good evening, wife. You're looking particularly ravishing."

"Flattery will get you nowhere, sir," she teased, crossing the room to him. As much as she'd never thought to be a wife again, she had to admit she enjoyed the sound of the title on Heath's lips.

"Devil take it." He caught her waist and hauled her against him. "I was hoping to bed you tonight. Is there any way I can change your mind, Your Grace?"

Tia enjoyed his banter. It was a side of him she'd never dreamt existed before getting to know him. She found herself smiling back at him, reaching up to run her fingers over the soft abrasion of his beard. Thinking about it grazing her skin made her instantly wet. She couldn't help it. "Perhaps there are ways you could persuade me," she suggested, relieved that their time of polite courtship was at an end. If she'd had to wait much longer, it would have driven her mad.

"Ah, a lady of reason." His gaze was brilliant and hot on hers, sending a frisson of desire through her. "How might I persuade you?"

"You may begin by kissing me," she told him boldly.

His hands slid upward, along the curves of her waist and higher, spreading fire in their wake. When he reached her breasts, he cupped them, his thumbs unerringly finding her hardened nipples beneath the thin barrier of fabric between them. He flicked over them once, twice, three times. It wasn't the kiss she had requested, but it was enough to send another stab of desire to her core. How was it that with a mere touch he could make her desperate for him? Desperate to be taken by him, loved by him, possessed by him. She didn't know what madness he wrought on her, only that she didn't want it to end.

"Where shall I kiss you, darling?" His voice was deep and dark and seductive, rolling over her senses like burnished velvet.

She moaned as he gently tugged at her aching nipples, arching into his capable hands. "Everywhere."

He lowered his head to press a soft, open-mouthed kiss on the side of her neck. "With great pleasure," he murmured before moving to the hollow at the base of her throat where her frantic pulse beat. His tongue darted against her skin. "You even taste of violets."

She had dabbed a bit of her perfume on that exact spot earlier. "I hope you don't mind. It's always been my favorite scent." Lord Stokey had detested violet water and had forbidden her from wearing it. After his death, she'd worn it every day simply because she could.

"Of course not." He dragged his mouth up to her earlobe, catching it between his teeth. "I can't smell violets without my cock going hard."

She shivered from his confession and his warm breath and the thought of his cock all at once. For some reason, his lips on her ear made her want him even more. His slow lovemaking was so seductive, so delicious, that she feared she wouldn't make it much longer without begging him to take her. She wanted him inside her, hard and deep and wonderful. She longed for him in a way that frightened her. It was new, foreign. Never before had a man been such a source of weakness for her.

"You're making me mad," she told him on a whisper. She ran her fingers slowly through his thick hair and rubbed her cheek against his. His neatly clipped whiskers were a welcome abrasion.

His tongue followed the whorl of her ear and he rolled her nipples between his thumb and forefinger again. "Good. I want you on fire for me, darling. Naked and wet and hungry."

Dear, sweet God. The things he did to her. He hadn't even kissed her mouth yet, for heaven's sake, and she was already quivering, a wanton woman in his arms. The attraction between them had not dimmed like a candle left burning too long. If anything, it had grown even more intense. How was it that a mere month ago, she had never given him a second thought and yet now, she couldn't imagine her life without him in it? She didn't know. But what she did know was that if he didn't soon kiss her, she'd perish from the wait.

She decided to be bold and turned her head so that their lips met at last. She opened for him, running her tongue against his. He kissed her deeply, holding her close, as if she were cherished. Heath cupped her jaw, keeping her still as he ravished her mouth. Slowly, he led her backward across the chamber, step by step until at last she felt the bed behind her.

He tore his lips from hers, gazing down at her. "Take off your gown for me, darling."

She gathered twin handfuls of silk and pulled the hem up over her body. The fabric slid over her already sensitized skin like a lush caress, heightening her arousal. Her eyes locked with his, she raised it higher, revealing first her hips, then higher still. His searing stare dipped.

"Shall I continue?" she asked with feigned innocence.

"Yes," he said without hesitation, his voice thick and low with desire. "Don't stop."

Tia shimmied, lifting her gown slowly to bare her breasts before whipping it over her head and tossing it to the floor. It fell behind her in a scarcely audible whisper of sound. She cupped her breasts, watching the way his eyes went heavy-lidded and darkened to the color of the sky just after sunset. "Is this what you wanted, Your Grace?"

"God yes," he groaned. His hands went back to her waist, lifting her gently onto the bed. He tugged open the knot on his dressing gown and shucked it, leaving him naked and glorious before her.

She allowed herself the luxury of admiring his lean, powerful body. He was not a man who sat about eating muffins all day, that much was certain. His chest was carved of muscle, his stomach taut and lined with whorls of golden hair that ran directly to his rigid cock. He was hers, she thought.

He joined her on the bed then, straddling her and lowering his head to suck a nipple. She arched and moaned as the wet warmth of his mouth shot a flame of desire directly to her core. His fingers slid between them, exploring her slick folds with an expert touch. Somehow he knew exactly how to touch her, how much pressure to exert, where she ached the most. He toyed with the bud of her sex, rubbing it fast and just hard enough to make her moan again as he sucked her other nipple. Looking up at her, he caught it between his teeth and tugged.

The delicious sensation of a climax built within her. She was very near to the edge. When he sank a finger deep inside her, touching her exactly where she longed to be touched, she lost control. The pleasure was as swift as it was sudden, claiming her with such force that she shook against him and cried out.

"Damn," he muttered, kissing the side of her breast as he withdrew his finger "I wanted to go slowly, but I can't wait. I need to be inside you now."

"Yes," she agreed, spreading her legs wider in welcome. She wanted him, all of him. Tia took his cock in hand and guided him to her ready entrance, tipping her hips to bring him deep. Her mind might not be entirely at peace with the notion of once again being a wife, but her body was more than sure. This was what her body wanted. Needed. Desperately. Oh yes.

"Ah, fuck." He braced himself over her, the tip of his cock just far enough inside her to make her desperate for more. "Tell me what you want, wife."

"I want you," she said, breathless, the wicked words making her even more wild with need. She rather liked being called "wife" by the handsome man atop her. "Inside me."

He thrust home, sending a delicious spear of pleasure

through her. "Like this, darling?" He kissed her before she could answer, his tongue plunging into her mouth in the same claiming.

She wrapped her legs around him, drawing him deeper. When he began a fast, hard rhythm, she met him thrust for thrust. He slammed into her again and again, his hand going back between their bodies to once again pleasure her. A few flicks of the sensitive button hidden within her folds, and she was coming undone again, clenching on him in a series of spasms. And then, he too was losing himself, sinking deep within her and spending his seed.

After five long years as a widow, she was indeed a wife once more, and at the moment, that didn't particularly feel like a bad thing to be.

Heath had spent the night in his wife's bed. It confounded him that he'd fallen asleep there with her rather than returning to his chamber as he ought to have done. Even as he flipped through the *Times* over eggs, kidneys and kippers the next morning, his reaction to Tia irked him. While he intended for them to get on well as husband and wife, and he certainly meant to take her as often as possible, he didn't wish to become—damn it all—*attached*.

In the short time he'd spent courting her, he'd realized that he needed to rein in his recklessness where she was concerned. He had loved once, madly and desperately, and he had lost that love. He didn't care to repeat his experience. Indeed, he'd gone to great efforts to close off that part of his life forever. The evidence was sealed up in a chamber in the east wing, for Christ's sake.

And last night, he'd taken one look at Tia standing in her chamber in that frothy confection, her breasts and waist on display like his personal Venus, and he'd lost control. His plans for an unhurried seduction had been dashed the moment he'd felt her soft, nude curves beneath him.

He stabbed at his plate with extra vigor and attempted to focus on the news rather than allow his already hard cock to once again rule him. He needed to take care, or he'd be following Tia about like a lovesick swain and writing maudlin poetry to her hips. He'd accomplished what he'd set out to do. He'd gained a wife. Now he simply needed to regain his senses.

The door of the breakfast room swept open to reveal the very object of his frustrated musings. She was pretty as an angel in her violet morning gown, her curls piled high on her head. The smile she sent his way when their gazes met sent an arrow of heat directly to his groin.

Devil take it.

They exchanged formal greetings, more for the sake of the servants than themselves, and he pretended not to watch her from the corner of his eye whilst she fixed her plate and was seated. In truth, he couldn't *not* stare at her. She was such a gorgeous creature, every bit the butterfly, vibrant and exotic and delicate all at once. If he had still painted, he would've captured her a hundred ways. With morning sun filtering over her while she slept, buttoned up in a formidable silk gown, beautiful and nervous on their wedding day, naked and flushed beneath him.

"Your Grace?"

Oh bloody hell. She was talking to him and he was mooning over her as if he were a lad seeing his first woman. "You may call me Heath, my dear," he reminded her. He'd been the duke for several years already, but he still sometimes looked about for his grandfather whenever someone addressed him as "Your Grace". And his profligate grandfather was not a man he ever wished to be.

"Heath, then." Her lips curved in a shy smile. "I fear you were engrossed in your newspaper and quite forgot I was here."

No. He'd merely been too busy imagining her in various poses. Particularly the nude ones. "I'm dreadfully sorry. What was it that you said?"

"I wished to thank you for making me feel at home." Her gaze was warm on his, trapping him in her thrall. "I daresay you went to a great deal of effort on my behalf, and it is most appreciated."

He had written ahead and seen to the redecorating of her chamber with her tastes in mind. Apparently, she'd found it to her liking. But it wouldn't do for her to continue staring at him as if he'd plucked the sun from the sky and handed it to her on the Cavendish family silver. She was doing wicked things to him with that frank, sensual look. And he was doing his damnedest to keep the wicked to a minimum and his raging emotions under tight rein where they belonged.

He cleared his throat, feeling uncomfortable. "It was no trouble at all. Mrs. Rhodes is an expert at seeing to the comfort of the household."

"I see." Her smile faltered. "I shall have to thank her as well, then."

A silence fell between them then, broken only by the clink of cutlery on china. He had disappointed her. He hadn't meant to, had only meant to diffuse the heaviness of the moment. Hadn't he just told himself that he needed to act with more restraint where she was concerned? That he couldn't afford to continue allowing himself to lose his head over her?

Yes, damn it. Of course he had. And now he was feeling badly when he'd done nothing wrong. He needed to escape the room and put an end to this foolishness. He stood abruptly, startling Tia from her concentration on her breakfast.

"I prefer to take my ride each morning," he told her, deciding that it would be best that they spent little time together during the course of the day. Some distance would do well to douse his inconvenient passions. Or at least, he hoped it would. "I shall leave your morning schedule to your preference. Today, Mrs. Rhodes will be giving you a tour of the house to better acquaint you with your new home. She will collect you after you finish breaking your fast."

"Yes, of course," she murmured in a tone of voice he couldn't quite decipher. But a tiny frown drew her brows together, and he suspected that didn't bode well for him. "Will you be joining me for tea?"

"No," he decided quickly. "I have some pressing matters to attend to, I'm afraid. Being away from the estate has left me with much work to do. I've a meeting with my steward."

In truth, he hadn't a meeting with his steward, who was a more than capable man he'd entrusted with the running of the estate in his absence. But perhaps it would be a convenient time to arrange one. He couldn't bloody well spend all day at his wife's side, sniffing at her skirts.

"Of course," she said again. "Enjoy your day, Your Grace."

"Heath," he gritted out just before stalking from the room.

He wasn't certain, but he was fairly confident he heard her say, "Yes, Your Grace."

The minx would be the death of him.

If there was one thing that drew Tia's interest as surely as a fly to a barn, it was a closed door. Closed doors and sealed-off rooms were meant to be opened and investigated. At least they were in Tia's estimation. But she hesitated outside the chamber she'd been warned away from in the east wing during her tour with Mrs. Rhodes, her hand poised over the knob.

Tia knew she was likely intruding, but one of her flaws was an unquenchable sense of curiosity. When she'd been a girl, she'd snooped through every room in her father, Lord Northcote's, country estate. She'd found nothing of interest save for a few spiders and the dusty journal of her great-grandmamma. But oh how she'd adored those days of adventure.

Given her history, she supposed it was hardly surprising that she should be entertaining herself by snooping about in Chatsworth House. After all, her husband was off riding after being rather aloof at breakfast, she'd done the necessary with her housekeeper and she'd even answered all her correspondence for the morning. She'd never been the sort to quietly sit and read books or—worse—engage in embroidery.

She cast a quick look about the hall before she opened the door and stepped inside. Though windows lined the far wall, curtains had been drawn, bathing the spacious chamber in shadows. Tia stalked across the room and made short work of the drapes, pinning them open to allow the beautiful late-morning light to illuminate the space she'd just invaded.

Everything in the room was covered with cloths, but the shapes beneath their coverings were unmistakable. Large, framed canvases.

"Paintings?" Her brow furrowed, Tia moved to the nearest stack, uncovering it.

Dust billowed forth, causing her to sneeze. Apparently, no one had entered this room or bothered with its contents in quite some time. Years, unless she missed her guess. Odd, that, especially considering Heath was so proud of the restorations he'd made to his country seat. Why would he seal away an entire room and its contents?

She looked down at the paintings she'd discovered and was instantly shocked. They weren't fusty, old Cavendish family portraits as she'd expected. Instead, they were beautiful works of art. The first was a landscape. Italian, unless she missed her guess. With bold strokes and rich, warm hues, it was so dreamy and inviting that she felt as if she were standing in the midst of the painting itself.

She flipped to the next, a scene of a nude man and woman embracing beneath a tree, presumably Adam and Eve in the Garden of Eden. The attention to detail and the lush representation quite took her breath. It was exquisite, and each painting she found was equally impressive. She skipped past a beautiful angel to another landscape, this one decidedly English, before stopping at the portrait of a woman who looked somewhat familiar to Tia. She was seated, her hands clasped, and had been represented with an almost loving attention to her beauty. Tia wished someone would paint her in that same way.

Indeed, whoever had painted these works possessed true, inspiring talent.

"What are you doing in here, Tia?" demanded her husband, intruding so suddenly on her thoughts and the chamber both that she gasped and spun about to face him, nearly knocking over the paintings she'd just revealed in the process.

"Heath." She flattened her palm over her racing heart, forgetting to annoy him by calling him "Your Grace" in her surprise. "I didn't hear you approach."

"I daresay not." He entered the room, looking rakishly handsome in his riding clothes, and rather a bit irritated as well. His full lips were drawn in a tight, disapproving line. "You were too busy riffling through rooms you have no reason to be intruding upon."

It would seem that the cool, aloof duke of the breakfast table was to continue. She supposed she couldn't entirely fault him. For all that they were wed, she was yet an interloper here. He hadn't wanted this room opened. The otherwise kind, round-visaged Mrs. Rhodes had been very firm on the matter of leaving the chamber as it was. Tia had ignored her husband's wishes, and perhaps it had been selfish of her to do so, she worried now as she watched him.

There remained much of him that she needed to know. She well understood that Heath had welcomed her into his bed, had proclaimed her the lady of the manor before his servants, but had yet to allow her fully into his confidences. He had certainly not revealed more of himself to her than his sexual needs. Heavens, she may as well have been his mistress and not his wife.

"I'm sorry," she said quickly, only half meaning the apology. After all, he couldn't very well go about closing up rooms without expecting her to investigate them. She was a leopard who couldn't entirely change her spots.

"You should not have come here," he told her. "I'll have the servants set the room to rights. Come." He held out his hand for her to take, his intention clearly to lead her from the chamber as if she hadn't just uncovered an extraordinary cache of beautiful paintings. As if his behavior were innocuous and normal.

It wasn't, and she wasn't forgetting those paintings, either. She crossed her arms over her bosom and stared him down. "No."

He raised an imperious brow. "No?"

"Just so." Perhaps taking a stand against him wasn't precisely the wisest course of action, but Tia was stubborn to a fault. She wanted to know why he was overwrought over her discovery of the paintings and why he wished to keep them hidden away when they should be enjoyed. "I won't leave until you tell me where these pictures came from and why in heaven's name they're secreted away in here."

His eyes darkened and his expression hardened. "I'm afraid you'll be waiting here a frightfully long time, then."

She shrugged as if she hadn't a care, when in truth she was very much invested in his response. She didn't wish for them to be polite strangers as they had been this morning. She longed to know him—all of him—as surely as she knew his body and the pleasures it gave her. "Very well. I'm sure I don't have anywhere else to go."

He clenched his jaw. "I haven't the patience for this, Tia. Not today."

"Tomorrow, perhaps?" she couldn't help suggesting, tongue in cheek.

But he was not amused. "Damn it, this isn't one of your larks."

The smile fled from her lips. "I know."

Did he think she was merely toying with him because

she was bored? His face was impossible to read. He held himself stiffly, as if he weren't certain if he wanted to stalk from the room or stalk to her and shake her. It occurred to her that she'd never seen her husband angry before, and perhaps she had unwittingly enraged him with her little intrusion.

"They're mine," he ground out at last.

At first, she couldn't be certain of his meaning. Of course the paintings were his. Chatsworth House and its lands all belonged to him. But there was something in the way he'd spoken the declaration that was different. It was as if he were saying he'd painted them himself. But that was ludicrous. Surely if Heath painted so sublimely she would have known.

Still, he seemed deadly serious, and she had to ask. "You painted these?"

He raked a hand through his hair. "I did. Damn it all, I should've bloody well had them burned."

Tia didn't think she would've been more shocked if he'd announced he was planning on sprouting wings and flying into the sun. She could scarcely believe he had painted the stunning canvases before her. The talent he possessed was incredible. While Tia had never been the book lover her sister Cleo was, she had always adored the art of painting. She had seen some of the finest art of their age on display, and she could honestly say that Heath's work rivaled it.

"Why should you wish to burn them?" she asked, trying to gather her scattered wits. "These are some of the most talented pieces I've ever seen. To destroy them would be a travesty. Indeed, keeping them tucked away like this, as if they're some sort of awful family secret, is travesty enough."

He came to her then, startling her by taking up the cloth and flipping it back down over the canvases. "The real travesty is that I ever wasted my time painting them at all. It was a selfish lad's fancy, nothing more."

It was apparent to her that there was a rather large part of his story he was withholding from her. He had intended to keep this room, these pictures, from her. She'd never seen him display such an intensity before, other than when they were making love. Her heart gave a momentary pang as she couldn't help but wish that she could move him the same way even when they weren't caught up in the undeniable passion between them.

She caught his hand in hers on impulse. "Why do you hate them so?"

He stilled, his gaze locking with hers. "I don't hate them. I feel nothing for them."

"I don't believe you." She squeezed his fingers, imploring him with her eyes. "I may have had no business poking about in closed rooms, but I know you well enough to see that these paintings have an effect on you. Please tell me why, Heath."

Chapter Eight

*G*ODDAMN IT. HEATH HAD BEEN RIGHT EARLIER that morning. The minx he'd wed would be the death of him. Tia had found his paintings. She'd been looking at the portrait he'd done of Bess when he walked in. The sight of his fiancée's sweet face staring back at him had shaken him to the core. He'd begun the painting after she'd agreed to marry him. And he'd finished it after her death, in the days of drunken misery that had overtaken him. He'd intended to give the painting to her parents, but in the end, he hadn't been able to part with the last piece of Bess he'd ever have. Even if he couldn't bear to look upon it.

"Please," Tia repeated, "tell me."

His wife's expression was soft. Concerned. It chipped away at the ice in his heart. He had never confided in anyone after Bess's death. He had simply carried on, and when he'd been able to put down the whiskey and rejoin the world of the living, he'd never again spoken her name. Not to anyone. But there was something about Tia that undid him. Made him weak.

He pulled her against him, needing to feel her soft, warm, and alive in his arms. As she embraced him, he sank his nose into her hair, breathing deeply of the sweet scent of violets. "I was betrothed," he forced himself to say.

She stiffened in his arms. Clearly, she hadn't known. He hadn't been certain. Bess's family owned the estate neighboring Chatsworth, and their betrothal had not been announced in society. They had decided to wait until he had returned from Italy.

"When?" Tia asked simply.

"Six years ago," he began, unsure of how much he would tell her. Perhaps everything. Perhaps only just enough.

"It's her in the portrait, isn't it?" Her voice was hushed.

He supposed it wasn't much of a leap for her to make, but he couldn't help but be startled. "Yes." Emotions long buried rose within him. "Her name was Bess."

"You loved her." It was a statement rather than a question.

Heath swallowed, thinking of the compassionate, kind-hearted young lady he'd grown to know as a lonely young man who'd just inherited a dukedom. "Very much."

She didn't withdraw, continuing to embrace him. "I could tell by the way you painted her. What happened?"

"She died." Five years after the loss, he still felt it every bit as keenly. The shock, the bitterness. The guilt. "I was away in Italy when I received word of her illness. By the time I returned, she was being lowered into the ground."

"Oh, Heath. I'm sorry." She pulled back slightly, searching his gaze, and he swore he could detect the sheen of tears in her vivid eyes. "If I had known, I never would have intruded."

How could he hold onto his anger in the face of her kindness? He traced the curve of her cheek with the backs of his fingers. "You're my wife now. It's only right that we shouldn't have secrets between us any longer."

She turned her head to press a kiss to his palm. "I understand why you wish to keep her portrait tucked away. But why the others? Why didn't you tell me that you paint?"

"I don't paint," he told her, careful to keep his roiling

117

emotions from his voice. He hadn't discussed his past with anyone, and resurrecting it was not without its share of pain. "Not anymore."

She gently trailed her fingertips over his beard. The urge to take her away from this chamber full of ghosts was strong. He longed for her. Needed to lose himself inside her, to blot out the misery of old wounds. She was silent, studying him for what seemed an eternity.

"Does painting remind you of her?" she asked at last.

There was something damn awkward about discussing the woman he'd loved and lost with his wife. But there was also something comforting about it. Something freeing.

"It reminds me of the way I betrayed her." Devil take it, he may as well lay it all before her, all the ugliness, the scars. Let her see him for who he truly was. "I was a selfish bastard, so consumed by my desire to paint that I nearly allowed it to destroy me. We were going to be wed, Bess and me, but I wanted to take a trip to Italy to study the great artists. I asked her to wait for me, and I left her behind. Months passed by, and then one day, the letters from her stopped. I received a letter from her sister instead, telling me that Bess's condition was grave."

"You hardly betrayed her by traveling to Italy, Heath," Tia told him firmly. "Was she ill when you left her?"

"No." He thought back to the last day he'd seen Bess. She'd been laughing, her cheeks pink, wearing a bright-green day dress. He still recalled the way she'd worn her hair, the way her warm, brown eyes had laughed at him. "She was in perfect health."

"You couldn't have known something would befall her in your absence," she said softly.

Of course he knew that. If he'd had the slightest inkling on the day he'd said goodbye to Bess that it would be the very last time he'd see her, nothing could have stopped him from staying by her side. Except that he hadn't known, and he had merely kissed the back of her hand as he'd done a dozen times before, and left her without a backward glance.

No, his lack of knowing what was to come didn't mitigate his culpability.

"I should never have left for Italy in the first place," he countered. "I was a fool, chasing a dream that could never be mine. Dukes don't paint. They wed and produce progeny for the future of their estates."

Tia stared at him. "Is that why you married me? For your heir and a spare?"

Christ. He didn't know what to say to her. Surely she'd realized that he hadn't wed her solely to bed her every night? She was a widow and the daughter of an earl. She could hardly be ignorant of the ways of the *ton*. But he saw the hurt glimmering in her eyes, and it cut through the grief that had returned to him the moment he'd caught sight of his paintings.

"Tia," he began, hating the way she was looking at him.

"Of course it is," she answered for herself, her tone cool. She slipped away from his grasp, setting some distance between them.

"It isn't the only reason for our union," he tried, taking a step toward her. Without the comforting warmth of her in his arms, he was suddenly bereft.

She shook her head. "No. You needn't prevaricate on my account. I suppose I was a fool for thinking differently."

"You're not a fool." Damn it, he felt like the worst sort of cad. "You know I desire you."

"Yes, that is most reassuring." She flashed him a smile that held no mirth. "If you don't mind, I find I'm feeling quite exhausted. I'll leave you to your memories."

"Please don't go," he called after her, but she spun on her heel and fled anyway, leaving him standing alone in a chamber laden with dust and the remnants of the man he'd once been.

Her husband was in love with a dead woman. And not just

any dead woman, but a woman with the face of an angel. An incomparable beauty who would forever be perfect in his eyes because he hadn't known her intimately enough to recognize her failings. A woman whose death he felt somehow responsible for.

Tia had spent a few days considering precisely what, if anything, she could do with this unsettling information. Following her confrontation with Heath, their interactions had grown considerably colder. Meals were stilted and polite. On the first night, he had come to her chamber and she had turned him away. He hadn't returned since, and she felt his absence like an ache.

The sudden wedge between them needed to be removed. Tia knew that as well as she knew her own reflection. She didn't wish for a tepid union with Heath for the sake of securing his duchy only. She had spent herself on just such a marriage already, and it had ended with her more alone than ever, nothing but a widow's portion to call her own.

Tia was not the sort of woman to simply wait about for life to begin going her way. No, indeed. She was a woman who took action. When Denbigh had thrown her over to marry another, she had gathered up the pieces of her broken heart and had in turn wed Lord Stokey. When Heath had invited her to be wicked with him, she'd followed him to his chamber.

Yes, Tia was a woman of action, which was precisely why she had requested a meeting that morning with her new housekeeper, the ruddy-cheeked Mrs. Rhodes. The door to Tia's sitting room clicked open to admit the woman's bountiful gray skirts.

"Mrs. Rhodes," Tia greeted her with as much calm as she could muster. In truth, she was more than a bit uncertain of the plan she was embarking upon. "Please do have a seat."

"Thank you, Your Grace." Mrs. Rhodes did as she asked, the chatelaine she wore at her waist tinkling merrily.

She appeared hesitant, almost as if she didn't know what to expect from her new mistress. And Tia couldn't blame her, for they'd only collaborated on a handful of menus thus far and their interactions had been frightfully limited.

"Mrs. Rhodes, I hope you don't mind if I ask you a few questions now that I've settled in here at Chatsworth House," she began, hoping she'd meet with little opposition. Some retainers could be dreadfully loyal to their old masters. Indeed, Lord Stokey's housekeeper had never truly accepted Tia's position in the household. The old bird had been bitter and unfriendly to the end.

"Of course not, madam," Mrs. Rhodes said cheerily. "I hope you're finding Chatsworth to your satisfaction."

Tia harbored no complaints as to the running of Chatsworth thus far. It seemed that Mrs. Rhodes and the butler, Burnes, were eminently worthy of their stations. The servants were efficient, the household ran like a clock and there wasn't even a dust mote to be seen in the sunlight.

"I find it most excellent," Tia reassured her. "My questions aren't concerning the household, I'm afraid. Rather, they concern the duke."

Twin gray eyebrows shot upward, the only outward sign of surprise, before Mrs. Rhodes was able to firmly remove all expression from her face. "His Grace?"

"Yes." Her husband was currently off on one of his customary morning rides, which provided her with ample opportunity to put her plan into motion. "I understand you've been the housekeeper here since His Grace was but a lad."

"I have, Your Grace."

Her lady's maid had garnered that bit of information for her, bless Bannock's dear heart. "Then perhaps you can tell me about Lady Elizabeth Robbins."

Bannock had also employed her belowstairs skills to ferret out Bess's full name. Tia was vaguely familiar with the family, but didn't recall ever running across Lady Elizabeth in London. She presumed the girl's family preferred the country, as some lesser lords were wont to do, few though they were. It seemed odd that she'd not been presented at court, but perhaps she had been too young, and her illness had claimed her before she'd had the opportunity.

Mrs. Rhodes considered her, perhaps carefully crafting her response. "What do you wish to know of her ladyship, Your Grace?"

Ah, here came the delicate part. "Mrs. Rhodes, I presume you are aware of His Grace's...tender feelings toward Lady Elizabeth?"

"I cannot say to be privy to His Grace's innermost thoughts, but I do know he and Lady Elizabeth's father had an understanding. That was before His Grace left for Italy, and before Lady Elizabeth took ill." The housekeeper looked distinctly uncomfortable with the vein of conversation.

But Tia was far from offering her a respite. "What can you tell me of His Grace after he returned from Italy?"

"I'm sure I shouldn't carry tales, Your Grace." Mrs. Rhodes appeared positively disapproving now.

Yes, of course it wasn't proper to gossip about one's master, but Tia rather hoped that when the gossiping was being done to said master's wife, all was forgiven. "I applaud your loyalty, Mrs. Rhodes, but I merely wished to ascertain what His Grace's reaction was."

Mrs. Rhodes gave her a searching stare, seemingly determining Tia's motivation. "He was devastated, madam," she said at last, her voice quiet. "He has not been himself since the day of his return." She almost said more but appeared to catch herself.

Tia had already suspected what the housekeeper had just grudgingly divulged. Her husband possessed great hidden depths she hadn't known existed. He was ever-changing. Once, she had thought him horridly boring. Then, he had been a temptation she couldn't resist, a handsome man with wicked kisses. When she'd agreed to become his wife, she'd imagined a life of shared passion and respect, not one marred by a past she hadn't realized had been haunting him. But she'd meant what she'd said to Miss Whitney in the library that long-ago night. *I'm brave enough to make anyone's ghosts flee in terror*, she'd told her charge.

And that was precisely what she was about to do with Heath's ghosts. Beginning with the paintings he kept hidden away in the east wing. She took a deep breath and proceeded, hoping to heavens she was making the right decision.

"Mrs. Rhodes, I'd like you to direct the servants to air out the closed chamber in the east wing. Have the footmen take an inventory of the contents and bring it to me. In the meantime, I'd like to see one of the landscapes hung in the drawing room and the Adam and Eve in His Grace's study." There. She'd done it, put the plan into motion.

Mrs. Rhodes had either swallowed a gnat, or she was most aggrieved by the suggestion. "But Your Grace, His Grace has explicitly requested that the chamber remain closed and that its contents not be removed."

Here it was, the opposition. But Tia was ever a wily opponent. "Oh, dear me. I'm surprised he hasn't told you himself. He's changed his mind," she lied smoothly, batting nary a lash.

"He has?"

"Why, yes. It was His Grace's idea that I meet with you today, in fact," Tia continued, hitting her stride. Heavens, this was easier than it should be. "He has reconsidered the notion of the pictures moldering away forever in an unused chamber. Indeed, he told me he would like to see as many of his paintings on the walls as possible."

Mrs. Rhodes blinked. "As many as possible, Your Grace?"

"Yes." In for a penny, in for a pound, as always. "With the exception of the portrait of Lady Elizabeth," she amended. No need to push him that far. She'd already be trying him enough as it was. "Please have the footmen consult with me as to the placement."

The housekeeper was silent for a moment. "I'm not certain of what to say, Your Grace."

Tia beamed at her. "It's simple, Mrs. Rhodes. Say yes."

Heath was bloody well seeing things. Yes, that was the reason for the painting of Adam and Eve on the wall of his study. Either that, or he'd drunk too much whiskey in an effort to drown the double portions of guilt that had been eating him since Tia had awoken the old feelings in him by unearthing his paintings. He'd hurt her, and it still bothered the hell out of him.

Of course, there was a third option for the seeming appearance of one of his works on his study wall. And that was the golden-haired trouble-maker who had been setting him at sixes and sevens since he'd looked down at her in the gardens at Penworth. His wife.

He blinked, just to be sure the painting remained.

It did, damn it all.

"Burnes," he hollered.

His worthy butler appeared at the door, almost as if he'd been hovering about, awaiting his master's outburst. "Yes, Your Grace?"

"What, precisely, has happened to the portrait of the fifth Duke of Devonshire?" Not that he'd cared for the portrait—the lines had been all wrong, the shading abysmal—but it had been hanging in the study for his entire life. While he'd made his mark on Chatsworth, there were some things a man didn't change. Family portraits were one of them, regardless of their dubious artistic merit.

"Her Grace required it to be removed," Burnes intoned.

The devil she had. "Pardon?"

Burnes, who ordinarily had one expression—dour—looked irritated. "At your request, Her Grace directed the footmen to remove some of the Cavendish family portraits and replace them."

At his request? The minx. She knew very well that he'd directed her to leave those paintings, his paintings, exactly where he'd left them in the east wing. He'd thought to give her time to collect herself after the day he'd found her there. She'd turned him away from her chamber, and he'd been willing to allow her some distance. He knew he likely should have told her about Bess from the start, but somehow, it hadn't seemed necessary. He'd never thought Tia would uncover that part of his life. But she had, and instead of allowing him to keep it locked firmly in the past as he preferred, she seemed hell-bent on hauling it into their midst. One of his paintings was staring back at him, and if Burnes was to be believed, it was only one of many.

"Did the duchess happen to say when I made this request?" he asked as calmly as possible given the emotions roiling within him, anger chief among them.

"I regret to say she did not, Your Grace."

Of course she hadn't. He'd thought her silence had been caused by hurt, but she'd been orchestrating this the entire time, using his own servants and his own supposed requests against him. He had underestimated her. He'd known she was flighty as a butterfly, but he hadn't realized she was also cunning as a fox.

"Do you know where Her Grace is at the moment, Burnes?" he asked next.

"I'm afraid I cannot be certain, Your Grace," Burnes told him before hesitating. "But I do believe she may be dressing for dinner."

Catching Tia half-dressed would certainly have its merits. He tossed back the remainder of his whiskey and stood. His ledgers and correspondence could damn well wait. He had a meddling wife to attend to. "Thank you, Burnes. If you will excuse me, that will be all."

Tia stood before her mirror, wearing nothing more than her

drawers and chemise, watching Bannock as she approached from behind with her corset in hand. She held out her arms as her lady's maid placed the corset around her waist and began fastening the hook-and-eye closures on the front.

Hours had passed since she had finished overseeing the placement of Heath's paintings, and she hadn't heard a word. He had returned from his ride and closeted himself away in his study. Perhaps he hadn't noticed the removal of the abysmal family portrait. Perhaps he was poring over ledgers, oblivious to her machinations.

"Are you certain there was no mention belowstairs of His Grace and my, er, efforts to decorate?" she demanded of Bannock, disappointed to have been denied a reaction.

"I'm sorry, Your Grace. No one said a word." Bannock finished the last closure and went to Tia's back, her fingers working on the laces. The familiar crush of her corset squeezed the breath from her.

"Not even a word?"

"Well, there was a bit said about the paintings. One of the maids was saying how His Grace had requested the room to be sealed and she didn't think he would want his pictures all over the walls." Bannock continued cinching.

It would seem the servants were not entirely convinced by Tia's claim that Heath had requested the paintings to be hung. They weren't wrong, but it warmed her that they had observed her wishes despite their reservations. She was beginning to feel at home at Chatsworth, and it was most welcome.

"Thank you, Bannock." Her dear lady's maid could always be counted on for the belowstairs gossip, and it certainly worked in Tia's favor now that they were both virtual strangers in a new household.

Suddenly, the door to Tia's chamber flew open. With a start, Tia turned to see her husband stalking inside. His handsome face was chiseled in stone. Their gazes met, and a mixture of dread and heat shot straight through her.

"Your Grace," she objected, finding her tongue. "I'm

dressing."

"So it would seem." He stopped when he was a scant few inches from her. "That will be all," he told Bannock, dismissing her.

"But Your Grace," Tia sputtered. She was dressing for dinner. He couldn't just dismiss her lady's maid, leaving her in her undergarments. She couldn't dress herself, for heaven's sake. "Cannot the matter wait until I've finished my toilette? I have need of Bannock."

Her lady's maid hesitated, casting her gaze from Tia to the duke, then back again.

"You are dismissed," Heath told Bannock in a firm, ducal, no-argument-allowed decree.

"Bannock, you must stay," Tia countered, quite vexed with him for his high-handed behavior. She knew she had gone against his wishes, and it was apparent that he was most displeased by her actions. But that didn't mean he had to act a bore before her lady's maid. Moreover, Tia hadn't intended to face him in such a state of *dishabille*. It was dangerous to her ability to make an argument. Damnation, she required layers. Corset covers, petticoats, buttons, and skirts.

Bannock's eyes were wide. She was loyal to Tia, that much Tia did not question. But she was also likely aware that the duke possessed the purse strings now. "Your Graces, I will leave you to your conversation."

"No," Tia cried, tempted to clutch Bannock's arm in an effort to make her stay but not wanting to seem desperate before her husband.

"Very good," Heath said approvingly, offering Bannock a nod before turning the force of his stare back on Tia.

The urge to wilt was strong. Tia tore her gaze from Heath's to helplessly watch as her lady's maid disappeared from the chamber, leaving her alone with the towering, angry male before her. Blast.

"Now that we're alone at last, I believe an explanation is in order," Heath told her in tight, clipped tones.

Tia searched his gaze as she took a step in retreat. She couldn't read him, and it made her ill at ease. "What sort of explanation?"

He raised an imperious brow and took a step toward her, effectively diminishing the safe distance she'd put between them. "I've been informed that the duchess directed the servants to rearrange the family portraits at my request. And yet, I made no such request. Therefore, someone is being deceitful." He stalked even closer and reached out to trail a finger over her jaw and down her throat. "Is it you? Or is it Burnes?"

His touch sent fire skittering through her. She wanted him, and if the smoldering in his eyes was any indication, the feeling was mutual. But as much as she longed for him to take her in his arms and kiss her into submission, she knew there would be a reckoning first.

She swallowed. "Mrs. Rhodes wouldn't comply unless I told her the directive came from you."

"As I thought." He traced the angular sweep of her collarbone next, stopping at her shoulder. "Why, Tia?"

She struggled to keep her wits about her. "I suppose she's a loyal retainer," she answered, deliberately misunderstanding him.

His gaze narrowed. "Why did you disobey me?"

Because he couldn't simply lock away his past and expect it to disappear. Because the man he was now needed to confront the man he'd been. Because she wanted him to be free to love her.

The last realization came to her with a pang. She hadn't expected to develop tender feelings for him. Lord knew she never had for Lord Stokey, but she was beginning to understand that her first marriage was entirely different from her marriage to Heath. This was a union born of passion and necessity, but it was also a union that could become much more. She wanted that for herself, for Heath. She longed for happiness, so strongly that it frightened her. Never before had she felt such a conflict of emotions.

"Have you nothing to say for yourself?" he demanded, gripping both her shoulders in his hands now and giving her a shake that was gentle enough not to hurt but forceful enough to let her know the seriousness of the moment.

"Your paintings should not be hidden away as if they're shameful," she managed. There was much she wanted to say, but her mind was working faster than her tongue, and it was in greater disarray than a library after a fire.

"The decision is not yours, Tia," he reminded her, his voice hard as his jaw. "You had no right to defy me and to make my household your unwitting dupes."

He made it sound as if she'd just sold all the Cavendish family heirlooms to a London street vendor for a few pennies. "I own that I should not have misled the servants, but I don't think any harm came of it. As far as they know, they were merely doing your bidding."

"They shall be disabused of that notion when they must remove all the paintings they've just hung and restore the house to its rightful order." His palms slid down her arms, his fingers gripping her tightly. "Damn it, woman, what can you have been thinking?"

"I was thinking that you can't hide from the past forever," she blurted. "I saw the pain in your eyes that day when you spoke of what had happened. Surely you don't think you'll assuage your grief and guilt by keeping your paintings hidden away in the east wing?"

"I've managed to do so for five years," he reminded her, releasing her suddenly before his fingers went to the fasteners at the front of her corset.

"You've managed to avoid it for five years," she corrected, growing equal measures aroused and alarmed by the progress he was making. "What do you think you're doing to my corset?"

"Opening the bloody thing," he demanded, reaching the top hook and eye, undoing it and whipping the undergarment to the floor.

Oh dear. It would seem that his ire had developed into

desire. Her mouth went dry and her heart kicked into a mad gallop. "I require a corset to dress for dinner," she tried.

"You're not dressing for dinner." He caught the skirt of her chemise and began dragging it over her head.

"Heath." Her vision went white for an instant as he removed the garment from her. "You're being rather imperious."

"I learned it from you, my dear." The smile on his sensual mouth was positively feral. He unbuttoned her drawers. "Step out of them."

She deemed it best to heed him. His mood seemed dangerous indeed. Watching him, she shimmied her hips. Her drawers fell down over her bare skin with a whisper of fabric before she did as he asked, taking a step back once more. She was nude before him while he was fully clothed. "What are you doing, Heath?"

"That should be obvious, my dear." His eyes glittered into hers with wicked promise. "I'm punishing you."

Punishing her? As if she had been a naughty child causing household upset because she'd put a frog in the governess's bed? Of course, that was a sin she had been guilty of in her youth, but those days were long gone.

"You're punishing me by taking away my undergarments?" she asked, aware of the chill air on her nude body.

"Not precisely," he murmured, his gaze lowering to her breasts. "Your nipples are quite hard, darling."

Somehow, the mere utterance of the word "nipples" from his beautiful lips sent wetness straight to her core. That didn't bode well for her determination to stand her ground without waving the white flag of surrender.

She crossed her arms over her breasts, obstructing them from his view just to spite him. "Of course they are. It's dreadfully cold in here, and I haven't any clothes. An ogre has taken them all."

He laughed. "An ogre, am I? My, you've a fanciful imagination, Tia. First dreaming up my wishes to redecorate

Chatsworth and now imagining me a monster." As he said the last, he shrugged out of his coat.

"I was doing my utmost to help you," she said quietly. "That is all."

But Heath wasn't paying her any attention. He was diverted by something on the settee to his left. "Ah, stockings," he said, pulling the stockings Bannock had laid out for her from the gilded back. "How thoughtful of your lady's maid to assist me."

Tia was beginning to rethink the wisdom of her grand plan to help her husband overcome the pain of his past. His calm demeanor was troubling. Had he raged at her, she would have simply raged back at him. But this deliberate, almost ominous, progression of events was as vexing as it was titillating.

"Why do you need my stockings?" She took another wary step in retreat.

"Get on the bed, Tia," he ordered, ignoring her query.

"No." She stepped back again, wondering precisely what he intended to do with the stockings.

"Yes." He followed her, stockings in hand, expression impassive. "On the bed. Now."

She wondered what he would do if she defied him and decided to give it a try. "I won't."

"Very well." Grimly, he closed the distance between them in a step and a half. His hands settled on her waist. "Then I shall do it for you."

Tia stared as her ordinarily imperturbable husband bent and hauled her over his shoulder. "Oh!" The air fled from her lungs, and suddenly her view was of the carpet at her husband's feet and his trouser-clad rump. And though his rump was tempting indeed, she didn't particularly care for being tossed over his shoulder as if she were an old coat. "Put me down at once," she demanded, finding her voice.

"In time, my dear. I don't think you'd like to be dropped on the floor just now." His tone remained eerily composed.

He traveled with her across the chamber, and she felt the

bedclothes tickling her calves before he unceremoniously dumped her in the middle of her bed. She landed in an ungraceful sprawl, conscious of the dreadful way she must look, limbs sticking this way and that. She adopted as ladylike a pose as she could manage while utterly naked and met his gaze. He was watching her rather the way she imagined a starving man would eye a freshly roasted pheasant. Oh dear.

"That was most unkind of you," she said, breathless.

He knelt on the bed then, joining her. "I would apologize, but I daresay I'm not any sorrier than you are for your misdeeds."

"I hardly think that moving about some pictures qualifies as a misdeed," she couldn't resist arguing.

"No more talking," he said, pressing a finger to her lips. He hooked a leg over her hips so that she was effectively trapped beneath him. "Not until I say you may speak."

The devil. He couldn't order her about in such a boorish fashion. "Heath, you've made your point. I understand you're vexed. Can we not conduct a reasonable conversation?"

He took one of her wrists and tied a knot around it with her stocking, pulling until it was good and tight. "You seem to be intent upon being uncooperative. I require your silence, madam."

"Well, you shan't have it," she promised, tugging at her wrist. "And you shan't tie me up, either. I'm not a prisoner, sir."

"Yes," he said, stilling in his ministrations to look down at her. "You are."

Dear, sweet heavens. Precisely what was he intending to do to her? She'd imagined that perhaps he intended to make love. Or at the very least lock her in her chamber. But this? Perhaps she had pushed him too far. Yes, she must have, for he seemed quite mad.

He took her other wrist and tied a knot around it as well. "You must pay the forfeit for your unwise actions." And then, he held her wrists above her head and secured them to the post on the intricately carved headboard. "There. Is it too tight, my dear?"

It seemed strange indeed that he would think of the niceties when he was binding her as if she were a common thief. "Yes. Do let me go, Heath."

"Not yet." He brushed his fingers lightly over one of her puckered nipples. "You don't truly think I'll let you off that easily, do you?"

She gazed up at him as he straddled her. He was devilishly handsome, his darkened eyes locked on her breasts, his jaw rigid. He looked almost dangerous, and she couldn't help but be aroused. "What are you planning to do to me?" she asked, daring to hope it involved him sliding home inside her until they were both mindless.

He cupped her breasts, rubbing his thumbs in lazy circles around the peaks. "At first, I thought about spanking your delectable bottom."

The concept didn't entirely appall her as it ought to have done. She caught her lip between her teeth, watching as he plucked at her aching nipples. "You changed your mind?"

He frowned down at her. "I distinctly recall telling you to silence that wayward tongue of yours."

"I don't do well with commands," she returned unapologetically, punctuating her claim with a sigh as he lowered his head and raked his beard over one breast. Oh, that felt nice. Too nice. It would seem he had decided to forego the spanking in favor of pure, unadulterated sensual torture.

"So I've noticed," he murmured before flicking his tongue over her nipple and then sucking it into his mouth.

Tia couldn't quite repress the moan of pleasure that rose in her throat. He skimmed a hand over her stomach, his fingers dipping into her sex to find the sensitive nub hidden within. Her ability to resist him was utterly dashed. She arched into him, seeking more as white-hot desire ricocheted through her. If this was his idea of punishment, she was a willing sinner.

He stroked through her already damp folds, making her even wetter as he turned his attention to her other nipple. He caught her with his teeth, lightly tugging. "At last, silence," he said against her skin. "It would seem I've discovered the way to keep you quiet."

He sank a finger inside her to the hilt. Oh dear heavens, yes. He most certainly had. She worked her hips against him, urging him into a faster, maddening rhythm. He sucked her breast again, working her into a fine frenzy as he curled his finger ever so slightly. The change in angle somehow undid her. A climax claimed her, hard and swift, coursing through her like a bolt of lightning.

"Damn it, what you do to me," he groaned, withdrawing from her to fumble with the fastening of his trousers.

Tia would have assisted him but for her bound wrists, still holding her captive. In truth, she didn't mind being at his mercy. Rather, she found it heightened her arousal. Watching him bring her to climax was like too much wine to her senses.

His cock sprang free, rigid and ready. He was inside her in one long, hard thrust. She tipped her hips up to meet him, bringing him as deep as she could. Nothing else mattered in that moment other than that he was man and she was woman, and they were joined in the oldest and purest way. Thoughts of his betrothed and the paintings fell from her mind.

His mouth was on hers as he began a frantic rhythm. His kiss was fiery as he took her. Possessive. He pumped into her again and again. As his tongue swept into her mouth, she came undone once more, the desire building to a keen crescendo. She tightened on him and a breath later felt the hot spurt of his seed as he lost himself within her. He thrust into her again and again as he found his release.

When he was spent, he withdrew from her, rolling over onto the bed and righting his trousers. Still quite breathless from their frantic lovemaking, Tia watched as he rolled to his feet and stalked away from the bed. Surely he would untie her now, she thought as he bent to retrieve his discarded jacket. But he didn't even spare her a glance as he shrugged it back on.

"Heath," she called out tentatively. "You've forgotten to untie me."

"No." He tossed her a glance at last. "I haven't. I'm not finished with you yet, my dear."

Good heavens. He couldn't expect to leave her trussed and naked. Could he? He appeared quite grave. She tugged at her wrists. "You cannot be serious. It's positively frigid in here."

"Oh, I'm serious." He straightened his jacket, his eyes flicking over her nudity. "I daresay you won't grow icicles until I return."

With that, he spun on his heel and began walking from the chamber.

"Heath!" she cried. "Release me at once."

"No." He didn't even bother to look in her direction as his hand settled over the doorknob.

"Please don't go," she tried, desperation mingling with horror. What if her lady's maid should return? What if Heath left her stranded for hours? Or worse, an entire day? Her stomach grumbled, reminding her she had been about to dress for a dinner that it now appeared she would not be partaking in. "Heath!"

"Ah," he said smoothly, casting her a sidelong glance. "It's frustrating when someone defies you, isn't it, my dear?"

He opened the door, stepped over the threshold and closed it with rather more force than necessary. Tia winced, staring at the space where he'd been. Yes, she decided firmly, the man she had married was hopelessly, unutterably mad. If only she wasn't beginning to feel the faint stirrings of a more tender emotion for him.

Dear, sweet heavens. She couldn't possibly be falling in love. Could she?

Chapter Nine

EATH FOUND HIMSELF IN A BIT OF A predicament. He took a healthy gulp of whiskey, savoring the fiery burn it sent down his throat. To be more precise, he was in any number of predicaments. He tipped back his glass again.

First, there was the matter of his wife, nude and tied to her bed upstairs. He couldn't very well leave her that way forever, and he knew it. But the devil of it was, that if he entered her chamber once more, he was reasonably certain he'd be tempted to fuck her senseless all over again.

Which brought him to his second predicament. He had intended to punish Tia, and he'd wound up bedding her instead. Not precisely a punishment, even if he had thoroughly enjoyed taking her and reminding her that she was at his mercy, not the other way round. He hadn't meant to abandon his sense of control. Hadn't meant to strip her bare and drive himself inside her. But by the time he'd caught her half-dressed in her chamber, the potency of his emotions had overwhelmed him. He'd lost his head.

Finally, there was the uncomfortable matter of his paintings being strewn about all over the bloody place at his supposed request. Seeing them had shocked him. Angered him. But he was alarmed to discover the hatred he'd once felt for himself whenever he'd looked upon them and remembered what he'd done had dissipated in the intervening years. Perhaps there was something wrong with him, some sort of damnable crack in his brain, for he was gazing at Adam and Eve on his study wall and noting the corrections he would make.

Worse, he itched to take up paint and brush and add some final touches to Eve's face. He hadn't painted her with enough sensuality. And for some bloody reason, he could not quite shake the notion that surely she had possessed a tempting Cupid's bow of a mouth.

Damn Tia.

She had opened doors that should have remained firmly shut. Why could she not merely be content to leave things as they were? Had he not provided her with the best of everything? She was allowed to keep her funds to spend as she chose. She was allowed lazy mornings to correspond with her harridan sister and God knew who else. She was the mistress of a vast estate, the wife of a duke. And yet, she had not seen fit to merely leave his past where it belonged.

Instead, she'd dragged it out for him and all his servants to see.

He tossed back the rest of his whiskey, not even pretending to contemplate the ledgers and letters before him. He was too rattled to bother with the mundane. He needed to figure out what the hell he was going to do next. He was drowning in a mire of his own making. Nothing made sense. Tia's words echoed in his mind, taunting him.

You can't hide from the past forever, she'd said. And blast it all, part of him knew she was right. He had been hiding from the pain of losing Bess. From the guilt of knowing that things may have ended differently had he not left her. For then, he had always told himself, she would have been happily ensconced in Chatsworth as his wife, and may never have taken ill at all.

One thing was certain. Locking away the paintings and reminders of who he'd once been had not lessened the pain or the guilt he'd tried so hard to ignore. Perhaps it had only delayed the inevitable. After all, he couldn't deny that painting still called to him. It always had, but the crushing guilt had been enough to drown his passion. Now, it called to him still, with a far more strident voice than ever before. He was a man bereft, the sands shifting about him into a new landscape.

Maybe, just maybe, Tia was right. Maybe it was time to reconcile the man he'd been—the past he'd lived—with the man he had become. He couldn't very well hide forever, or pretend that Bess had never lived, that he had never loved her and that he had never been consumed with the desire to paint.

Adam and Eve stared at him, their temptation mirroring his. Damn it, there was only one thing he could do, really.

"Burnes," he bellowed.

The ever-efficient butler appeared at his study door. "Yes, Your Grace?"

"Please see to it that the footmen have my painting supplies and canvases moved to my chamber at once." His paints and pigments were the finest available. He had no doubt they would still be usable. But just in case, he had another plan. "See to it that they get me fresh supplies as well."

Burnes stared at him for a moment. "You are certain, Your Grace?"

The ordinarily sacrosanct butler had seen Heath in his lowest moments. While most servants wouldn't dare gainsay their masters, however politely, Heath knew that Burnes was acting with a familiarity born of mutual respect. Burnes had saved him five years ago from certain death. Mindless in his grief, Heath had consumed far too much whiskey and he'd taken out his shooting rifle, ready to put an end to it all. Burnes had found him. They'd never spoken of the low moment since that day.

Heath closed his eyes for a moment, still shamed by his long-ago actions and grateful his loyal butler had discovered him in time. He hoped that he wasn't making the wrong decision. He opened his eyes once more, meeting his butler's gaze. "Yes, Burnes. I'm quite certain. Have it all arranged as it once was."

"Of course, Your Grace." Burnes bowed. "Forgive me."

Heath nodded, watching as the man quit the room once more. Forgiveness. It was a hell of a thing. Perhaps it was time he went about the business of forgiving himself. Certainly, it was time to go about the business of forgiving his wife. The thought of her waiting for him, her wrists bound and her breasts high and full, her beautiful body on display for him, made him incredibly hard.

And he knew it in that moment. The time he'd always known would come had arrived. He was going to paint her.

Tia didn't know how much time had passed since her husband had unceremoniously left her tied to her bed in complete *dishabille*. But her fingers felt as if they were being pricked by a hundred needles at once, and it was a good sign that Heath had abandoned her for the better part of an hour. She'd tried to nap, but her position was deuced uncomfortable. She'd tried to escape, but her efforts had only served to tighten the knots binding her.

Drat him. She dismissed the tender stirring of feelings she'd felt earlier. She wasn't falling in love with the arrogant blighter. Of course not. Indeed, when he finally deigned to release her, she was going to give him an earful. Perhaps even box his ears. Yes, that sounded like a retaliation most excellent.

She was beginning to despair he'd ever return for her when the bedchamber door abruptly opened. He strode into the room, as debonair and unruffled as he'd been when he'd left. His gaze settled on her, sending an unwanted lick of fire down her spine.

"Madam."

Lovely. It seemed she was still the object of his ire, even after his disappearance. "If I had known what a cad you'd be, I'd never have agreed to wed you," she pronounced with a regal sniff.

"I can see your time alone has humbled you," he said wryly, stopping as he reached her bedside.

"I can't feel my fingers, Heath." She glared at him, cursing her body for responding to him as it did. Already, she felt a tingling in her breasts and between her thighs. Despite herself, she couldn't help but hope he might join her on the bed for another wicked romp.

He knelt on the bed, reaching above her to gently touch her hands. "They seem to all be in their proper place."

"Are you going to untie me, or do you intend to prolong this torture?" she asked, trying to dampen her ardor by closing her eyes and imagining her most ferocious governess, Miss Hullyhew.

She felt the knot loosening. "This wasn't meant to be torture," he told her, his voice low and silky. "It was meant to be a lesson."

"Was it a lesson for you or a lesson for me?" she couldn't resist asking. After all, it hadn't escaped her notice that while he'd intended to punish her, he'd wound up pleasuring her instead.

The knot on her right wrist came undone. "Perhaps it was for both of us," he said cryptically.

Tia opened her eyes again, glancing up at his handsome profile as she flexed her fingers. "What did you learn?"

"That I've married a most vexing woman." He untied her other wrist.

"A most vexing woman?" Freed at last, she scrambled into a sitting position, unmindful of her nudity. "At least I didn't strip you and tie you to a bed."

"I'd gladly give you the rope." A smoldering grin curved his lips. "Besides, I didn't hear you complaining earlier, my dear."

"I confess I enjoyed the first portion of your lesson," she conceded. Why hide from the truth? Their relationship had been founded in their mutual desire, after all, and she was no milk-and-toast miss. "The latter portion was severely lacking, however."

He startled her by leaning closer and catching her chin to take her mouth in a fierce kiss. She melted, opening to him. So much for her plan to box the wretch's ears. All he needed to do was look at her, and she was helpless as a babe in his hands. His tongue tangled with hers and she moaned, moisture pooling between her thighs.

"Damn," he muttered, tearing his mouth from hers. He ran a hand over his neatly trimmed beard. "If I don't stop, I'll have you flat on your back again."

Tia didn't particularly see a problem with that at the moment, but her husband appeared to have other plans. He turned away and stood, attempting to straighten his trousers. The rigid outline of his arousal was clearly visible. "I didn't hear you complaining earlier, my dear," she returned with a knowing smile, repeating his words of just a minute before.

"Touché, darling."

The unmistakable sounds of thumping in the chamber next door reached her ears, piquing her curiosity. Unless she was mistaken, something was being moved about. But what? "What is happening?"

"You shall see. Dress and meet me in my chamber." He paused. "Nothing too elaborate. A dressing gown should be all you require, I think."

Tia stared at him. "We aren't going down to dinner?"

"No. We're having a different sort of dinner this evening. One more appropriate to the day." With that, he turned on his heel and headed for the door joining their chambers together.

Good heavens, what had he planned? She dove under the bedclothes lest one of the servants responsible for making the commotion in his chamber catch sight of her. The door clicked closed on her husband, leaving her alone again. She supposed she'd have to wait and see what mischief he had in store for her now.

By the time she'd finished some perfunctory ablutions and wrapped herself in a dressing gown as he'd requested, the thumping next door had quieted. She surveyed herself in the mirror for a moment, feeling unaccountably nervous. After his alternately passionate and angry responses to her, she didn't know what to expect from Heath. Perhaps she'd gotten more than she'd bargained for when she'd married him. If she had expected their union to be quiet and ordinary, she'd most certainly been mistaken. The desire burning between them was as hot as ever. Perhaps more so. And whereas she'd thought she'd known him, she was beginning to realize there were hidden depths to her husband of which she'd only just caught the faintest glimpse.

She smoothed her wild hair, pinched some color into her cheeks, straightened her dressing gown and decided she had tarried long enough. Her natural inclination toward curiosity was clamoring to discover what Heath had been about in his chamber. She padded back across her chamber to the connecting door, hesitating long enough to knock.

"You may enter," he called from within.

She wasn't prepared for the sight that greeted her when she crossed the threshold. His previously dour, masculine chamber had been rearranged to accommodate a stack of stretched canvases, two easels and an assortment of paints, pots and brushes. In the midst of it all, he stood watching her, looking very much unlike himself in only trousers and a partially unbuttoned shirt. His gaze trapped hers.

"What is all this?" she asked hesitantly, though she well knew. She wanted to hear him say the words aloud. It would seem he hadn't won their little skirmish after all.

"I want to paint you," he said, denying her the admission of defeat.

She faltered, stopping halfway across the room. "You wish to paint me? I'm hardly a proper subject."

"I cannot think of a more suitable subject." He stalked toward her.

"I've never been painted before," she protested, taking a step back. "Surely you could paint a landscape instead. Your Italian landscapes are divine, Heath."

"No." He stopped before her, shaking his head. "I'm painting you."

Very well. Playing along with him wouldn't hurt her. At least he was willing to paint again. Earlier, she would have sworn he'd never again take up brush and paint. "You truly want to paint again?"

A grim smile stretched his sensual lips. "I'm afraid I haven't much choice in the matter. It is either paint again or go mad."

She tried to read his expression and failed. She couldn't discern if he was still furious with her or if he was merely resigned. "I merely want you to be happy," she said, meaning the words. The only way to accomplish his freedom from the past was to move beyond it, to stop hiding it away and pretending as though it had never happened. He'd locked up a vital part of himself along with his paintings and it was time he reclaimed it.

"Take off your dressing gown if you please," he ordered suddenly, startling her with the abrupt shift in subject.

She raised a brow. Was he ready for another round of heated lovemaking? She couldn't deny that the notion held great appeal for her. "I thought you said you wished to paint me."

"I do." His smile turned wicked. "In the nude."

"Dear heavens." Her hands went to the belt securing her dressing gown in place, a defensive gesture. "You cannot be serious."

Dukes didn't paint their duchesses in the nude. For the love of all the angels, what if someone were to happen upon it? While she was reasonably well-shaped, that didn't mean she wanted the world to see her *en dishabille*.

"I'm utterly serious, darling." His hands covered hers, warm and strong. "Off with the gown. I want to see every inch of you."

"You already have," she reminded him. "I'll be pleased to show you any time you like, but I'd rather not be on display for the world as if I'm a common doxy."

"You'll not be on display for the world." His nimble fingers worked at her belt despite her best effort not to allow it. "It will only be for me."

She stared at him. "Is this some sort of punishment? That's it, isn't it? You're still angry with me for ordering the servants to hang your pictures."

"It's not a punishment," he said, voice low and seductive. "I've been wanting to paint you since I first saw you in the gardens at Penworth."

"In the nude?" She couldn't help but ask.

"Yes." He pried her hands away at last, opening her belt. Her dressing gown gaped, revealing to him that she wore nothing beneath, not even a chemise. His gaze slid over her like a caress. "And a hundred other ways. Your beauty is captivating, Tia. I've never wanted to paint anyone more."

Not even his beloved betrothed? She didn't dare ask the question, though she longed to know the answer. For now, it would have to be enough that he'd been willing to shed some of the manacles keeping him prisoner. He was ready to paint again. She could scarcely believe it.

Perhaps the ice around his heart was beginning to thaw. The notion filled her with a brash sense of determination. She shrugged out of her dressing gown entirely, standing before him without a stitch just as he had asked.

"Well," she demanded with a bravado she didn't entirely feel, "where shall I pose?"

Hours later, Heath was consumed by the canvas before him.

Though it had been years since he'd last painted, it had all come back to him almost as if no time had passed. His decision to move his painting supplies to his chamber had been sudden, driven in part by an irrational need, in part by desperation. The emotions Tia had unwittingly unleashed in him were as fierce as they were dangerous. But he had to admit that taking up brush and paint once more felt incredibly right.

Painting Tia felt even more right.

God, she was a beautiful creature. Her form was perfect for painting. He'd always been interested in art that represented a private glimpse into the everyday. It was why he'd been drawn to painting nudes. But he'd never had the opportunity to work with a nude model. Until today.

His wife was draped across a gilded settee he'd had brought into his chamber for just this purpose, her golden hair unbound. She held a book in one hand and rested the other in an indolent pose. She looked like a goddess come to life.

Tia sighed just then, ruining the illusion. "My bottom's growing quite sore."

"I shall kiss it to make it better." He worked a bit more pink onto one of her nipples before glancing back at her. "I've nearly finished for the day."

They'd taken a break to eat the supper trays he'd had brought to his chamber, but she'd been posed for the better part of three hours. The light was far too low for proper work at this point anyway, but he'd found that once he'd started he was loath to stop.

Painting had always been that way for him. Consuming. Raw. A part of his very soul. It seemed almost impossible to him now that he had fought it for so long. Although he still objected to her method, he had to admit to himself that Tia had been right to shake him from his stubborn insistence to lock it away. He had painted before Bess. And the stark truth of it was that he couldn't have known Bess would take ill when he'd left for Italy. Perhaps his time of punishment was done.

He glanced back up at the minx who had become his wife, and tried to imagine Bess resting in her place, nude and allowing him to paint her as he wished. But he could not. He couldn't imagine his life without Tia in it. Didn't want to.

Jesus. A whole new rush of emotions came barreling down on him like a locomotive. If he were brutally honest with himself, he had to say that he was damn happy he'd gone to Thornton's hunting party. Everything he wanted was before him, waiting patiently. It scared the hell out of him. He couldn't—wouldn't—be vulnerable again.

He met Tia's gaze just as she shifted her pose, moving her right arm and wiggling her fingers. "I cannot help it, Heath. I'm not meant to be so still."

Her tone was distinctly unapologetic. He found himself grinning at her. He couldn't have managed to wed a woman more the opposite of what he'd set out thinking he'd wanted. But he admired her determination and her daring. Her ease with her body and lovemaking both was unusual for a woman of her station, and he loved every second of it. Just thinking about making love to her again had him instantly hard. Any thoughts he'd had of completing the shading on her breasts dissipated.

He put down his brush and stalked toward her. "You've ruined the pose, my dear."

"Perhaps we could take a break?" she suggested hopefully. "You didn't warn me how dreadfully difficult this would be."

"It would seem the most difficult thing for you to keep still is your lovely mouth," he said, leaning over her. "But I think I know just the remedy for such a quandary."

Her tongue ran along the seam of her lips, driving him wild. "You do?"

"Oh yes." He wedged a knee onto the cushion alongside her and caught her chin, tipping her face up to his. Christ, but she was a beauty. And his. "This." He lowered his mouth to hers for a kiss that was as long as it was deep and possessive.

"That could prove very beneficial," she murmured when at last their mouths broke apart.

"I want you," he told her, not bothering with the niceties of seduction. Desire was clawing through him, a rampant beast. He had to have her. Now.

"I thought you were determined to finish painting," she said, and though her tone was mild, her voice was breathless.

It would seem he wasn't the only one affected. He caught her hand and pressed it to the demanding ridge of his cock. "Does it feel as if I want to paint at the moment?"

Her eyes darkened, her fingers working on the fastening of his trousers. "No."

Though he was in a fine frenzy, he allowed her to undo his trousers and remove them, enjoying the play of her small hands over him. He tore his shirt away, not having a care for the buttons. And then, the sweet suction of her mouth all but brought him to his knees.

His fingers sank into the silken, violet-scented skeins of her hair. He watched as the Cupid's bow that taunted him so unmercifully worked over the tip of his cock. She swirled her tongue around the head before taking him deep into her throat. He was already on the brink. The sight of her, nude and glorious and pleasuring him, was enough to make him come.

But he so badly wanted to lose himself inside her. He wanted to bring her to the same dizzying heights of desire. One more prolonged pass of her tongue down his length and he gently extricated himself, grabbing her arms to haul her to her feet. Their fingers tangled in an echo of that day in the drawing room at Penworth. Now they no longer needed to hide their desire. They were man and wife. He was hers and she was his.

They moved to his bed as one, both eager for each other. Desperate for skin and mouths and the fleeting sense of heaven on earth they could find together. He helped Tia onto the mattress and joined her, settling between the tempting curves of her thighs so that his cock nestled in her wet folds. He ground against her, enjoying both the tease and the way she responded, her legs opening and wrapping around his hips. A low, seductive moan rumbled from her sweet lips.

He bowed his head and sucked a hard, pink nipple into his mouth. He'd discovered that Tia's breasts were highly sensitive. The more he played with her, the wilder she became. And he couldn't deny that he preferred Tia to be on fire for him, the same way he was for her. He nibbled at her other breast gently and reached down to flick the bud between her legs that was already plump and slick for him.

"Oh Heath," she groaned. "Please. I want you inside me."

He tugged at her nipple and sank a finger into her tight channel. *Yes.* This was what they both wanted. What they needed. This mad release, this gorgeous frenzy. Good Christ, she was so hot, so ready. He ran his tongue around the peak of her breast and worked his finger in and out of her. She jerked beneath him, tightening, trying to bring him deeper.

His cock was hard, his ballocks tight. He didn't think he'd last for much more sensual torture, which was a pity because his Tia was such a willing participant. He tore his mouth from her breast and kissed her. As she opened for him, his tongue slipped inside, claiming her. She moaned again, raking her nails down his back with just enough force to almost make him come.

With a groan of his own, he withdrew his finger and replaced it with his cock in one swift thrust. He was buried to the hilt, and it still wasn't deep enough. He didn't think he'd ever grow tired of fucking his beautiful, maddening wife. Or painting her. God, yes. He'd paint her every day. Naked. And then he'd take her every way he could think of. Against the wall. On a settee. In the bath. On the floor.

From behind. As the wicked images swirled through his mind, he plunged into her again and again, the pressure within him building to a crescendo.

She constricted on him as she found her release. And then he was losing control too, that quickly. He cupped her luscious bottom, lifting her to the angle he wanted, and thrust into her one more time, driving as deep as he could. His seed left him in a hot, pulsing rush. Heath jerked into Tia one last time, kissing her again as he emptied himself inside her.

He collapsed against her, his breathing heavy, heart thumping madly. His entire body felt suddenly as if it had been depleted of all its strength. All the fight in him was gone, replaced by a pleasure-soaked languor. He kissed her cheek before rolling onto his back.

She rested a hand lightly on his chest. "Heath?"

Blast. She wanted to talk. His mind was a muddle of spent emotions. He sighed. "Yes, darling?"

"You still love her, don't you?"

Christ. She didn't have to elaborate. He knew precisely who the "her" was that Tia spoke of. The thought of his betrothed was akin to a bucket of Wenham Lake ice being dumped directly on his cock. He didn't want to think about Bess. Not now, not when he was sated and naked and in bed with his wife.

"Heath?"

She was, as ever, persistent to a fault. There would be no dancing around the matter, and she was far too clever for him to bother with prevarication. She'd only see it for what it was. He closed his eyes and gave her the only answer he could. "Yes." For the truth of it was that he hadn't stopped loving Bess. In his heart, she was still the sweet, innocent girl he'd known. Her death had not diminished what they'd shared.

Tia withdrew her hand, tensing at his side. The mattress shifted beneath him, and he knew what was happening without having to look. But he opened his eyes anyway to watch as she left the bed.

"Tia," he called out to her, not wanting her to leave. Not like this. "I've never lied to you about my past."

"No," she said sadly, keeping her back turned to him. "You haven't."

Why did it feel as if he'd done something wrong? Damn it all. She shrugged into her dressing gown without looking at him, and he knew she was deeply wounded by his admission. What had she wanted? For him to lie to her? Loving Bess didn't preclude him from caring for Tia. Surely she understood that.

"Don't leave," he implored, not wanting the evening to end on such a discordant note. Not after what they'd shared.

But his wife, in typical form, wasn't listening to him. She marched from the chamber, the door closing loudly at her back. He flinched and pressed his fingers to his newly throbbing temple. The silence in her wake was nearly deafening.

She was gone.

The next morning dawned grim, gray and cold for Tia. She woke from a fitful sleep at dawn and couldn't force herself to remain abed. Too many thoughts were whirling through her mind, leaving her emotions in a horrid hodgepodge from which she very much feared there would be no return.

She rang for Bannock and requested breakfast in her chamber, intentionally eschewing the private breakfasts she'd often been sharing with Heath. It wasn't that she meant to punish him, but that she needed time to sort out her feelings. She supposed she'd brought on his agonizing concession and thereafter her own agony with her foolish questioning. Why ask when she'd been petrified of the answer?

Tia didn't know. She scarcely ate any of the ample selection of fruits, eggs and meats Bannock had brought her to devour. She didn't even touch her chocolate—a rare event indeed, for Tia adored her chocolate in the morning. Instead, she'd completed her toilette and simply sat alone at her writing desk, staring out the window in search of solace that wasn't forthcoming.

At last, she took up pen and paper in an effort to distract herself. She wrote to her sisters Cleo, Helen and Bo. She wrote to Miss Whitney to inquire after the girl's latest societal jaunts and marriage prospects. She wrote to her dear friend Bella, who was likely about to perish from boredom as her lying-in approached. She even wrote to her mother and father, which was even rarer than foregoing chocolate. For while she loved Mama and Papa dearly, her every letter was invariably met with a long list of whisperings they'd heard concerning her reputation.

"Pish," she said aloud as she finished her last letter, signing her name with an artful flourish. Her hand was cramped, her fingers ink-stained and her heart in no better form than it had been at the onset of her correspondence. Her paltry attempts at distracting herself had failed.

She had fallen in love with her husband.

There. She'd admitted it to herself, weak-willed, foolish creature that she was. She had allowed herself to be wooed and won and seduced. Initially, her attraction to him had been primal, laced with lust and the excitement of doing what she knew she ought not. But it had quickly become different. Deeper. More dangerous. The time they'd spent together had only drawn her to him even more. He was handsome, a skilled lover, charming when he wished to be. He made her heart flutter and her body hunger. And now that she had seen his beautiful paintings, she couldn't deny it any longer.

She loved Heath, as frightening and awful as it was.

Because he distinctly did not return the sentiment. No indeed. That tender feeling was solely reserved for the paragon Bess. His dead betrothed. Tia frowned, thinking herself horrid for knowing an instant of stabbing jealousy toward the woman. It was dreadfully small-minded of her, she knew. She simply couldn't help the way she felt.

A sudden knock on the connecting door startled her then. She stood hastily, straightening her skirts. It would be Heath, likely returned from his ride. And while she wasn't certain how she would face him after last evening's debacle, she knew that it wouldn't do to look a bedraggled mess. Tia took great pains to look her best at all times. Perhaps it didn't do much for her ability to win her husband's heart, but it certainly couldn't hurt.

"You may enter," she called out, steeling herself.

And then, there he was, standing at the threshold in his riding clothes, sinfully handsome as ever. "Tia," he greeted her, unsmiling.

The air between them fairly cracked with awkward tension. "Good morning, Your Grace," she returned, equally polite. "I trust you enjoyed your ride?"

"No." He passed a hand through his hair and stalked into her chamber. "I daresay I didn't."

"I own it is rather dreary," she commented, trying to hold her wits about her as he stopped close enough for her silken skirts to brush his trousers.

"That wasn't the reason for my lack of enthusiasm." He caught her chin, tipping it up so that he could better search her gaze.

"Then what was?" she asked, daring to hope that he felt something for her, however small, beyond mere desire.

"You." He traced her jaw with his thumb. "I'm sorry, Tia. I never meant to hurt you last night."

She swallowed, choosing her response with care. After all, she well knew she was partially responsible for what had transpired with her ninny-headed question. Why had she had to ask it? If only she had not. "I shouldn't have pried when I already knew the answer."

"I don't want the past to come between us," he said gravely, giving her spirits even more buoyancy.

"Nor do I," Tia agreed readily, even if she very much

feared it would be inevitable. After all, it already had to varying degrees. Sadness crept through her. Why couldn't they have met years before? Dash it all, why couldn't she have met him when she'd been a starry-eyed girl fresh off her comeout? But she hadn't. Instead, she'd given her heart to Denbigh, and Heath had given his to Bess.

Now they were two halves facing each other. Two halves she wasn't certain could make one whole. Not when she loved him and he loved another.

"Do you suppose we can begin again?" He cupped her cheek, his bright eyes pinned to hers.

She couldn't look away. "I wish we could," she murmured, knowing too much muddled the path before them.

"We can," he vowed. "I care for you, Tia. Very much."

"I—" she began, only to falter. She had almost confessed she loved him. Good heavens. "I care for you as well," she said instead.

He leaned closer, smelling of a maddening combination of himself, leather and the outdoors. "Will you sit for me again today?"

He still wanted to paint her? She hadn't been certain after last night. But she was certain of so little these days, it seemed. She turned her head, pressing a kiss to his hand. "Yes of course. I would be happy to sit for you if you'd like me to."

He smiled down at her, looking more at ease than she'd seen him since their arrival at Chatsworth House. "I'd like nothing better, darling." And then he pulled her to him for a kiss that, while unable to erase the misgivings swirling through her, at least gave her the expectation that perhaps one day he would be able to lay his past to rest at last.

Chapter Ten

TWO MONTHS LATER, TIA SAT AT HER WRITING desk once more, engaging in her daily morning ritual of reading and responding to letters from her sisters, friends, and family. She and Heath had settled into a routine of sorts at Chatsworth. It was a life of comfort and ease. There had been no more arguments, no more talks of suitors past, living or otherwise.

She wasn't fool enough to think that Heath had forgotten Bess, or that he even ever would. But for now, the tentative bond they shared was enough. They spent their days mostly together. She sat for Heath while he painted, and their sessions were frequently ended with or interrupted by frenzied bouts of lovemaking.

With a happy smile, Tia flipped through her tray of letters to the next in line and promptly froze as she looked at it more closely. Her heart picked up its pace into a mad gallop at the familiar seal. She turned it over, fingers tracing the precise, masculine script she knew too well.

She tore open the letter and confirmed what she had already known. It was from the Earl of Denbigh. Her first instinct was to tear the note into shreds without bothering to read it. Time had passed but had failed to assuage the pain he'd dealt her in throwing her over. It still hurt to know that while she'd been helplessly in love with him and he'd been sneaking away with her for secret kisses, he'd been wooing another.

Lady Evelyn Landers.

Tia frowned, the name bringing back memories she'd preferred to keep buried. Lady Evelyn's smug smile after her engagement to Denbigh had been announced. The new Lady Denbigh looking satisfied and with child not long after their nuptials.

But that had all been years ago, which begged the question of why the earl would write her a letter now. She couldn't help but be curious even though she knew she ought to pitch the letter into the nearest fire. Tia had never been the sort who did what she ought to do. She began reading.

He longed to see her, he wrote. He was out of mourning for his wife and there was an old secret he wished to air. He hoped it would change everything. Would she meet him at her father's estate?

Hands shaking, she folded the letter as it had been, staring unseeingly into her lap. Lady Evelyn had died. Tia hadn't even known. But that shouldn't have come as a surprise. Denbigh had been something of a rare sight in town. He'd retired to his country estate shortly after his nuptials.

She had to admit that the temptation to see Denbigh one last time was strong. But whereas once she would have been elated at the possibility of rekindling their romance, she now felt merely a curiosity for the old secret he mentioned. Her loyalty was to Heath. He was her husband, and she loved him, regardless of whether or not he returned that love. It was her most fervent hope that he one day would.

No, she resolved. She wouldn't respond to Denbigh's letter. Nothing he could say would be of import to her any longer. The adjoining door clicked open, revealing Heath.

He was informally dressed in a white shirt, trousers and bare feet. Dear God, the man was sinfully handsome. She hastily stuffed the letter into a Trollope book Bella had sent her. The silly woman refused to believe that Tia preferred not to waste her time wading through voluminous manuscripts in her spare time.

"Good morning," she greeted him cheerily, hoping he wouldn't notice the letter. It wouldn't do for him to know she'd received word from an old suitor. The dust between them had largely settled. No need to stir it up once more.

"Have you finished your correspondence, darling?" he asked, sauntering across the chamber to her.

She couldn't help but admire just how wonderful her husband looked, completely at ease as she'd rarely seen him. "Quite finished. Are you ready for me?"

"Always." He grinned as he stopped before her writing desk. "You ought to know that by now."

Tia was at eye level with his very obvious arousal. The imp in her prompted her to reach out and cup him through his trousers. She heard his sharp intake of breath and couldn't suppress a smile at his response. "I would certainly say you are," she told him archly.

"Ah, wife. You'll be the death of me." He caught her wayward hand and raised it to his lips. "I'm tempted, but I very much fear that if I linger here with your lovely hand on my cock, I'll forget all about showing you the portrait I've finished."

That caught her attention. "You've finished my portrait?"

He nodded, looking suddenly nervous. "I believe I have. I worked on it this morning instead of going for my ride. Will you come have a look?"

"Of course I will." She shot out of her seat as though someone had pinched her bottom. "You must show me at once."

"Promise to be gentle on me," he said wryly, leading the way back to his chamber. "This is the first painting I've completed in years."

Tia smiled at his back. She was more than aware, and she was quite honored to have been chosen as the subject of his first painting since Bess's death. Surely it had to mean something. She didn't imagine the passion between them, and she continued to hope that it would grow into something stronger. Love, should she be fortunate enough.

She followed Heath in silence to the work area he'd set up by the large windows on the far wall, the better to catch the most sunlight. When she rounded the easel and caught sight of the canvas, she lost her breath. The painting itself was stunning. He had rendered the oils so effortlessly, the colors he'd chosen all cast with a golden glow. Instead of painting her in the chamber as she'd assumed he'd done, he had painted her draped over rocks in the midst of a beautiful forest. The trees were whimsical, intertwined in a lush landscape. And she scarcely recognized the goddess staring back at her as herself.

"What do you think?" Heath asked, an uncharacteristic uncertainty evident in his tone.

He had painted her with reverent strokes, had made her beautiful. Dear heavens. He'd painted her in much the same way he had painted Bess. She was so moved that it took her a moment to find her voice. "It's incredible, Heath."

"I know it could use a bit more work."

She turned to him, thinking that if anything, his painting was even stronger than it had been before. Tia wasn't a stranger to art. In her wilder days, she'd hosted parties for some of the premier young artists of their day. She'd been a steadfast attendant at the Grosvenor Gallery and the Royal Academy both. She knew incredible pictures when she saw them. This latest work just confirmed what she'd already suspected.

Heath possessed an innate talent for painting that was as rare as it was magnificent.

"More work?" she repeated, incredulous. "Why, I believe this is one of the finest pieces I've ever seen."

"Of course it isn't." He scoffed. "This is the mere dabbling of a man with too much idle time on his hands."

"It's nothing of the sort." She turned her gaze back to the portrait, wishing that others could see what was before her. Naturally, the fact that he had painted her nude body with nary a stitch of clothing rendered that impossible. But that didn't mean his other pictures ought to be hidden away forever. "You should exhibit your work. I've seen the works of Mr. Burne-Jones, Mr. Millais and Mr. Watts," she told him, listing off some of the most renowned and revered artists she knew. "Yours rivals any of them."

"I'm gratified by your flattery, but it isn't necessary, my dear." He gave a derisive laugh. "I couldn't hold a candle to Burne-Jones or any of the others."

"Yes." She was adamant on the matter. "You can and do. You must send some of your work to the Grosvenor Gallery for this year's exhibition. Say you will, Heath."

"I'll do nothing of the sort." He was equally adamant. "I paint for myself, not for others. No good can come of opening myself to the ridicule of society and the acid pens of the critics."

"To Hades with the critics." Tia looked back to her husband. "You cannot mean to simply continue hiding your pictures away."

"They're not hidden." He raised a brow. "I'm reasonably certain you wouldn't wish this particular gem to be on display for all the world to see anyway, darling."

She flushed, thinking of the raw eroticism with which he'd painted her. "Of course not. But the others—"

"Are for me alone," he finished, his tone firm and ducal. No opposition would be tolerated. "Tell me, do you truly like the portrait?"

"I love it," she told him, utterly without artifice. But that didn't mean she wasn't determined to see that he received the recognition he deserved. He could very well take all his ducal decrees and stuff them. She'd never been terribly good at following orders. Just ask her poor old governess, Miss

Hullyhew.

He gave her a rare, unfettered smile. "Thank you. Though I'm afraid I didn't do the subject one bit of justice. Her beauty far exceeds my poor ability to capture it with oils and canvas."

"I'm gratified by your flattery, but it isn't necessary, my dear," she said, using his own words on him.

His smile turned into a grin. "Touché." He caught her around the waist and drew her against him, his eyes darkening in a way she found all too familiar. "Would you care to sit for another portrait for me?"

"I would be honored, Your Grace," she said, fluttering her lashes. "Shall I be dressed for this one?" She palmed his hard cock, feeling an answering blossom of desire unfurl within her. "Or would you prefer it if I disrobed?"

He kissed her swiftly. "Perhaps you ought to disrobe."

She met his gaze, feeling emboldened by the moment, the way he was looking at her, the way he had painted her. He had fashioned her into a Venus. And she liked it. "Perhaps you ought to help me," she suggested, presenting him with her back.

The gown Bannock had helped her don that morning was an elegant cream and navy affair, but alas, its buttons were not down the front bodice. But her husband, it seemed, harbored no concerns about playing lady's maid. His nimble fingers were already halfway to her bottom, unhooking the buttons from their moorings faster than even Bannock. She supposed Bannock hadn't quite the inspiration for haste that Heath had.

Wordlessly, he stripped her gown and undergarments, making short work of them. When he spun her back to face him once more, she wore only a chemise. His eyes roamed hungrily over the skin he'd revealed, his hands a hot brand on her waist through the delicate fabric. Desire swept through her at the sight of him, so intent, so beautiful. He was seeing her, she realized, through the eyes of an artist. The notion sent a pang of longing directly to her core.

"Something tells me I'm not about to sit for a portrait," she murmured wickedly. She caught his shirt and all but tore it from his body, desperate to feel him, to see his masculine strength.

"I've something else in mind for you first." He caressed her waist, then higher, cupping her full breasts through her chemise. Her nipples were aching and hard, poking into his palms. "If you don't mind."

Of course she didn't mind. She scraped her nails down the taut plane of his stomach, delighting in the excited groan it elicited from him. "Not a bit." She opened his trousers, releasing him. He was hard and hot in her hand, and an answering longing shot through her. She stroked him, knowing by now just what he liked.

"Damn it, woman." He shucked his trousers, divested her of her chemise and swept her into his arms before carrying her to the bed dominating the far side of the room.

When he laid her carefully upon it and joined her, she reached for him, thinking theirs would be a fast, furious coupling. But her husband apparently was of a different mind. He pressed her against the counterpane and knelt at her feet.

"This time, I want to worship you," he told her in a low, velvety voice that sent a frisson of anticipation down her spine. He pressed a kiss to first one knee and then the other. "God, I love the way you smell."

She hadn't known. "It's merely violets," she said on a sigh as he moved higher, kissing her inner thigh.

"Mmm." He continued his torturous trail, leaving her all but squirming beneath him. "And I love the way you taste." He pressed an open-mouthed kiss to her other thigh. "Here." He kissed her again, drawing ever closer to the place she wanted him most. "And here." Finally, he flicked his tongue against the swollen, slick bud of her sex. "But especially here." He sucked on her, then traced a path of fire over her folds. "Here, you taste just like pure honey."

Dear, sweet heavens. She jerked against him, moaning as

an unadulterated rush of pleasure assailed her. He continued his sensual assault, sucking and licking, sinking his tongue inside her. She grasped his hair, holding him against her. She simultaneously wanted more, and yet she wanted it to end. Wanted him inside her, his seed deep within her. She wanted that feeling of being one with him, the blissful surrender.

But her husband was determined to make her unravel for him. He toyed with her, alternating between gentle, whispers of touch and firm pressure. When his finger dipped into her sheath, she almost reached her pinnacle right then and there. She tipped her hips, bringing him deeper. His rhythm echoed the pulse of his tongue on her. Fast, then slow and lingering, then fast once more.

Her climax overtook her then, sudden and fierce. She shook against him, crying out, losing all control. Nothing mattered but his tongue on her, his finger inside her, the glorious sensations he evoked from her body.

Heath withdrew his finger, glistening with her juices, and sucked it into his mouth as if he were consuming the finest delicacy. "Pure honey," he repeated.

The action was so sensual, so deliberate. She was wet and hungry, ready for him. Ready to be taken by him. Tia couldn't wait a moment more. She clutched his shoulders and pulled him down atop her. His cock nestled against her, his strong chest against her sensitive breasts. He kissed her deeply, and she tasted herself on his lips.

"Take me, Heath," she whispered. "Take me now."

He thrust into her, sheathing himself completely. She matched him thrust for thrust, clawing at his shoulders, wild for him. When he dipped his head to take one of her aching nipples into his mouth, she came again, tightening on him, the waves of pleasure even more potent this time than the last. In another few thrusts, he too had lost himself, crying out as he filled her with his seed.

He collapsed against her and rolled them as one to their sides, fitting her head neatly into the crook of his shoulder. "Sweet Christ, woman. What you do to me."

He was breathless. Good. So was she. In fact, she was quite speechless as well. This time, she knew better than to ask questions to which she didn't wish to hear the answers. She settled against him, kissing his neck.

I love you, she thought. *I love you desperately.*

She didn't dare to say the words aloud.

Heath watched his sleeping wife in the early morning's light, brushing a tendril of golden hair away from her brow. He'd spent the night in her chamber, something he'd avoided doing since their wedding night. But she hadn't wanted him to leave, and he had been reluctant to revert to sleeping alone in his massive bed. An unsettling emotion curled through his gut as he admired the burgeoning glow of the sun casting her delicate features in a soft glow.

Contentment.

Yes, that was the word for it. He was simply content. More content than he recalled being in years, and he was man enough to admit to himself that the prospect scared the bloody hell out of him. It scared him as much for what he stood to lose as what he stood to gain.

He cared for Tia. What he felt for her had transcended the wild attraction that had initially drawn him to her side. She had become deuced important to him. He woke wanting to see her. He bided his time until she emerged from her chamber and he could touch her again, paint her again, hold her in his arms. Strip her nude for an impromptu lovemaking session. Catch a whiff of the maddening scent of violets.

Damn it all to hell.

He hadn't bargained for this when he'd wed her. He'd intended to have an uncomplicated society union. They would have mutual respect for each other, share their beds and desire, begin a family. That was all. That would have been—should have been—more than enough. But in the course of the last few months, everything had altered so far from his ideal that he was beginning to fear he'd never find his way back. Good Lord, he'd never meant to care for her so deeply that the mere act of watching her sleep turned him into a maudlin fool.

A cold, hard knot settled in his gut.

He needed to put distance between them. He couldn't afford to fall in love again. He had done so once, and it had ended disastrously. In love, there was far too much to lose. For if he lost the woman he loved again, he didn't think he would survive with either his sanity or his life.

The reminder of just how low he'd sunk after Bess' death was enough to have him tossing back the counterpane and sliding out of bed. He tossed a look over his shoulder to make certain Tia still slept soundly. She did, completely unaware of the tumult assailing him, gloriously beautiful and all his. She shifted as he watched, the bedclothes slipping to reveal the curve of one pale breast and the soft pink tip of a nipple.

He hardened instantly but forced himself to turn his back. Lingering would only weaken his resolve. He had come a long way from the naïve, passionate young man who had devoted himself to painting and love and nothing else. Now, he was a man with far more important matters on his hands. He had estates to attend to, the legacy of the duchy to uphold.

Stifling a curse, he stalked from the chamber, not even bothering to retrieve his discarded dressing gown. The chill morning air served its purpose, diminishing his arousal. He closed the door gently at his back and turned his mind to where it belonged. Matters of his estate. He would spend more time in his study, he vowed, and less time painting his beautiful wife.

Falling for her was a steep cliff off which he refused to allow himself to plunge.

Tia was having breakfast alone. It had rather become a habit in the last fortnight or so as her husband's duties on the estate had begun to require his attention far more than ever. She tried not to allow his recent defection to affect her, but she couldn't help but find cause for worry.

She stabbed at her poached egg with more force than necessary and forced a bite to her lips. She had hoped—perhaps naively—that time would draw them closer together. But it would seem that it had only led them further apart. His initial passion for painting had dissipated. He hadn't even put brush to canvas in days. And while he still visited her chamber most nights, he had never spent the night with her aside from the last occasion when she'd risen to find him gone. Only his crumpled dressing gown and the scent of him on her pillow had served as a reminder that he'd been there at all.

Inwardly, she could admit that she was dismayed by the turn of their relationship. Outwardly, she continued to pretend as if nothing was amiss. She was always pleased to see Heath. She was always pleasant and welcoming. She ran the household for him, making sure everything was arranged and ordered to perfection. But the cracks were widening in her veneer, and she wasn't certain how much longer she could go on pretending his detachment was enough.

Without a bit of warning, the door to the breakfast room was thrown open, revealing the very subject of her frustrated musings. Her husband stalked into the room, looking handsome as ever and completely infuriated.

Oh dear. She'd seen that expression before. It had been just before he'd tied her to the bed. Only, this time there wasn't a bed in sight, just a young footman watching in barely masked alarm.

Heath dismissed the poor fellow and barely waited for him to discreetly disappear from the room before turning on her. "Jesus, Tia. What have you done?" He dropped a folded missive in her lap with disgust, as if he'd found it out in the stables mired in dung. The vehemence in his voice startled her.

"I haven't the slightest notion," she said honestly, at a loss for his abrupt entrance and equally abrupt anger. "Perhaps you could enlighten me?"

"Enlighten yourself, madam," he bit out. "Read the letter, if you please."

She unfolded it with care, scanning the contents as understanding dawned along with apprehension. Good heavens. She turned her gaze to her fuming husband, hoping she could snuff the flames of his rage. "I merely sent away a few of your pictures to the Grosvenor Gallery."

She had preyed upon those she knew in the art world for assistance when it had seemed clear that Heath wanted no part of exhibiting his work. And judging from the letter, they had more than come through for her. Of course, they hadn't known that she had sent the paintings without Heath's approval, and now they had rather upended the teapot.

"Without my consent," he gritted, his eyes snapping with blue fire. "And now they're bloody well going to display them to the masses. You've overstepped your bounds."

She faltered. This truly was not the reaction she had intended when she'd chosen to send off a few of his pictures in secret. "I hoped you'd be pleased."

"Pleased?" He was incredulous. "Pleased that my wife has gone behind my back to make me a laughing stock before the world?"

"A laughing stock?" Good heavens, she certainly hadn't anticipated the level of his rage. She'd imagined he might initially be displeased at having his paintings sent away without his knowledge. After all, she hadn't forgotten his reaction to her decision to have his pictures brought out of hiding. But still—this—his naked fury, she hadn't envisioned. "No one will be laughing, Heath. 'Tis high time you allow the world to see precisely how talented you are."

"Did it ever occur to you as you were in the grips of your

self-absorbed meddling that maybe I bloody well don't want the world to see my paintings?" he all but bellowed.

Tia flinched at his cruel words before pushing her chair away and standing so that he could no longer hover over her like a wraith. Perhaps she had overstepped her bounds this time, but that didn't excuse how hurtful he was being. "Do you truly think I've done this for myself?" she demanded. "How dare you?"

"How dare *you*, Tia?" He caught her about the waist, trapping her against him. "Why did not you not ask me, damn you?"

"Because I knew you wouldn't allow it," she said honestly. "Your work is beautiful."

"It's private." His grip tightened on her. "You sent them the picture of Bess."

Ah, there it was. The true reason for his anger. She had sent away the painting of his precious betrothed. The paragon to whom Tia could not compare. "Pray, be honest. You're angry with me because I sent away her painting, not because I sent away any of the others."

"I didn't paint it for all of London to critique," he said, his tone dark. "It was meant for her, and when she died, it was all I had left of her."

She couldn't deny it. She was hurt by his revelation. Of course, she'd suspected that despite his decision to begin painting again, he hadn't entirely let go of the past. Of the woman he'd loved. She had to wonder now if he ever would. It seemed that Bess's hold on him was as sure and strong as if she were alive.

"You will always love her," she said quietly, hating the fact. Hating herself for the jealousy that sliced through her. How could she be jealous of a dead woman? It made no sense, but there it was. She had married a man whose heart would forever belong to another.

"I've made no secret of the fact that I was in love with Bess," he said, some of the heat leaving his voice. "We've spoken of this many times."

Yes, they had. And yet Tia continued upholding the delusion that one day he would love her too. It was plain to her now that such a day would never arrive. Her heart gave a painful pang in her breast. It was torture, plain and simple, to love a man who would never love her at all.

"The painting will be returned to you at the end of the exhibition," she forced herself to say. "You'll have it back. You needn't worry on that account."

"You don't understand the severity of this, Tia." He raked a hand through his hair, the rage still emanating from him. "This isn't some frivolous lark at a country house party. My painting—that painting in particular—is a private matter. I told you that I never wanted to exhibit it, and you ignored me."

She couldn't argue with the latter portion of what he'd said. She had ignored his wishes, but it was only because she'd thought that he needed that final push. She'd known quite well that he would never exhibit the work on his own. But not only did his paintings deserve to be seen by the public, Heath deserved to realize the part of his life he had sealed off all those years ago. He had traveled to Italy to study painting. She could see very well in his work that it had been his driving passion. She saw now the joy it returned to him. Why shouldn't he completely cast off the shackles he'd allowed the past to close around him?

But his other words sliced her deeper, creating an uglier wound than any blade could. He thought her too stupid to understand? He'd accused her of being frivolous, of thinking it all a lark. How very wrong he was. She had never been more serious about anything in her life.

She stared at him, numbed and at a loss for how to respond. Indeed, she feared that were she to speak, she would ruin her composure by bursting into tears.

"Have you nothing to say for yourself?" he demanded.

"Nothing, it would seem, that would alter your opinion of me," she said quietly. "You have already decided that I am nothing more than a stupid interloper here."

"This time, you've gone too far." His fists were clenched at his sides.

She found herself wishing she produced such emotion in him, instead of a mere portrait of his dead betrothed. And the awful realization hit her then with the weight of a brick to the chest. He would never even care for her, never mind love her. He'd never been able to care for her from the first. He had desired her, that much was apparent. By his own admission, he'd been in search of a wife. But to him, their union had been an arrangement for his benefit. He gained the mistress of his house, possible mother to his heirs. And she had gained only the heartache of thwarted hopes.

"I begin to think you never should have wed me at all," she told him, her voice breaking against her will. She didn't want him to see how low he'd brought her, just how weak she was for him. Her pride didn't want to allow him to know just how much he'd come to mean to her.

Everything.

And yet he was looking at her now as if she were a stranger, as if she were nothing to him. Her heart broke waiting for him to say something, anything. To heal the fissures that were growing between them into a massive chasm. How had they come so far together only to fall into such disrepair?

"Perhaps I should not have," he agreed at last, his tone frigid. "But the deed has already been done."

She recoiled. His words were like a slap to her cheek. Somehow, she stood strong before him, unwilling to let him see that he had broken her. "If you will excuse me, Your Grace. I find I'm quite finished with breakfast."

It was the biggest understatement she'd ever spoken.

She didn't dare await his response before all but running from the room lest he see the tears already coursing down her cheeks. He'd just confirmed her greatest fear. She had trapped herself in a second loveless marriage. Only this time, her fate was far worse. Because this time, she loved and would never be loved in return.

Tia hesitated outside her husband's study door while Burnes announced her. She hadn't faced him in three days. While she wasn't certain of what her ultimate course of action would be, she was sure of one thing. She needed to get away from Chatsworth House and Heath. She needed time to gather herself, to heal. Bannock had overseen the packing. It was all done. The only thing that needed to be finished was this formal audience with her husband.

It loomed before her, daunting as mounting a horse again after she'd been thrown. Terrifying but necessary. Burnes returned, expressionless as ever.

"His Grace will see you now, Your Grace," he intoned.

"Thank you, Burnes." With a deep breath, she swept past him and into her husband's lair.

He was seated behind his desk, imposing and regal as any duke might be. Looking at him now, it was almost difficult to reconcile him to the passionate lover she'd known. The man who had set her aflame with his passion stared at her now as if he scarcely knew her. She might as well have been another piece of furniture in the room.

"You required an audience?" he asked when she faltered, unable to find her tongue.

She stopped a short distance from his desk, clasping her hands. "Yes. I have packed a few trunks. I'd like to go to Harrington House for a time."

"Harrington House?" He raised a brow. "I wasn't aware of any such plans. It's the midst of winter, Tia. You know as well as I that the roads can become impassable quite easily."

She had already foreseen such an argument. "Snow has yet to fall. The journey will be a short one, and I'm expected. I've sent word ahead of my impending arrival."

"You arranged all this without my knowledge."

"Yes." She paused. "I thought that you wouldn't mind

to see me gone after our last words."

"I'm sorry for the way I reacted," he surprised her by saying.

"Thank you," she said simply. But it didn't change what had happened. It didn't change the disparity between what he felt for her and for Bess. It didn't change what she must do. "And I'm sorry for going against your wishes. My leaving for a time is best, I should think."

"I don't want you to go."

She hadn't expected that either. "You don't want me. You made that clear."

"I desire you," he told her.

Ah, so they were back to that old story once more.

Desire was not love. Tia knew well enough to understand the vast ocean of difference between the two. Sadness swept through her, for she knew for certain that she couldn't continue in this manner, with the ghost of Bess between them. She loved Heath, but his heart belonged to a dead woman, a woman with the face of an angel, and a woman with whom Tia could not dare compete. She couldn't bear to love him while he loved another.

"Desire is a fleeting thing," she said slowly, numbed by the direction of her thoughts. She was going to have to leave him, to leave Heath and the life they'd been building together at Chatsworth House. It was the only way. "You love another."

His expression was pained, his jaw clenched. "I've made no secret of my past. I cannot change it now, nor would I wish to."

Of course he wouldn't wish to change his past with Bess, she thought with more than just a trace of bitterness. His time with her had made him happy. His time with Tia had merely been duty combined with desire. Not love. Never love.

"I wish to leave this morning," she announced.

"Why now?" he demanded.

Because her poor heart was breaking, but she couldn't

tell him so. "I daresay some time apart would be a boon for us both," she lied. "I find that I miss my family, and I'm sure you would like to attend to the estate without my interference."

"How long?" he asked, clearly not liking the idea.

"A fortnight," she said. "Perhaps more."

"A fortnight," he agreed grimly. "No more. I won't have us living apart, Tia. You are my wife."

She longed to rail at him, ask him why he didn't treat her as his wife anywhere other than in the bedchamber. How could he expect her to carry on while he carried the flame for his lost love? "I'm aware of my duties," she told him coolly. After all, he had made it abundantly clear to her that she was just that to him. A duty. His heart would forever belong to another. "I will return whenever you wish it of me."

In truth, she didn't even know if he would miss her. Beyond the bedchamber, that was. But as much as she reveled in the undeniable passion they shared, it simply wasn't enough. She wanted more from him. All he had to give. And that included his love, even if she knew she'd never receive it.

"You will come back to me in a fortnight's time," he repeated.

If she'd longed for tender words, none were forthcoming.

Chapter Eleven

"**D**ARLING, YOU LOOK HORRID."

Tia grimaced at her older sister Helen. She'd arrived at the familiar, imposing façade of her childhood home and was immediately bombarded by her boisterous family, brothers, sisters and all. Helen, ever the perceptive one of the Harrington clan, sensed something was amiss and hadn't waited long to take her aside. She'd marched into Tia's chamber at the first possible opportunity, not bothered in the least by Tia's assertion that she required a rest after the hardship of travel that day.

"How sweet of you to say so," she told her sister wryly. "I'm sure I'm quite flattered by your kind words."

"Oh pish." Her sister, who was just as blonde as she and possessed their mother's fair beauty and stubborn temperament, waved a dismissive hand. "You needn't feign injury on my account. I'm your sister. I can read you like a book, and you've got to be Friday-faced for a reason."

"I don't know what you're prattling on about," she lied, not wishing to delve into the depressing tale of her marriage. Not now. Perhaps not ever. She preferred to wallow in her private misery, thank you very much. She had come to

Harrington House to be distracted, not dissected. "I'm merely worn out from pitching about in the carriage."

"It's the duke," Helen guessed, not about to allow Tia her privacy. "What has he done? I'll box his ears if he's done you ill."

"He's done nothing wrong," Tia was quick to say, mindful of the ears of the unpacking maid. She raised a brow at her sister, communicating silently.

"You may go, Dobbs," Helen dismissed the girl, taking Tia's cue. "Thank you. That will be all."

The maid dropped into a curtsy and disappeared. Her sister scarcely waited for the door to click closed before returning to her quest for information. "Now, you must tell me all at once. I've scarcely had the opportunity to speak with you since your wedding, aside from letters, that is."

"Oh, Helen." Now that they were alone, Tia's every intention to keep her misery to herself seemed to vanish. Her sisters had always been her best friends and trusted confidantes. Faced with Helen's sisterly concern, her resolve crumbled. So did she, tearing up and turning into a water pot. "He's in love with his betrothed."

"Don't cry, my dear." Helen wrapped a supportive arm about her waist and led her to a settee. "How can he have a betrothed? You're his wife."

Tia longed for a handkerchief, but she hadn't any so she sniffled instead. "He doesn't have a betrothed. Not any longer. She died years ago."

"Ah, I begin to see." Helen patted her consolingly. "It can be difficult indeed when one's rival is a ghost."

"She was a paragon of beauty and kindness and all other manners of perfection," Tia said, feeling hideous for even saying the words aloud. Her jealousy of Bess was a constant source of shame for her.

"I'm sure she was, but she couldn't hold a candle to you, my dear." Her sister paused, searching her gaze. "You've grown to care for him, haven't you?"

"I love him," Tia confirmed on an awful wail. She didn't

know what had come over her. She couldn't seem to gather herself now that the dam had burst within her. The tears were slipping fast down her cheeks. She was an utter mess. "I didn't want to love him, but I do now, and it's ruined everything."

"Oh dear." Helen pressed a handkerchief into her palm. "If love is as bad as all that, I consider myself fortunate never to have fallen prey to it."

Like her namesake Helen of Troy, Helen was exquisitely beautiful. But she was also formidable as a dragon. She didn't tolerate romance or lovelorn suitors. She was far too elegant for something so lowering. Tia wished she were made of the same stern stuff as her sister. But alas, she had been cursed with a weakness for a sinfully handsome duke who wanted her in his bed but not his heart.

"You are fortunate indeed." Tia wept before burying her nose in Helen's handkerchief and blowing away.

"Gads." Her sister eyed her distastefully. "Do keep that, dearest. I shan't be needing it back."

Tia tried to formulate a response, truly she did, but for some reason she couldn't seem to make the great racking sobs stop. What had become of her?

"I know of something that may brighten your spirits," Helen said suddenly and rather loudly over the din of Tia's wailing.

"You…you do?" Tia sniffed, trying to calm herself.

"Why yes." Her sister beamed, the effect making her look positively radiant. Tia was sure she looked no better than a bedraggled street urchin in comparison. "The Earl of Denbigh is visiting us. I can't think of why I didn't tell you sooner. He'll be here in just a few days."

Denbigh.

The shock of the name, the shock that she would see him again for the first time in years, halted her tears. But still, she had no desire to revisit that portion of her life. "I don't wish to see him."

"But I have a feeling he would dearly love to see you."

Helen patted her shoulder again. "He's written so fondly of you in the letters he's been sending me."

Denbigh had been writing to Helen? Tia frowned at her sister. "Since when are you friends with the earl?"

Helen actually flushed. "We ran across each other at a garden party a few months ago."

"I see." Tia wasn't sure she liked her sister befriending the man who had once jilted her, but she supposed it wasn't any of her affair. "Well then, you can visit with him if you like him so much. I haven't come here to observe social niceties."

"No indeed," Helen agreed sagely. "You've come here to escape the husband you've fallen in love with, who also happens to be in love with his deceased betrothed."

The urge to cry again was strong. "Thank you for the reminder."

"Come now, buck up." Her sister gave her a gentle shake. "You always used to be the bravest amongst us when we were growing up, remember? What was it you used to say when Cleo and I would run to your chamber in the midst of the night?"

Tia thought of what she'd told Miss Whitney what seemed like so long ago now. "I'm brave enough to chase the ghosts away."

"That's right, and don't you forget it. For I have no doubt that in time you shall chase this ghost away as well."

If only she had as much faith in her abilities as her sister did.

Heath wandered through Tia's chamber, feeling like an interloper for even entering without her being present. But he couldn't help it. He needed to remind himself that she hadn't been a flight of fancy, that she was a living, breathing woman. He needed to smell her, feel her, touch her. He needed, quite simply, her.

He missed his wife. By God, he was a fool. He'd been so determined not to suffer the pain of losing her, and he'd pushed her away. When he'd discovered she'd sent his paintings away without his permission, it had been the ammunition he'd needed against her. He'd seized it like the desperate man he was, using it as a weapon to guard his heart. Yes, he'd been so damn determined not to suffer the pain of losing her that he'd forced her away.

He'd lost her.

And losing her, he'd discovered in the days since she'd departed for her father's country seat, was not something he was prepared to do. He loved her. He didn't know the precise moment his feelings had shifted and strengthened. He didn't know the whys or hows of it. But he did know that his minx of a wife had turned his life upside down in the very best way. She'd made him whole again, brought him back from a cold and lonely existence.

He loved her so much that he couldn't bear to keep her at a distance any longer. He was ready to face whatever fate befell them. If she took sick, he would be at her side. If she lived to ninety and a day, he would be there too if God and fortune willed it.

Realizing he loved her had meant reevaluating his feelings for Bess. Initially, he'd been beset by guilt. He'd almost been afraid that loving Tia would somehow besmirch Bess's memory. But Tia's words had come back to him, chiding him. She was right. He had attempted to avoid what had happened five years ago, sealing it away in his mind as surely as he'd sealed away the room containing his paintings. Lingering in guilt would not bring Bess back. Denying the love he felt for Tia would not bring Bess back.

Nothing would.

But he did have the power to bring his wife back.

She didn't belong at her father's estate. She belonged with Heath. By his side. In his arms. And it was entirely up to him to find a way to win her back. He picked up a bottle of her scent and inhaled deeply. Violets. Somehow, it smelled sweeter on her soft skin. Just thinking of it made him harder than a hunk of coal.

Perhaps groveling would be in order.

He replaced her scent bottle, thinking that he would gladly swallow his damnable pride and win her back in any manner necessary. He'd been an ass, plain and simple. He had been cruel to her, had hurt her. Hell yes, he would grovel.

He cut a path past the writing desk where she so often spent her mornings. Her cream-colored, monogrammed paper was stacked neatly alongside a pen and a sheaf of envelopes. The entire vignette looked as if she might return, bustling through the door with a beaming smile on her lovely face at any moment. The only item that was out of place was a tome perched precariously on the edge of the desk's glossy surface.

Perhaps it was his painter's eye that drew him to the book, righting it so that it was parallel to her stationery. As he did so, the corner of a letter slid from beneath its cover. His interest was piqued. He knew very well that his wife was not a reader. The book had likely been a gift from one of her sisters. Before he could think twice, he flipped through to the frontispiece where the letter had been left.

The dark scrawl visible through the paper did not appear feminine. A gnawing pang of worry in his gut, he went against his conscience and unfolded the letter. Hastily, he scanned its contents, hands shaking with rage by the time he'd finished. By God, he was the worst sort of fool. Not only had he driven his wife away, but he'd driven her straight into the arms of another man. Unless he was mistaken, it was none other than the man she'd spoken about loving. The Earl of Denbigh.

Heath knew that Denbigh had lands bordering the Earl of Northcote's estate. Tia had gone to her sister at Harrington House, her father's country seat.

Damn and blast.

"Burnes," he bellowed, before realizing he was in his

wife's chamber and the butler wasn't likely to hear him. "Devil take it," he muttered, going to the bell pull.

He was going to have his carriage readied. He had a wife to collect and an earl to beat to a pulp. He just prayed that he wouldn't be too late.

Against her better judgment, Tia had agreed to share tea with Denbigh the afternoon of his arrival. Helen had persuaded her that she needed the distraction and that the earl wished to impart something important to her. And so she'd relented. Her misery at having left Heath hadn't abated. She missed him dreadfully.

With a sigh, she pressed her forehead to the cool pane of glass in the drawing room as she awaited her guest. From here, she had an excellent view of the east gardens and trees beyond. The day was as gray and cold as her mood. She had resigned herself to her fate, but it wasn't without more than her fair share of misery. Heath would never love her as he'd loved Bess.

But she was beginning to fear it didn't matter. She loved him regardless of the way he felt for her. A fortnight apart suddenly seemed far too much.

"Tia."

The voice was familiar. She turned from the window, bracing herself for the first sight of him. He was just as she remembered, tall and handsome with midnight hair and a rake's practiced air. But he appeared a bit older now, a handful of silver threaded through his thick mane at the temples. His green eyes met hers, and part of her expected the same tingling sensation to travel through her at the indirect contact.

But instead, she felt only sadness. "Denbigh," she greeted him, holding out her hand for him to take.

He raised it to his lips for a lingering kiss. "You're every bit as lovely as you were when I first saw you at the Granville soiree."

The Granville soiree. She'd been sixteen, hadn't yet been presented to the queen, and had been testing her mettle at a gathering in the country on a neighboring estate. He'd been two-and-twenty, handsome and hopelessly debonair. It was hard to believe it had been nine years ago when she'd been a naïve miss with stars in her eyes and diamonds in her hair, believing in love and forever.

"You look very well," she forced herself to say, for aside from the silver in his hair and the slight grooves bracketing his mouth, he was the same perfect earl he'd always been. "I'm sorry that we don't meet under happier circumstances."

He inclined his head, releasing her hand. "As am I. But I won't pretend that it isn't lovely to see you after so long."

She felt the same way, but she found that it was only in a nostalgic sense. He was a part of her past. A part that had been dear to her. A part that had shaped the lady she'd become. But a part that was where it belonged. In the past. "Please," she said, gesturing to the *Louis Quinze* settee, "do sit and let's chat. I'd dearly love to hear all about your daughter."

He sat while she rang for a tea tray to be brought around. They settled in with their steaming teacups before them, happily talking about the balls where they had danced all night long, about their old friends—who had married, who had not—about the past that had seemed so very far away and now suddenly seemed once more within each.

Truly, it was as if no time had passed, as if she'd blinked and the nine years between them had fallen away.

"Do you recall Lady Chesterfield falling asleep at the Nightingale soiree and snoring over her soup?" Tia asked, chuckling as she recalled the sight of the august matron nodding off.

"How could I have forgotten?" Denbigh laughed. "She snored as loudly as my dog. Old Lord Chesterfield was quite put out with her when her wig nearly fell off." He took a sip of his tea before grinning at her. "Truly, I've missed you, Tia. You never failed to make me smile when I most needed it."

"I was not the one who went away," she pointed out, for she found that the anger she'd carried toward him for years had dissipated but the need for answers had not.

He lowered his teacup to its saucer with a rattle. "I can explain."

"I'm not sure it matters now." And truly, it didn't. She loved Heath. She always would. It seemed she certainly had a knack for loving men whose hearts belonged to another.

"Lady Evelyn came to me because she was carrying another's child," he said baldly.

His revelation shocked her so badly that her tea spilled onto the saucer and her silk skirts. She paid it no heed. "But you told me the babe was yours."

"I lied to you. The child belonged to my brother."

His younger brother had died suddenly after a hunting accident. Tia hadn't known him terribly well, but he'd been known as quite the rascal. Suddenly, it all began to make sense. "She came to you when he died?"

"Yes." He deposited his tea on the tray spread before them, no longer pretending to indulge. "I didn't want the child to be born a bastard. I felt I owed it to my brother to do our family's duty by Lady Evelyn and the babe both."

An awful clarity overtook her as she recalled the day he'd met with her to tell her he was wedding Lady Evelyn. She'd been so shocked by his abrupt change that she hadn't noticed how somber he'd been. How distressed. How his smile when he'd proclaimed his feelings for Lady Evelyn had been fragile at best, insincere at most. She could see it now, without the cloud of hurt that had enveloped her then.

"You didn't love her," she said quietly, the realization hitting her. She wondered for the briefest of moments what she would have done, how she would have reacted, if she had known the truth then. Would she have begged him to stay with her? Run off to become his mistress? She supposed she'd never know, and in the end, that was a good thing indeed. For she hadn't belonged with Denbigh. She hoped that she belonged with Heath, but after the way they'd left things, she couldn't be certain any longer.

"I never loved my wife, Tia," he told her, his tone equally soft. "Now that she is gone, I'm free to tell you the truth at last."

"You're a bit late in your confession." She thought then of her miserable marriage to Lord Stokey. "I wed Lord Stokey because of you."

He closed his eyes for a moment. "I'm sorry for that."

"I'm afraid an apology doesn't quite erase it all." She too deposited her teacup before her. "Why didn't you simply tell me the truth when it would have made a difference?"

"It wouldn't have done you any good. You would have wanted to follow me, and I couldn't bear for you to ruin your life for me."

Of course she knew he was right. She would have made quite a cake of herself, chasing after the grand love she'd thought they'd shared. But there remained a very salient question he'd yet to answer. "Why are you telling me this now?"

"You've arrived in good time, old boy," Bingley, one of Tia's three brothers, said cheerfully, thumping Heath on the back.

The Harringtons were an eccentric lot, he was discovering. He'd been greeted upon his arrival at Harrington House not by a butler or even a footman but by Tia's evidently inebriated sibling. He was dressed as if prepared to go riding, but he held a half-empty glass of whiskey in his hand. Apparently, he hadn't made it that far from the bottle.

Heath raised a brow, bemused by the younger man's air of familiarity. He'd known Tia had three brothers—indeed, he was familiar with Lord Adrian Harrington, who was of an age with him as the eldest Harrington son. But Adrian was rather subdued compared to the raucous young fellow before him. "Oh?"

"We've a housheguesht," Bingley elaborated, taking another swig of his whiskey. Before frowning and making another attempt at the word. "Er, houseguest."

A houseguest? Heath prayed it wasn't who he thought it was, that his wife had not come to Harrington House for an assignation with the blasted Earl of Denbigh. "Who might that be?" he asked, surprised at how calm his voice sounded, belying the rage and dread swirling in his gut.

"Why the Earl of Denbigh, of course," Tia's unwitting brother enlightened him. "He's only jusht arrived."

"Where the devil is he?" Heath bit out. He was going to thrash the bastard.

"I say, not a friend of his, are you?"

Heath had rather endured all he could of inebriated, foppish younger brothers. He caught Bingley by the shirt. "Where?" he demanded.

"Taking tea in the drawing room," Bingley choked out. "With my sister."

The hell he was. Heath released his brother-in-law and turned on his heel, not even bothering to offer an explanation. It was time he interrupted his wife's *tête-à-tête* with her past.

Denbigh stood, coming to Tia and dropping to his knees, taking her hands in his. "My feelings for you remain the same. I know you've married Devonshire, but I was hoping we might renew our acquaintance."

Dear heavens. He wanted to become lovers. She stared at him, thinking that several months ago, she would have thrown herself into his arms. Marriages in the *ton*, after all, were built on alliances and not on love. Dalliances were commonplace as long as they were conducted in secret.

"Denbigh," she began, not knowing what to say. Her emotions roiled within her, a wild tumult. "I'm in love with my husband."

His grip on her tightened. "Have you no tender feelings for me?"

She thought she understood him then. He was a man who had lived for nine years with a wife he hadn't loved. He'd been trapped by his own sense of duty. And now, he was finally free. But she wasn't. "I cared for you then," she admitted softly. "I care for you now. As a friend."

He brought her hands to his lips again before rising. "I understand. I daresay it was too much to hope for. It would seem I'm too late."

"Yes." She stood as well, opening her arms to him for one last embrace. He accepted it, catching her against him, and it took her back, just for a breath, to a chapter that would now be forever closed. "Thank you for telling me. I'm glad to know you weren't the awful cad I've always thought."

Before he could respond, the door to the drawing room burst open. Tia started, peering around the earl's shoulder to see which of her brothers had dared to intrude upon her privacy. Likely it was Bingley. He'd been in his cups for two days solid, the blighter. There'd been some sort of contretemps with an opera singer, according to Helen.

But it wasn't one of her brothers.

It was her husband, and his blue gaze met hers. Disbelief settled over his features before his face became carefully blank. "Lord Denbigh," he said grimly, "may I ask why you're holding my wife in your arms?"

She disengaged herself hurriedly, aware of how the tableau must present itself. She was sure she appeared horribly guilty. "Heath," she said, starting toward him. "Denbigh and I were having tea, and we were just now saying goodbye."

"It's good that you've exchanged your farewells," he

returned, looking past her to the earl, "for now I'm afraid I'm going to have to thrash him to within an inch of his life."

"No." She took hold of his arm, thinking she might restrain him. Images of him and Denbigh bruised and bloodied rose to her mind. "We were embracing. Nothing more."

"You're right to want to thrash me," Denbigh said, stalking toward them. "I came here in the hopes of making your wife my mistress."

A low, primal sound emerged from Heath's throat. He shrugged Tia away and started for Denbigh, fists clenched and ready to pummel. He swung, his fist connecting with the earl's jaw.

"I deserved that one," Denbigh said, rubbing the reddening skin of his chin. "But not another. She wouldn't have me, Devonshire. She's in love with you."

"Yes," Heath scoffed. "And that's why she ran to you the moment you sent her a bloody letter."

Dear heavens. He'd found the letter. Tia had quite forgotten about it after tucking it away in the book Bella had sent her. "I didn't run to see him," she defended. "You pushed me away after I sent your paintings to the Grosvenor Gallery. I needed some time."

"Time during which you plotted to meet your old lover." His voice was cold.

"There was no plotting, you dullard," Denbigh said, unwisely drawing Heath's attention back to him. "I heard she was in the country from her brother and I asked if I might pay her a visit. She merely acquiesced."

Tia took the opportunity to throw herself between the two warring men, staring up into the face of her irate husband as she braced her palms on his chest. "Please, Heath," she pleaded. "Your quarrel is not with the earl. It's with me."

He stared down at her, fury swirling in the depths of his eyes. "From what little I've seen, it would appear that my quarrel is with the both of you."

"Please," she said again, not wanting any more violence on her account. "You mistook what you saw when you entered the room. None of this is as it seems."

"You told me you wished to visit your sister," he said, his tone accusatory. "You lied, damn you. How could you?"

"I didn't lie." Tears of desperation pricked at her eyes. She had been wrong in leaving him, she realized now. Far from making the chasm between them bridgeable, it had only served to make it wider. Perhaps unsurpassable. "You must believe me."

"This is a dialogue best reserved to husband and wife," Denbigh intoned behind her. "I'll take my leave of you both."

Tia didn't bother to watch him leave. She knew he was gone the moment the door clicked closed. There would have been a time in her life when nothing would have stopped her from following. But now, the man she loved stood before her, and he was all that mattered.

"What Denbigh said is the truth," she said quietly. "He and I are not lovers. I didn't run away from you to meet him here. I merely thought that some time and distance between us would give us both a new perspective. You were so angry with me, and I didn't know what to do."

"He is the man you loved, isn't he?" Heath demanded. "The man you spoke of that day in the yellow drawing room at Penworth. It was Denbigh, wasn't it?"

Part of her wanted to deny it, but the rational part of her mind knew that subterfuge would only lead to further ruin. "Yes," she whispered. "It was him."

His jaw tightened. "Tell me again that what transpired between you and him today was innocent."

"It was."

"I wish to God I could believe you."

The raw bitterness in his tone struck her as cleanly as any slap could. He stood so stiff and so still, holding himself apart from her. The gap between them was indicative of so much. She wanted it gone. She wanted to touch him, to soften him. To remind him of what they shared. To bring him back to her.

She brushed her fingers over his whiskers, noting that they were long, not neatly trimmed as he usually wore them. Perhaps he too had suffered in their time apart. "You must believe me," she said, refusing to allow him to break her gaze. "I hold no love in my heart for Denbigh. Indeed, I begin to think I never did. It was a mere girlish infatuation that became so much larger for my imaginings than it ever could have been. I'm not meant for him, nor he for me."

"Then why did you agree to meet with him here?" he asked, his voice harsh, his expression grim and unyielding.

Why had she? Oh, it seemed such a foolish whim now. Not at all worthy of the trouble seeing Denbigh had caused. Knowing the truth was a small solace. Alienating Heath was an insurmountable obstacle. "He wanted to tell me the truth of why he threw me over all those years ago," she admitted softly. "I was curious to hear it. I certainly had no intention of beginning where we left things off. You are my husband, not he."

"And yet you ran from me, Tia. The first sight I have of you in days is you wrapped in another man's arms. What am I to think, damn you?"

He was still angry. She supposed she couldn't blame him. The tableau upon which he'd intruded had been suspicious indeed. If she had been in his place, and she had walked in upon Heath embracing Bess, she would have been jade-green with jealousy. She was already jealous enough of her predecessor without ever having even met the woman.

"Please, Heath," she tried again. "It was as Denbigh said. He came here hoping to rekindle what we once shared, but I let him know that the time for such a thing was long past. We were saying goodbye. That is all."

"I'll not share you with him," he vowed, his voice vehement. His hands clamped onto her waist in a possessive grip. "Do not ask it of me."

186

How ironic that he could not bear to share her with another man when Tia had been forced to share him with Bess's memory from the start. She longed to point out the disparity to him, but with his emotions so ragged after what he'd just thought he'd witnessed, she didn't dare.

"I would never ask that of you, Heath. I'm yours." She caressed his jaw, eager to touch him now that he was back in her life. The last few days had been interminable. She had missed him so very much.

He crushed her against him, his mouth swooping perilously near to hers. "Say it again."

She knew instinctively what he wanted to hear. And it was true. There was no sense in denying him. He had her heart as surely as if he held it in his hands. "I'm yours."

"You're goddamn right you are."

And then his lips crushed hers. At first, the kiss was punishing, but it quickly changed. His tongue slid inside to claim, and her knees nearly went weak. Suddenly, need coursed through her. She wanted him with a desperation that all but swallowed her whole. This was where she belonged.

He dragged his mouth from hers and down her throat, devouring her. His palms skimmed upward from her waist, cupping her breasts through the thick barrier of her garments and corset. Her nipples hardened instantly, pebbling against her chemise as he pressed against her. A moan escaped her. She longed for him to touch her everywhere, to take her right there in the drawing room.

"Tia," he murmured against her skin, licking the frantically beating pulse at the hollow of her neck. "I need you so damn badly."

An echoing hunger unfurled within her, moisture pooling between her legs, her sex aching for him, for his touch. But reason reminded her that they were, after all, in her father's drawing room. Anyone could happen over the threshold at any moment, creating all manner of scandal. "Someone could walk in," she reminded him breathlessly as he caught the line of buttons decorating the bodice of her tea gown and ripped without mercy.

Oh dear. Her bodice hung open in two shreds. Her husband's eyes roamed over the skin he'd revealed. "I don't give a damn."

Tia knew she should be shocked. She should be horrified, really, to be in *dishabille* and cavorting with a man—husband or no—in the drawing room in which she'd grown up. Her brothers could intrude. Her sisters could intrude. A maid. The butler. Anyone. And yet, the desire between them was almost palpable, hot and heavy. Somehow, the notion of letting him take her right there in the middle of the day, of doing the forbidden, made her yearning increase tenfold.

She shrugged out of the sleeves of her gown and turned for him to loosen her corset. He nipped at first her neck, then her earlobe, sending a wicked shiver through her. His anger had burned into a roaring, raging fire of passion instead. Her laces came undone, and she opened her corset cover and undid all the closures she could reach. He spun her back around and peeled her chemise, the final barrier, down to her waist. When his mouth closed over a nipple, she arched into him, need blazing through her like a bolt of lightning cutting through the sky. As he sucked the other nipple, tugging at it with his teeth, his hands fisted in her silken skirts, raising them to her waist.

His trouser-covered leg pushed hers apart. Through the slit in her drawers, she could feel the fine fabric encasing his strong thigh directly against her. She arched, the delicious friction teasing her already swollen folds. Everything fell away but the man before her, the desire to become one. Their argument was forgotten. Their pasts ceased to matter. She rocked against him, wanting more.

"Heath." His name left her lips, half plea, half moan.

He flicked his tongue over one exquisitely sensitive nipple while rolling the other between his thumb and forefinger and pinching. "Tell me who you want, Tia. Tell me."

She was worked into such a frenzy that she scarcely could manage a coherent thought. "You."

Heath caught her up in his arms and hauled her against the nearest wall, trapping her so that she was suspended above the floor. With one hand, he untied the tapes that held her bustle in place. He shifted her just enough so that it fell away, no longer pressing uncomfortably into her bottom. His other hand sought out the slick flesh revealed by the slit in her drawers.

"My God," he said on a groan. "You're so wet for me." He worked the tender button of her sex, exerting just enough pressure to make her mad. "Do you want me?"

"Yes." He slipped a finger into her passage and she moaned, her head lolling back against the papered wall. "Please, yes."

She found the fastening of his trousers and undid it, releasing his rigid length into her hand. Tia gripped him, thinking about the way he would feel in just a moment, buried to the hilt. "Now, Heath," she demanded, unable to wait any longer.

In the next breath, he thrust into her, ramming home. She cried out, nearly finding her release. He kissed her as if he were ravenous for her, simultaneously driving deep and then withdrawing, only to sink inside her once more. Tia tried to hold onto her control, to stave off the wild unraveling that threatened to overtake her. But she was no match for the wicked sensation of her husband just where she wanted him. He pushed within her again, with so much force that her head hit the wall, but she didn't mind. This time, she exploded, tightening on him, glorious pleasure whirling through her. Heath sank into her one more time, kissing her again, the sweet pulse of his seed mingling with the subsiding waves of her climax.

He tore his lips from hers, staring down at her with that intense blue stare. "You're coming home with me tonight, Tia."

Her wits were still befuddled by what they'd just shared. Indeed, she felt quite certain that were he to release her, she'd crumple into a puddle of ripped silk at his feet. "Tonight?" she repeated, trying to reawaken the rational portion of her brain.

"Tonight," he repeated grimly.

"Can it not wait until the morning? I fear my parents will be overset if we simply disappear." She worried her lip, knowing that her mother and father would think the worst. Not to mention poor Helen.

He withdrew from her and lowered her to her feet, keeping her steady when she would have lost her balance. "You either leave tonight with me, or you stay here forever."

She blanched, not expecting an ultimatum from him, not after what had just transpired. "You cannot be serious."

"I'm deadly serious, Tia." His mouth was set in a grim line. "Make your choice."

Chapter Twelve

ER CHOICE HADN'T BEEN DIFFICULT. Indeed, it had scarcely been a choice at all.

Tia had said hasty goodbyes to her family— not that poor Bingley would recall it, for was still quite befuddled with drink—and Heath had whisked her away back to Chatsworth. Her homecoming had been bittersweet since her husband had chosen not to ride in the carriage with her but to brave the increasingly wintry weather on his own mount.

And he'd scarcely spoken more than half a dozen words to her in the day since their return.

She'd breakfasted that morning alone. She'd taken tea alone. And now she sat alone in the small drawing room she preferred for its cheery, striped wallpaper. Beyond the windows, the countryside was covered in the peaceful mask of snow. Flurries continued to fall, rendering the ground of Chatsworth House quite picturesque. Perhaps a turn in the gardens was in order. At the very least, it ought to do something to cut away at the listlessness that had been dogging her ever since the day before. She rang for her jacket, hat, and muff, and in a trice she was stepping out into the cold air. The snow fell around her as she walked.

The passionate Heath who had taken her so boldly in the drawing room at Harrington House had gone back into hiding. She began to wonder why he had even come to fetch her. Had it been mere possessiveness? Rage at the possibility of her taking a lover? She supposed she'd never know, for he refused to enlighten her beyond his pronouncement the evening before of, "Madam, we are home."

Tia didn't know which was worse, his silence or his anger. Her shoes crunched in the snow as she meandered around a fountain, her thoughts heavy. Anger she could manage. She almost wished he would rage at her, yell at her, anything other than his calm avoidance. It was as if she had ceased to exist.

Perhaps for him she had.

The notion gave her pause, sending a shiver through her that had nothing to do with the frigid air. His sudden arrival at Harrington House and his demand that she return with him had filled her with foolish expectations once more. She'd thought that it had meant something, that she meant something to him. Something more than mere chattel. She'd hoped too that it would ease the tension between them, but that hadn't happened. Instead, the tension had only seemed to grow worse.

"Tia."

Startled, she turned at the sound of his voice. Her husband stalked toward her through the snow, his expression determined. He wore only his shirtsleeves, trousers and waistcoat. Snow clung to his golden locks. Her heart fluttered as he approached her. She couldn't help it. She would always love him so, regardless of whether or not he would ever forgive her or even care for her at all.

"Heath," she greeted softly, her breath making a delicate fog on the air before her.

"Why the hell are you wandering about in the snow?" he demanded, his tone as surly as ever. "You'll take a chill. Come in at once."

"I'm properly dressed," she argued, uncertain if she should be warmed by his concern or if it was merely driven by a selfish need not to feel responsible for another woman's illness. "If anyone is in danger of taking a chill, surely it's you."

He held out his hand to her. "Come in at once."

Tia could be every bit as stubborn as he when she chose. She shook her head. "No."

"Tia." He caught the crook of her arm. "Come inside."

"I'm enjoying the snow," she insisted, digging her heels into the snow in protest. "It's very beautiful, don't you think?"

"It's cold is what I think. You can admire it from the window, wife. Now come along, blast it."

"You haven't called me that in quite some time," she said, still ignoring his request. She wanted to shake him, bring him back to her. Do anything to snap him from this frozen state. "I thought maybe you'd forgotten."

"I'm more than aware that you're my wife," he said grimly, as though the fact gave him no pleasure. "I'd never forget I wedded such a wrong-headed minx."

She searched his gaze, so vivid, so blue. "Perhaps you regret marrying me. I daresay I've caused you nothing but trouble."

He ran his thumb along her jaw, tipping up her chin. An errant snowflake settled on her nose and melted. "I regret many things that have come to pass between us, Tia. But marrying you isn't one of them."

She longed to believe him, oh how she did. Unable to help herself, she reached up to run her fingers along the abrasion of his neatly trimmed beard. The sensation was as familiar as it was beloved. "What do you regret?"

Heath stared down into the beautiful face of his wife. The woman he loved. Words clamored to reach his tongue. He'd spent the last day alternately chastising himself for once again playing the ass, and formulating what he would say to her. How he could attempt to win her.

What did he regret, she had wanted to know.

He would begin with the simple. Seeing her with Denbigh had brought out the savage in him, and he had no wish to lose control in such a manner again. He'd had ample time to consider precisely what he'd seen, and while he was certain that Denbigh's motives hadn't been innocent, he was equally certain that Tia's had been. But still, he wasn't yet ready to believe the earl's claim that Tia loved him. Surely she would have told him herself if it were true.

Admittedly, he'd done little to earn her love. He would begin now and continue for the rest of his days.

"I regret my reaction to discovering you'd sent away my paintings to the Grosvenor Gallery," he said at last. "I'm sorry I was so harsh and unyielding."

She smiled softly, snowflakes studding her lashes. God, she was a beauty. "I never should have sent away your paintings without your knowledge. It was wrong of me."

He shook his head. "You were right to do what you did. I've decided to allow my pictures to be exhibited."

She raised a brow, looking startled. "Even the one of Bess?"

"Even that one." He cleared his throat, attempting to find the proper words. After he'd removed his head from his own arse, he'd come to the realization that there was no harm in displaying his work for all to see. Indeed, it had once been his dream to do so. In many ways, Tia had helped him to reconcile the man he was now with the man he'd been. "After the exhibition is complete, I'll have it delivered to her family. I should think they might find joy in it."

"Truly?" Tia searched his gaze in that way she possessed, seeing more of him than he wanted her to see.

"Truly." He paused, searching for the proper words. "Someone once told me that I cannot hold on to the past forever. I find she is right."

"She will be very pleased to hear that." She ran her fingers across his mouth and he couldn't resist catching them there. He kissed them once because he couldn't help himself and twice to help temper the sting of the cold air.

Damn it, she made him weak. He wanted nothing more than to take her in his arms and carry her to his chamber. That long-ago day in the gardens at Penworth returned to him. She had been an ethereal beauty then. He'd been drawn to her, ignorant of just how much she would come to mean to him in the ensuing months. Just how much she would change his entire world.

But there was something he needed to know for certain. It wouldn't alter the way he felt for her, but a man needed to know the lay of the land. He rubbed his thumb lazily over her lower lip. "Tell me, Tia. Do you still love Denbigh?"

"No," she denied without hesitation, warming his heart with reassurance. "I loved him with a girl's naïve infatuation. Now I am older and wiser. I know the difference between true love and a mere childish fancy."

He kissed her then, taking her mouth the way he longed to take her body. With passion and possession. She tasted of the sweetness of her morning chocolate, the fresh coldness of snow and something that was uniquely her. Their tongues tangled, and she stepped closer, her corseted curves pressing into him in a way that made him go rigid in spite of the nip in the air.

She didn't love Denbigh. Thank Christ, because if she did, he would have had to ride to the bastard's estate and beat him to a bloody pulp. She was his, damn it, and he wasn't about to lose her. He'd almost lost her once because of his own foolishness. He wouldn't be so stupid ever again.

A gust of wind blew against them and Tia shivered into him. Blast her, she was going to catch her death out in this wintry weather. With great reluctance, he pulled away from her, ending the kiss. Her Cupid's bow was perfectly pink and slightly swollen from his kiss. Her eyes sparkled up at him with a mixture of unshed tears and the effects of the wintry air.

She blinked and a tear slipped down her cheek. He caught it on his thumb.

"I'm sorry," she murmured. "I don't know what's gotten into me lately. I've never been such a watering pot before."

It occurred to him then that he'd never—not when she'd injured her ankle, not when he'd found her shivering in the hunting cabin in East Anglia, and not even when he'd been unkind to her—seen her weep before. The sight cut at his heart. Damn it, he would never again be responsible for her tears, he vowed. Nothing and no one would be the cause of her pain ever again. Especially not him. She shivered again, reminding him that they had tarried in the elements overly long.

"We've lingered in the cold long enough," he told her. "Come inside with me."

When she looked as if she would have argued, he took her hand and tugged her along with him as he beat a hasty path back to the doors. He'd be damned if he allowed her to take ill now that he had her back where she belonged. Besides, if she was chilled, he had more than one way to warm her.

A slow truce had begun blossoming between Tia and Heath. She smiled to herself the next morning as she made her way to the breakfast table. She put the slight upheaval in her stomach down to her fluctuating emotions. Lord, she'd been a ninny lately, crying one moment and laughing the next. She didn't know what had gotten into her, but she had a feeling it had everything to do with being in love.

And in love she was.

She was more hopeful now than ever that she wasn't alone in her feelings. She was certain she'd spied a glimmering of something in his eyes yesterday in the snow. He had kissed her with so much sweet passion that it had made her cry. And last night, he had made love to her so tenderly, holding her long afterward almost as if she were precious to him.

She smiled again as she entered the breakfast room to find him waiting there for her, handsome and grinning back at her like a lovelorn suitor. She hadn't dared to believe that he would come for her at Harrington House. Indeed, she hadn't dared to believe he would even miss her. But he had. And she was back where she belonged.

"Good morning, darling," he greeted her softly, standing to acknowledge her entrance.

"Good morning," she returned, thinking that it was indeed a very good morning. She'd awoke to his kisses and they'd made slow, heart-melting love before he'd left her to get ready for the day. Gone were his hours of poring over estate matters in his study. It even seemed that the tension between them had lifted like a fog.

As she crossed the room to join him, something odd happened. Her head suddenly felt too light for her body. She swayed, dizzied, and a wave of nausea assailed her. Oh dear. She pressed a hand to her stomach, thinking that Bannock had laced her far too tightly that morning.

Heath's gaze met hers as she stilled, uncertain if she was going to cast up her accounts or faint dead away. She'd never felt anything like it.

"Tia?" Worry creased his features as he hurried toward her. "What's wrong?"

She didn't know. Her mouth opened, but she couldn't find the words. Any words. And then, her ears began ringing and her vision darkened round the edges. The last coherent thought in her mind was that her dratted corset must surely be the culprit.

Then, everything went black.

"Are you certain?" Tia asked the village physician Heath had summoned to her side against her protests to the contrary. She'd told him that her corset had merely been too tight, but he'd reverted to his ducal arrogance and had ignored her completely.

It would appear now that Heath hadn't been wrong. Something more than a mere corset was at play. Something wonderful. Something she hadn't so much as considered.

The kindly elder man closed his doctor's bag with a snap. "Quite certain, Your Grace. All the signs are here. I expect His Grace will be most relieved."

"Yes," she agreed, feeling dazed by the news he had just delivered to her. "I daresay he will."

She wasn't ill. She was with child.

She was carrying Heath's babe. The knowledge filled her with wonder, excitement. Contentment. She had never conceived during her marriage to Stokey, and later, she had made certain her lovers took precautions. She and Heath had been intimate for months without change in her courses. She had simply closed off that part of her mind, the fragile maternal hope that she might one day bring a child into the world. It had been far better to think it impossible and avoid disappointment than to anticipate an event that would not be forthcoming.

But now it had.

"You will want to rest, Your Grace," the doctor reminded her, gathering up his bag to see himself out. "Fainting is quite common for a woman in your condition, but we don't want you to injure yourself."

"Yes," she agreed, scarcely hearing the man with her mind whirling. She wanted to see Heath. "Will you send the duke in to me on your way out? I should very much like to tell him the news."

"Of course, Your Grace." The older man smiled. "And may I be the first to offer my felicitations?"

"Thank you." She smiled. She knew women who had been *enceinte*. So much made sense to her now. Her weepiness of the last few weeks, her changing moods. What a fool she'd been not to notice.

The door had scarcely closed on the doctor's back when it flew open once more to reveal Heath. His hair was askew, his eyes clouded with worry, a frown curving his sensual lips.

"Tia." He rushed to her side and took her hands in his, bringing them to his lips. "My God, I can't lose you. Not now. Not ever, damn it all. You must get well. Tell me you'll get well."

"I shall get well," she reassured him, struck by how very concerned he was for her. Her heart gave a pang in her breast. She caressed his bearded cheek. "You needn't fear."

"Whatever it is that's caused this, we will get through it together." He kissed her palm.

"Of course we will," she began, only to be interrupted.

"No, darling. Let me finish. I need to tell you what I've been meaning to say for days. I should have told you a long time ago, but I was too bloody stupid to realize that what was right before me was what I'd wanted—what I'd needed—all along." He paused, seeming to collect himself as the tears she'd been attempting to squelch sprang free. "I love you, Tia. You've brought me back to myself in ways I never imagined possible. You've helped me to heal, to move forward. I love your stubborn, infuriating ways. Devil take it, I even love that you never listen to me when you think you know better. I love you so much, and I can't bear to lose you."

"Oh, Heath." She swiped at her cheeks with the back of her hand. "You're not losing me. I'm not ill."

He stared at her as if she'd suddenly announced her desire to jump out the nearest window. "You're not ill?"

"No." She smiled, her heart so filled with happiness that she feared it would burst. "I'm with child."

"With child?" A slow, beautiful grin spread over his face. "You're having my babe?"

"Yes." She nodded, unable to say more past the emotion clogging her throat.

"My God." He let out a whoop and crushed her in a hug. "That's wonderful news. Why the devil didn't you say so sooner?"

Tia laughed. "I would have, but someone interrupted me."

"I suppose I did," he said wryly, drawing back to search her gaze. "Are you happy, darling? I know we haven't always had the smoothest of rides, and I know I've been an utter ass, but I swear I shall make it up to you."

"I'm very happy," she assured him, framing his face in her hands. "Happier than I've ever been."

He kissed her swiftly, and it was passionate, open-mouthed. His tongue slid against hers and she welcomed the invasion, wanting more. When at last he tore his lips from hers, they were both breathing heavily, staring at each other with a newfound connection.

"There's something else I must tell you," she told him, ready to say the words she'd been keeping to herself for far too long.

"Good Christ woman, what can it be?" he demanded, every inch the duke. "I'm not certain my heart can withstand any more scares."

"I'm in love with an arrogant, domineering duke who is too stubborn for his own good and who creates the finest paintings I've ever seen." She smiled as comprehension dawned in his eyes. "I think I've loved him since the moment he carried me off to my chamber and undid half my bodice."

"That is most fortuitous," he drawled, "because I have it on good authority that the same duke is in love with a lady who has a penchant for spraining her ankle and redecorating his house."

She laughed, thinking back on the twisted path they'd taken to get them to where they were today. Their two halves had made a perfect whole after all. "Well then, the duke is a very fortunate man."

"Oh yes," he agreed, lowering his lips to hers for another kiss. "He's a very fortunate man indeed."

Epilogue

London, five months later

"TURN A BIT TO YOUR LEFT, DARLING."

Tia sighed and did as Heath asked, shifting so that more light fell across her face from the morning room window. She had agreed to sit for another portrait, but she hadn't taken into account just how uncomfortable sitting still would be now that her stomach had grown quite round and the babe was intent upon wielding his feet and elbows upon her so unmercifully.

"How is this?" she asked.

"Perfect." He glanced up at her, the look of concentration on his face that she'd come to know well in the last few months. "You needn't looked so aggrieved. I only need you to sit for a few moments more."

"I'm sure I don't look aggrieved," she felt compelled to argue, even though she was reasonably certain she did.

"And I'm equally sure you do." He raised a brow at her before turning his attention back to his canvas.

The reception to his paintings at the Grosvenor Gallery had been exceedingly positive. More of his work was in demand, and Heath had been steadily painting ever since the winter.

She sighed again. "I know you said you wished to represent a maternal goddess in nature for this picture, but I daresay I resemble a cow far more than a goddess."

She was very conscious of her burgeoning shape. Soon, she would no longer be able to conceal her condition in the clever drapery of her custom gowns. Heath couldn't seem to keep his hands from her growing belly. He was constantly caressing her there, telling her how beautiful she was. And if his lovemaking was any indication, he was telling her the truth. She supposed that love, at least, was blind.

"Nonsense," he said. "You're the most gorgeous woman I've ever seen."

"And you're possessed of the smoothest tongue I've ever heard," she returned archly.

"You seemed to enjoy it last night," he reminded her, making her flush as she recalled precisely what his tongue had been doing to her the previous evening.

"Naughty man," she scolded without heat. In truth, she found his frank, sensual nature incredibly attractive. She always would.

Their days since her return from Harrington House had been nothing short of wonderful. Time had only brought them closer, their passion burning hotter than ever. And with each moment that passed, she swore that her love for him grew.

A knock at the door interrupted the comfortable silence that had descended between them. Looking askance at her, Heath called for the butler to enter.

"Lady Helen Harrington has arrived, Your Graces," the august man announced.

Tia brightened at the prospect of an unexpected visit from her sister. "Do send her in, please."

But the moment her sister crossed the threshold, Tia knew from Helen's troubled expression that this wasn't an ordinary social call. Oh dear.

"Lady Helen," Heath greeted her cheerfully, not having been blessed with the same sense of sisterly discernment. "What a pleasant surprise."

"I'm sorry to intrude," Helen murmured, hesitating a few feet away, wringing her hands. "It is merely that I haven't anywhere else to go."

Tia rose from the settee, and not without a bit of effort on her part. These days, it seemed that every part of her body ached. She went to her sister, putting a soothing arm around her shoulders. "Come and sit, dearest. What do you mean when you say you haven't anywhere else to go?"

Helen allowed herself to be led to the settee. She'd barely seated herself before she burst into tears. "Oh Tia, I've done something horrid."

It occurred to Tia that the scene before her was the exact opposite of the one that had played out at Harrington House. Then, it had been Tia in need of reassurance and Helen the one with the ready handkerchief. With a dawning sense of dread, she realized that the tables had seemingly turned.

She handed Tia a handkerchief. "What is it, sister? What can be so bad?"

"I'm with child," she revealed on a shuddering wail.

Good heavens. Helen, her spinster sister, was having a babe. Out of wedlock. She patted her sister's shoulder, shocked. "Who is the father, dearest?"

"Don't ask me. Please." Helen's eyes pleaded with her. "I've come to you because I need help finding a cottage somewhere far away. Somewhere I can go so that no one will know."

Tia met her husband's gaze, an unspoken understanding passing between them. *Thank you*, she mouthed to him. *I love you*. He nodded, mouthing the same words back to her. Thank heavens she had a sympathetic husband. Helen would need them both in the months ahead.

"Of course we shall help you, Helen," she promised her sister. "We shall help you in every way we can."

Helen's only response was more miserable weeping. Heath was at their side then, a protective presence. He wrapped them both in a warm embrace, pressing a kiss to the top of Tia's head.

"You needn't worry, Helen," he said. "Tia and I are here for you."

Tia gripped her husband's hand, feeling more grateful than ever for the day she'd sprained her ankle in the maze at Penworth and he'd come to her rescue. Sometimes, love was simply meant to be.

Read on for an excerpt of Book 4 in the Heart's Temptation Series, *Sweet Scandal*.

Sweet Scandal
Heart's Temptation Book 4

Lady Helen Harrington is a spinster by choice. She hasn't any desire to entangle herself in romantic nonsense. Instead, she prefers to spend her time championing the causes nearest to her heart through writing articles for the *London Beacon*. When a ruthless American tycoon suddenly buys the struggling paper with plans to turn it into a business journal, Lady Helen isn't about to stand idly by or put down her pen. Even if the ruthless tycoon in question happens to be the most maddeningly handsome man she's ever met in her life.

Levi Storm built his empire the hard way, spending years working his way out of the slums where he grew up. He won't allow a spoiled aristocrat like Lady Helen to interfere with his plans to further his brand with the newspaper he's just acquired. It doesn't matter how lovely she is or how persuasive her arguments or how perfectly she fits in his arms.

When scandal looms and Helen discovers a shocking secret about Levi, she does what she must to protect herself. But Levi isn't the sort of man who admits defeat, and he's not ready to give up on the plucky Lady Helen, especially when he discovers that she has secrets of her own...

Chapter One

London, 1882

*J*UST AS SHE HAD DONE EACH MONTH FOR THE last three years, Lady Helen Harrington stepped into the offices of the *London Beacon*. But on this day, something was frightfully out of the ordinary. She clutched her latest article, a piece on the shocking plight of London's poor, to her promenade dress as though it were a shield.

The *Beacon* had never been a bustling hub of activity. Indeed, as a journal concerned with egalitarian matters rather than societal gossip or daily news fodder, it had suffered from both lack of staff and funds. Often, the only soul in the office was the owner and editor, Mr. Bothwell.

And yet, somehow before her swarmed a veritable hive of activity. Men were everywhere. Boxes and plaster dust and papers littered the quarters. There was banging and clanging and shouting and strangely, the entire building itself seemed to be buzzing.

No one appeared to notice her as she stood in the entryway, gawking at the commotion. A man bearing tools almost crashed into her in his eagerness to reach his destination. She sidestepped him and managed to run smack into a hard wall of chest instead.

Her papers and her reticule went flying and she nearly fell to the floor with the impact of the collision. Large, masculine hands caught her around the waist, pulling her far too close to an equally large, solidly muscled male form.

"Oh dear," she muttered, hastily stifling any quickening of her pulse that was inspired by the rather indelicate position.

"Steady," the man commanded in a distinctly American accent. One word and he'd given himself away.

She looked up into his impossibly blue gaze and her pulse exerted a will of its own, kicking back into a gallop. Good heavens, he was beautiful. There was no other way to describe him. His wavy, dark hair was swept back from his forehead, perhaps a bit too long for fashion, his lips molded with enough perfection that even she, dedicated spinster, was not unaffected. The finely trimmed beard covering his strong jaw made him appear intensely masculine in the very best way possible. If ever Helen had laid eyes upon a man who could shake her unwavering resolution to never be wooed or misled by a man, surely it was he.

"I trust you aren't injured?" he asked, his words managing to pierce the London-like fog that had taken up residence in her brain. Oh yes indeed, very American, that accent. There were certainly enough of them traveling in her circles these days. But not this man. She would not have forgotten him.

"Madam?" he pressed when she failed to respond.

"No," she hurried to reply lest he realize the cause for her lack of alacrity.

"Excellent." He released her and bent to retrieve her fallen papers and purse before handing them back to her. "Please see yourself out."

Helen almost gaped at him. It occurred to her that the tone of his voice was not one of concern but rather one of irritation. Had the man no manners?

"Who are you, sir?" she demanded, unnerved by his rudeness and determined to get to the bottom of the tumult before her. "What is going on here?"

He raised an imperious brow at her. "May I ask who *you* are, madam?"

She blinked, finding his arrogance and audacity most vexing. "Who I am?"

"That is indeed the question I just posed." His expression remained an icy mask.

He wasn't about to budge. Very well. She too could be persistent. "Where is Mr. Bothwell?" she asked instead of answering him.

He waved a dismissive hand as though to suggest that Mr. Bothwell's mere mentioning was as bothersome to him as a fly. "Bothwell is gone. Off happily counting his pounds somewhere, I'd suspect." His gaze flicked over her person, boldly taking stock of her in a way that had her cheeks heating. "What business have you with him?"

"Business?" She frowned then.

Ladies of her station did not have business. No, indeed. The articles she wrote for the *Beacon* had initially earned her a bit of pin money, but as time had worn on and the *Beacon's* pockets were increasingly to let, she had merely volunteered her services instead. After all, it had been the platform she relished and not any meager funds once associated with it. The opportunity to give voice to the causes that were important to her was of the greatest significance.

His sensual mouth compressed into a firm line. "Are you dimwitted, madam?"

The question took her aback. Of all the insolence she'd encountered in her life, the man before her surely took the proverbial cake. "How dare you?"

"Hang it, I haven't time to squabble with a woman who keeps repeating every word I say." He all but growled before hailing one of the men engaged in the industry of hauling away some battered old furniture. "You there, please see that this lovely, confused lady is taken to her personal conveyance at once."

And then without preamble, without even so much as another glance in her direction, he turned his back on her.

She had been dismissed.

Helen stared at his infuriating back, noting despite herself just how broad and well-muscled it appeared to be. Precisely who did he think he was? Did he not know she was a peeress? That she was the daughter of an earl? That she ought to be at least treated with a modicum of respect if not gallantry?

Oh no he didn't.

She sidestepped the poor fellow assigned with the task of escorting her to her carriage and hurried after the source of her discourteous dismissal. "Sir, I must insist on an answer. What in heaven's name is going on here?"

He spun about on his heel, surprise evident in every line of his visage. Perhaps he had expected her to meekly do his bidding. If so, he was bound to be sorely disappointed. "Madam, kindly leave my building as you've been instructed. I have a great deal more important things to do than answer your hen-witted questions."

His building? His arrogance knew no bounds. And now he was calling her hen-witted? Surely the man must be daft. Either that or he was utterly mad, for there was no other explanation for such an appalling lack of couth. "This building belongs to the *London Beacon*," she pointed out. "I write a monthly column for the *Beacon*, and I won't be going anywhere until I can speak with Mr. Bothwell directly."

"Damn it all," he muttered, startling her by taking her elbow in a firm grasp and propelling her toward Mr. Bothwell's office. "Come with me."

He said the last as though he was giving her an option. He wasn't. The man was all but dragging her across the floor and into the room that had once housed Mr. Bothwell's sturdy old desk and a bookcase laden with fine literature. He slammed the door behind them and she should have flinched or objected to the impropriety but she was too engaged in taking in her surroundings to notice.

Mr. Bothwell's office had changed. In place of his desk was a brand new and fine mahogany desk with intricate carving and an inlaid mother of pearl monogram bearing an 'S.' The carpet was lush beneath her feet and the gaslight had been replaced by gleaming electric globes. A fresh coat of paint had been applied, and it all looked very costly and very unlike any expense that could be afforded by the haphazard Mr. Bothwell.

Understanding began to dawn upon her at last. The handsome, forbidding man before her and his insufferable demeanor had so flummoxed her that she hadn't listened carefully enough to what he'd said. "Do you mean to say that Mr. Bothwell has sold the paper?"

The old rotter hadn't said a word to her when she'd last seen him. He had simply accepted her article and said he would see her in a month's time. Nothing had seemed out of the ordinary. Mr. Bothwell's fingertips had retained their typical ink stains, his thinning shock of white hair mussed as always. He hadn't suggested at all that anything was amiss.

"That is precisely what I mean to say." He towered over her, so near she could detect the faint, masculine scent of his soap. "I own this building and the *London Beacon* both. Mr. Bothwell won't be returning, and your services will no longer be required."

Dismay rattled through her. "But I have an understanding with Mr. Bothwell. I've been writing a monthly for two years now." Small circulation journal that the *Beacon* was, it had been the only publication where she'd managed to publish her views. Bothwell espoused reform, and he'd been willing to give her free reign in venting her sometimes *de trop* and sometimes shocking notions. The *Beacon* had always been a paragon of reform, albeit a small one, at least until the interloper before her had greased the old man's palms. She very much feared she couldn't find another paper that would dare to publish her work.

He remained impervious to her pleas. "Whatever

understanding you had with the former editor and owner is no concern of mine."

Well. It would seem that he was equal parts handsome and callous. He appeared quite impervious. But she too was made of stern stuff. One had to be when one possessed three minx sisters and three unruly brothers. "You needn't be so dismissive, sir. I've put a great deal of research into this article, and it's about—"

"I don't care," he interrupted. "I don't care if it's about butterflies or your grandmother's shoes. It won't be published by my paper, and nor will anything else you write. As I said, your services will no longer be required."

The blighter. Butterflies and an old woman's shoes indeed. As though she would have nothing of greater import, no topic weightier than fripperies and nonsense, to offer the reading public. Now her temper was rather beginning to get the best of her. "Sir, your manners are deplorable."

He flashed her a grin that wasn't polite or kind but somehow still had an effect on her. Dash it all, the man had dimples. "Madam, if I had ever concerned myself with manners, I wouldn't have a cent to my name. As edifying as I find this discussion, I truly do have more significant matters requiring my attention. Would you care for me to have you escorted to the door or would you prefer to be thrown over my shoulder like a haversack and carted to the door?"

"Are you threatening my person, sir?" Surely he wouldn't dare.

He closed the distance between them, setting his hands upon her waist. Apparently he was and he would. "You have until the count of three, madam. One. Two."

She placed her hands over his, trying in vain to tug free of his grasp. It was a mistake. Even through her gloves, the contact felt somehow oddly, delightfully intimate. She gazed up into those ethereal blue eyes and realized he'd stopped counting. Her corset had grown unaccountably tight and a disquieting sensation had taken up residence deep within her. None of it made a whit of sense since each time the man opened his mouth, the sentences he uttered were even more rude than the last. He was troublesome. Arrogant. Irritating.

Handsome.

"Sir, you must release me at once," she forced herself to say in her haughtiest tone.

For a moment, he simply stared, their enmeshed gazes yielding a simmering tension that was as undeniable as it was unwanted. His grip on her waist tightened, almost becoming possessive. She found it hard to breathe. His head dipped to hers, his mouth alarmingly near. He was going to kiss her, she realized.

"Three," he said. "You had fair warning."

Abruptly he bent and did as he'd promised, scooping her over his shoulders, voluminous bustle of her promenade dress and all. She was treated to an upside down view of his desk, shimmering in the other-worldly glow of the electric lights despite the gloominess of the outside day. She couldn't believe it. The man had actually thrown her, the daughter of the Earl of Northcote, over his shoulder. It was the outside of enough.

So she did what any lady in her incredible predicament would do. She made a fist and pounded on his insufferable back.

About the Author

Award-winning author Scarlett Scott writes contemporary and historical romance with heat, heart, and happily ever afters. Since publishing her first book in 2010, she has become a wife, mother to adorable identical twins and one TV-loving dog, and a killer karaoke singer. Well, maybe not the last part, but that's what she'd like to think.

A self-professed literary junkie and nerd, she loves reading anything but especially romance novels, poetry, and Middle English verse. When she's not reading, writing, wrangling toddlers, or camping, you can catch up with her on her website www.scarsco.com. Hearing from readers never fails to make her day.

Scarlett's complete book list and information about upcoming releases can be found on her website.

Follow Scarlett on social media:

www.twitter.com/scarscoromance
www.pinterest.com/scarlettscott
www.facebook.com/AuthorScarlettScott

Other Books by Scarlett Scott

Heart's Temptation

A Mad Passion (Book 1)
Rebel Love (Book 2)
Reckless Need (Book 3)
Sweet Scandal (Book 4) (Coming Soon)

Love's Second Chance (Coming Soon)

Reprieve (Book 1)
Perfect Persuasion (Book 2)
Win My Love (Book 3)

Wicked Husbands (Coming Soon)

Her Errant Earl (Book 1)
Her Lovestruck Lord (Book 2)
Her Reformed Rake (Book 3)

Made in the USA
Middletown, DE
26 December 2023